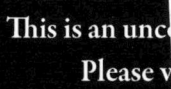

ABOUT

NORTH SHORE

Charles Jovanovic is known for being fun, loud, and a drama queen. That changes when he comes home after a six-month dancing gig on a cruise line and finds his boyfriend kissing a muscular tattooed stranger. He retreats into his Staten Island apartment and ignores the world . . . until he discovers that the man he'd found with his ex is his downstairs neighbor.

Luis Ramos hates cheaters. He had no idea his near hookup had a boyfriend, let alone a boyfriend as gorgeous as sassy, leggy Charles. His guilt leads to frequent groveling, but Charles's wrath won't quit. As soon as Luis decides to back off, he catches Charles watching him practice one of his stripper routines. Luis jumps at the chance to make peace, and Charles can't resist an invitation to dance.

Reluctant friendship turns to late-night dance sessions, intimate conversations, and flirtatious encounters in the dimly lit laundry room. Charles tries to ignore Luis's efforts to revive his dormant passions, but the sexual tension is undeniable. When Charles realizes he wants more than a rebound, he has to learn how to move past his jealousy and trust that Luis wants him, baggage and all.

Riptide Publishing
PO Box 1537
Burnsville, NC 28714
www.riptidepublishing.com

North Shore
Copyright © 2018 by Santino Hassell

Cover art: L.C. Chase, lcchase.com/design.htm
Editor: Sarah Lyons
Layout: L.C. Chase, lcchase.com/design.htm

ISBN: 978-1-62649-761-0

First edition
April, 2018

Also available in ebook:
ISBN: 978-1-62649-760-3

NORTH SHORE

SANTINO HASSELL

A FIVE BOROUGHS STORY

RIPTIDE
PUBLISHING

TABLE OF

CONTENTS

CHAPTER ONE
CHARLES

"Only you would get dramatically fired from a cushy job on a cruise ship."

Mere's low voice was music to my ears after months of intermittent cell phone access. Taking a job as an entertainment dancer on a cruise had sounded like a dream until literal cabin fever had set in.

It had been one of many many reasons I'd finally had enough. Unfortunately, my version of "enough" had led to me being bounced off the boat after I'd quit dancing mid-performance during one of the evening cabaret shows. Then I'd threatened to throw the entertainment manager overboard if he kept trying to forcibly shove me back onto the stage.

Apparently, threats were grounds for an insta-firing. Insta-firing with a side of "pay your own way home".

"Untrue," I grunted, dragging my enormous steamer trunk from the back of my Uber. Over a hundred bucks to get to Staten Island from JFK, and the assface driver could not even be bothered to help me remove my belongings. "Plenty of people got fired during the six months I was on the cruise. It *sucked*, Mere. They were borderline abusive. I just couldn't take it anymore."

"I'm sorry, babe. I was just trying to make..."

The rest of her sentence faded to a warble as my phone slipped from where I'd tried to balance it between my shoulder and cheek. I watched, almost in slow motion, as it fell on a slant against the curb. And *shattered*.

I inhaled sharply, closed my eyes, and tried not to roar my frustration so the entire block could hear. That was my thing—the thing that had started driving Landon crazy after we'd moved to this quiet street off Forest Avenue. I was so *fucking loud* that people could hear me out on the street even with our windows down. The people in the houses around us could hear me through the thin walls of each narrow house. It was one of Landon's least favorite things about me. Never mind the fact that I was usually yelling because of his passive aggressive bullshit.

My frustration turned to the kind of anger that also felt like regret. This was an omen.

My whole trip home had been an omen. Everything from the fact that a storm had delayed the flight from the Bahamas, I'd been later bumped from that same flight due to overbooking, then I'd been saddled between a family of screaming kids once finally on a plane, proceeded to get a shitty Uber driver after landing, and now... this.

The worst part was that I hadn't called Landon yet, so he wasn't expecting me. I'd called Caleb after being fired and sobbed into the phone as he calmed me down. Spoke to Ashton at the airport while losing myself in overpriced margaritas. Texted with Steph while waiting forever on a layover and asking her intrusive questions about Angel's dick, but... no Landon.

If I was honest with myself, I'd been afraid to tell him about how I'd hit a breaking point with my managers. He'd assume I was being dramatic, I'd get mad, and I didn't need his disappointed coldness or annoyed shouting turning me into me a nervous wreck while I was traveling.

"You done?"

I ripped my gaze from my broken cell phone to the Uber driver giving me the side eye out his window.

"Yo, if you would have fucking helped me, I wouldn't have broken my phone."

The dude kept staring at me, chewing gum, and looking unimpressed. "Bro, I have a cast on. I can't lift all that shit."

How had I missed that he was injured? I couldn't even put blame on people properly. Snarling to myself, I dragged my duffel bag out of the bag, tossing it with the rest of my crap on the sidewalk, and waved him away. He peeled out like he was escaping a fire, which—maybe he was. I was the walking talking embodiment of a major disaster area.

I grabbed my phone, shoved it in my backpack, and started

the arduous task of dragging my belongings up the narrow stairs. It sucked. Everything about it sucked. It was one and a half flights, but narrow as hell, and the carpet made it weirdly slippery under my flip-flops. Also, the walk-up to our floor in the two-family-house was *sweltering*. It was May, but felt a lot more like the middle of August. The early spring heatwave that had driven half of my friend group into serious, or broadened, relationships had seemingly come back just to torment me.

"Fuck life and suitcases and Carnival Cruise Line."

My breath was coming out in rough pants by the time I had half my bags lining the top few stairs, the other three still down on the sidewalk. I was so done with life that part of me did not care if I went outside to find them gone. If they wanted my assortment of costumes and hideous cruise uniforms, they were welcome to it. If I ever danced another manufactured piece of easily digestible crap again, it would be too soon.

Sighing, I shook myself and prepared to face my boyfriend's questions and potential wrath at me losing yet another job. There was music *blasting* from the inside of the apartment, which was good since Landon was home but annoying because I was not prepared for the shitty stereo system he'd insisted on putting in our bedroom. It was 90s era, and should have stayed there.

After fumbling with my backpack to find the keys, I let myself in and was instantly hit by a ferocious blast of hot air. Oh my *God*, he had every window open and no AC on. Cheap bastard had gone full-on old man thrifster in my absence. I bet he still cooked in the dark over paranoia about the electricity bill. The one time he'd returned from a weekend trip to find me home with the AC blasting and lights on in, oh gosh, *two* rooms, he'd shouted for an hour. As if he was even the one who paid the bills on a regular basis...

The memory made my stomach flip in the bad way. The bracing for it way. The way that made me stop and wonder why I'd come here instead of to Caleb's place, like he'd suggested as soon as I'd called. I took a deep breath, closed my eyes, and then pasted on a smile.

"Landon, I'm home," I sang, making my voice go into the high falsetto the musical director had commanded. "Surprise!"

There was no response, but I wasn't shocked. Knowing him,

he'd worked out in this blazing heat and was now blasting this trash electronic music as he showered.

I dropped my backpack and walked through the dining room (which I'd converted into a dance space and was now a... random Landon gym storage space, apparently), through the large kitchen, and into our open bedroom. I'd expected to find it a disgusting mess after Landon being left to his own devices for six months, but instead I found a spectacle I could only stare at.

Two people were pressed together. On *my* bed. On the AmeriSleep mattress I'd worked overtime at three jobs to pay for, just so I could have something that wouldn't further exacerbate my insomnia and screwed up back.

Landon was sitting up on his knees, only wearing underwear and a sleeveless shirt, as a ripped man with tattoos covering the dark golden stretch of his back pressed against him from behind. They were grinding against each other and kissing as they knelt together on the bed.

It wasn't real. It couldn't be. Because, Landon? He looked like he was ready to get on his hands and knees and get fucked, but he didn't bottom. He'd told me so even after I'd informed him I preferred to bottom, anyway. He'd made a federal case about it as if the very notion bothered him, and it was lucky that I was unlikely to try. He definitely never made these needy begging sounds while making out. He didn't even kiss me very much. He was... never...

"I can feel you through your jeans," he panted between kisses. "I need that big dick in me."

Everything went still and quiet around me. Things started to move in slow motion—one of those big hands pressed against the back of Landon's neck and shoved him facefirst down to the bed. I saw the tattooed man's lips move but I couldn't hear what he was saying. I couldn't even hear the music. I couldn't process anything except: *I finally caught you, you piece of shit.* It echoed in the back of my mind in increasing volume.

A savage breath tore out of me, and I whirled on Landon's monstrous sound system. It looked like a stack of eighty car stereos with two ugly-ass speakers on either side, and *oh wait*. Now it was on the *fucking floor*.

I put my foot through one speaker, then the other, and was so hellbent on trashing this radio that I didn't register the voices behind me.

"What the fuck is *this* drama?"

"Jesus, Charles, what the hell are you doing here?"

Snarling, I grabbed one of the speakers and spun around. The tattooed guy was hopping up and down in an attempt to fix his tight jeans, big dark eyes flicking between me and Landon in confusion. And Landon—he was still standing there in his underwear. And he looked mad. He. Looked. Mad.

"I *live here*, you *motherfucker!*"

Tattoos froze with his hands on his T-shirt, and cringed hard. He shot a dirty look at Landon, but I didn't care that he'd apparently been tricked too. Because he hadn't been tricked like I'd been tricked.

"You're not supposed to be back until next month," Landon said, voice strained. "I had no idea you would be here tonight."

"What—" I blinked at him, not comprehending. "*What*?"

"Charles." Landon's voice lowered. "Don't make a scene. After Luis leaves—"

"Fuck Luis."

My heart slammed into my chest, and I let that speaker fly. Landon ducked, falling sideways on the bed, before scrambling to his feet again. It didn't matter that he was caught. That I finally knew what I'd suspected for almost two years—he was cheating on me. He'd *been* cheating on me. In our own bed. I'd suspected it for ages. Honestly, since the beginning. Too many gut feelings and unexplainable events that had built up to an undeniable but unspoken truth, and now it was out in the open.

And it didn't matter, because he didn't care. I was still, somehow, the dramatic one. The irrational one. It was my fault for not calling to give him a heads up. I'd ruined his fun. I was making a scene.

Tears blurred my vision, and that made me angrier. A wave of heat swept through me until everything once again started to fade. Luis was a blur in my peripheral vision and so was the door leading to the kitchen. I could see nothing but Landon—my boyfriend. My live-in nightmare.

"I fucking knew it," I whispered. "All that time—you said I was being paranoid. You said I was making shit up and being paranoid. You made me *feel like I was crazy*."

"Because you are fucking crazy," Landon exploded. "You expected me to wait around celibate for eight months? That's not even reasonable, Charles. You are *never* reasonable. You go on your trips and your adventures, you work for twenty hours a day, you have all of these friends, and yet you're shocked when you come back and find me elsewhere?"

I shook my head, unable to process the barrage of accusations. Too much work. Too many friends. Too much... travel? *What*? He was the one who went away for random weekends with groups of suspicious looking white men.

"So, all this time..."

Landon's cheek clenched. He shot a look at Luis, who was still a muscular blur to the right, before glaring at me again. "Like I said, Charles. You've never been reasonable. Or realistic. You just expect and want and never think, do you? It's about what you want and never about anyone else's needs."

I'd heard these words before from him. But I'd never truly thought he'd also been talking about his ability to remain faithful. All these years, and I'd been waiting for definitive proof, and it turned out he'd been confessing all along.

"You promised," I whispered. "You told me if I waited, you'd wait too."

Incredulity spread over him. Pure genuine incredulity.

"We had that fucking conversation when we were drunk, baby. God, you thought I was serious? Jesus fucking Christ, Charles. I don't even know what to say."

A pitying expression crossed his face. I wanted to crack in half from mortification and the bloody explosion of my heartbreak, but I grabbed the other speaker instead. I cocked it back, fully intending to smash it over his head, but Tattoos was suddenly behind me. He crushed his strong sweaty chest against my shredded tank top with one big hand wrapped around my arm. I strained against him, but even though I was stronger than I looked, my sculpted dancer's body was practically a twig compared to his.

"Oye, lindo," Tattoos whispered in my ear. "Calm yourself."

I tensed, eyes wide and fixed on Landon. His face was changing now. From incredulous back to angry, his blue eyes flipping between me and Tattoos. Tattoos' hands on me. The lack of space between our bodies. The way Tattoos was rumbling in my ear, his lips brushing the sensitive ridges in a way that usually drove me out of my skin.

Oh my God. Even now, Landon hated to see anyone else touch me. Even the man he'd been writhing against only a moment ago. After he'd just called me an idiot for expecting him to wait.

Tears welled in my eyes even as a hysterical laugh burst out of my mouth, because what was this? What was any of this? How could I have kept doing this for so long?

"Charles," Landon said, voice low and serious, as he moved closer. "We need to talk about this. Just wait for Luis to leave."

Tattoos guided my arm down, causing me to drop the speaker, but he didn't let me go.

"We don't need to talk about shit," I said between rasping breaths. "You need to get the fuck out of my apartment because I am done."

Landon stopped walking a few inches away from me. "This is *our*—"

"This is *my* apartment, you broke no-credit having bitch," I choked through my tears. "My lease. My bank account that's auto-drafted for rent, utilities, and the fucking *cable*. So, you can *get the fuck out* with your metro card and your fucking fifteen-pound dumbbells."

Luis' chest shook against me, and he snorted back a laugh, but the rage that took over Landon was swift as a viper. By now, the signs were easy to recognize. His eyes turned to granite, his face a mask of disgust. The kind of disgust that led to him knocking the shit out of me.

His arm jerked up, but Luis went from restraining me to nudging me out of the way. He stood toe-to-toe with Landon, shoulders back and chin up.

Landon stared at me, red faced and enraged even as he hissed, "Leave, Luis."

"Mmm." Luis cocked his head. "Nah. You heard the man—you leave."

Landon's eyes bugged out of his head. He was breathing hard, the way he did before a rage blackout, but I noticed he suddenly had self-control when it came to a guy like Luis. A guy who'd relaxed onto the balls of his feet as if he was ready to dole out a casually thorough ass whooping.

"You don't have shit to do with this," Landon sneered. "So get the fuck—"

"Leave," I shouted so loud, it probably echoed in the streets outside. "Or I'll call the cops and tell them about your side job."

It was the wrong thing to say. I felt the blow even before he swung, muscle memory causing me to rear back and put my arms up to cover my face, but it never came. I sucked in deep gasping breaths, tears streaming down my face, and could barely make out the sight of Luis propelling Landon out the door.

"—wait outside while he packs your shit before you get yourself good and fucked up."

That rumbling voice said other words, words that would probably give me a clue about where Landon was going, what they were doing, and whether I needed to find my baseball bat in the mess he'd made of my bedroom, but I didn't move.

Instead, I sat next to the broken stereo and sobbed.

CHAPTER TWO

LUIS

Landon was easily the dumbest person I'd ever met, and I'd met some dumb motherfuckers in my lifetime. I'd half dragged his ass down the stairs because he'd found his bravado somewhere in the crack of his ass and had tried to fight me at the last minute. Now, he was limping around throwing his man's bags all over the sidewalk.

The dude had a *lot* of luggage.

"You look like an angry naked toddler," I said. "Literally like those tighty whities are your diaper, and this is a tantrum."

"*Fuck you.*"

Landon turned on me again, red faced and looking like he really wanted to hit me. It was the same way he'd looked at his boyfriend. I had no doubts this guy had a temper on him, and it didn't sit quite right with me. Not when he was apparently so quick to throw hands that his man reflexively covered his face.

"You remind me of another blond headed bully I knew back in the Bronx," I said. "He got the shit kicked out of him too eventually."

"You don't have a fucking thing to do with this," Landon hissed, getting in my face. "He was not supposed to be back until—"

"My guy, that's his apartment! The fuck? Are you dumb?" I looked up at the sky, and the brewing storm clouds in the distance. "Your trifling ass never even mentioned you had a boyfriend."

"Like it would have mattered," he said scathingly.

"You bet your narrow white ass it would have mattered," I countered. "I don't get in mess or break up relationships. I didn't even want to fuck a neighbor, my dude. Since I moved in, you had to beg me in like thirty-seven Grindr messages before I walked up those stairs."

"You dropped your pants really fast, though."

It was unbelievable that this piece of shit had just sent his boyfriend, the boyfriend he was obviously using, into a meltdown, and was still trying to talk shit to me.

"I'd have dropped them faster for your man." I smirked my filthiest smirk and winked for good measure. "What's his name? Charles? You're all right, but he's fucking beautiful. Has a nice culo on him too."

Landon went red and started to speak but before he could, the sound of a screen slamming up echoed on the quiet street. I ducked out of the way just as clothes began to rain down from the windows on the second floor of the house—an array of boxers, jeans, T-shirts, and flannel. When a weighted down gym bag narrowly missed nailing Landon, I retreated to the street. This was some Waiting to Exhale type of shit.

"What the *fuck*, Charles?" Landon shouted, jumping out of the way of the remains of his shitty stereo. "Just let me pack—"

"You thought that was a scene?" Charles' voice boomed from upstairs. "This is a scene, motherfucker."

I crossed my arms over my chest and watched in awe as Charles made a tapestry of the sidewalk, ranting loudly the entire time. It seemed like he'd shifted from horror to rage so loud that everyone on the block could hear him.

"—can't even keep a rhythm when you're fucking me!"

Wincing, I looked around just in time to see Mrs. Hernandez across the street standing in her driveway with Mr. Rosenblum. I waved, grinning, and they stared at me like I was surely the cause of this problem. This wasn't the chat with your neighbors type of neighborhood since it was a mish-mash of longtime home owners and homes that had been split up and rented out, but *man* they were wary of me. Maybe my moving-in BBQ had been a little too rowdy, but what was expected when I was finally given access to a real backyard?

"—find your mother and ask her to send you some more money!"

It started to drizzle, and Landon scurried around, shoving his clothes into bags and trying to get dressed in the process. It took twenty more minutes for him to haphazardly pack his shit, and by then I was drenched. I could have gone back into my own apartment mad long ago, but two things—I'd left my sneakers and my shirt up in their apartment, and I wanted to see Landon get gone. Part of me kept replaying the sight of Charles ducking and covering his face, and that part kept reminding me this shit was kind of funny, but it probably wasn't over. Landon was scum.

"I need my phone, you dumb bit—"

"I'll get it," I said, interrupting Landon's shout. "I left my sneakers upstairs, anyways."

He looked ready to argue, glanced up at the now quiet and closed windows, and nodded shortly. I thanked my lucky stars that I wouldn't have to beat his ass yet, and jogged up the staircase. Charles had already lined up the guy's Laptop, cell phone, wallet, and a backpack on the landing outside the door. Convenient for Landon because his shit wasn't smashed, but I still needed my stuff back.

"Coño..."

Grumbling, I shoved Landon's shit in his backpack, wondering how I'd become some kind of fucked up go-between, and shoved it at him. It wasn't until after he called an Uber and got in it five minutes later did I drag the rest of Charles' bags up to their—his——door. It was old, just like everything else in the house, but I couldn't help but notice a massive dent in it. Had it always been there? Or was it a sign of another violent altercation?

Maybe I should have hit him after all, but I wasn't trying to end up in jail...

Licking my lips and bouncing on the balls of my feet, I tapped at the door. It was completely silent. I tried again, pressed my ear to the door, and heard nothing. Not a single sound.

"The fuck..."

I closed my eyes and told myself to call the sneakers a loss and walk away, but... something about this whole thing felt wrong. What if the dude was hurt? Or planning to hurt himself? He'd looked absolutely defeated. Crushed to bits. And if I knew anything about the type of rage explosion he'd just had, it meant he was coming down hard right now, and probably feeling worse than he'd felt before. I could see it so clearly that I found myself turning the handle and slipping inside.

The place was a fucking wreck. There was shit broken and strewn everywhere. I walked around broken glass and other objects, moving slow on the creaky wooden floorboards, but there was no sign of the willowy man in the living room, sun room, kitchen, or their bedroom.

Wary, I stepped into my Nikes and grabbed my white T-shirt, but hesitated before slinking back to the door. Unless this Charles was a fucking wizard, there was no way he'd left this apartment.

I knocked on the bathroom door. "Hey, man. You alright?" He didn't respond, and worry upgraded to fear. "Look sweetheart, I know you probably hate me, but gimme a sign of life or I'm calling the cops. I'm not leaving you alone—"

"Mind your fucking business, dickhead."

My mouth twitched into a smile, but it quickly faded. The sass in that Brooklyn accent was still top notch, but there was a higher thread in it that sounded like pain. I shrugged off my mother's home training and looked into the bathroom.

"Damn, baby. What happened?"

Charles was hunched over the sink, letting water run over his hand, which was bleeding profusely. "I'm not—" His breath hitched, and he bit down on his lip before muffling out, "your baby."

"You're bleeding a fuckton. Did you... I mean, did you—"

"I didn't do it to myself," he growled. "I knocked over the bookshelf by accident, and broke this porcelain dancer figurine. It's... it was something my grandmother gave me before she died, and I fucking broke it by accident."

His voice cracked on the end, and I felt like a monster. Like somehow, him breaking it was my fault.

"I'm sorry. Maybe you can fix it or whatever." I glanced down at his hands again. "But you might need stitches, man. You should—"

"Just leave!"

My hands tightened around the side of the door, and I retreated a step. He was right. I was partially why he was in this state. I had no business here. No right. But...

"Look, you have any reason in the world to fucking hate me, but you're shaking really bad, and you're bleeding a lot. Just let me help you, and I'll go."

Charles kept biting his lower lip, brows bunched together. A beat passed, and he nodded jerkily. When he moved his trembling hands from the water, I saw why. Both his damn hands were bleeding. I hissed at the sight. "First aid kit?"

He jerked his chin at the medicine cabinet, and I quickly raided it. He didn't have a full kit the way I did, but there was gauze, tape, bandaids, and Neosporin, so that would work. I eyeballed all the blood, looked at his face, then asked, "Gloves?"

Charles' eyes narrowed defensively, and I held up my own hands.

"Hey, we don't know each other from a hole in the wall. Safety first, lindo. I'd do the same with, y'know, an eight-year-old on the— okay, maybe not. But like, any other—"

"Just shut the fuck up." His jaw clenched, and he cut his eyes away to stare at the window. He looked *so angry*, but he said in the same strained tone, "Under the sink."

I quit talking and found a mostly empty box of rubber gloves, slapped them on, and went to work. I was good at pretty much everything I did in life, but taking care of injuries was one of my ultra-important skills. Considering I'd come up in boxing clubs since I was a kid, and had had more than my fair share of injuries gained in legal and illegal rings, it was a necessity.

Charles kept his eyes on the window the whole time I carefully tended to each cut. They didn't look as deep as I'd assumed, so I found myself sneaking glances at him from time to time. The look on his face made my entire heart hurt. He was biting his lower lip and every now and then, a tear tracked down his cheek. He pressed his lips together tighter as if to keep from sobbing.

Guilt filled me, and an intense need to somehow make this better. Not just that, but I wanted to pull him against my chest and squeeze him. Rub his back while he cried and run my fingers through those wild glossy curls, even if he cursed me the entire time. Intense feelings of compassion weren't exactly rare for me, but usually self-preservation won out over just about everything else, and there was a good ass chance he would go full alley cat on me if I touched him wrong.

I knew that, but I couldn't stop staring at him. Even after I'd finished and he jerked his gaze back to me, I didn't turn away. I kept tracing his features, the big lips and huge dark eyes framed by thick lashes, his high cheekbones and thick arched eyebrows. Even with his skin blotchy, nose red, and eyes swollen from crying, he was one of the most striking people I'd ever seen.

I waited for him to tell me to leave, but when his lips parted he ended up sucking in an aborted sob.

"I don't think they're cut too bad," I said. "It just looked like a lot."

"Good. You can leave now."

I nodded, but didn't move. The need to do something kept bubbling up in my chest, and I continued to search him for a sign as to what could even be done.

"Look—"

"No," he whispered. "Just stop. I don't want to hear you."

"Listen," I pleaded. "I'll fuck off if you want me to, but I swear to God I had no idea he wasn't single. I've been living here for five months and never seen you once. And what you saw on the bed? That was as far as we got. First time I ever touched him. I can't speak for what else he did while you were gone, but all me and him did was kiss."

Charles shook his head slowly, but he didn't look incredulous. Just angry and tired. He didn't even wipe the frequent single tears sliding down his face.

"Why do you care?"

"Because I would never fuck up someone's—"

"No," Charles said. "You—why do you *care*? You're—" He looked me over, sniffling. "You're... *upset*."

"I just don't like hurting people."

Charles' gaze snapped up to meet mine and for just a minute, the hostility faded. He leaned against the sink and didn't cringe when I slowly put one hand on the counter beside him and lifted the other to gently wipe away one of his tears. He inhaled sharply, but didn't shove me away.

"What can I do?"

"Nothing," he whispered. "There's nothing."

"I can help you clean up," I said. "Since you have battle wounds?"

A choked sound escaped him that almost sounded like a laugh.

"Order you a pizza from Brothers? A sandwich from Hot Bagels?" I waited for a twitch, a glint in those damp eyes, a sign that he liked *something*. "Cookies from the Cookie Jar?"

For some fucked up reason, this caused him to cry *again*. I was either the worst at being sweet, or he had no idea how to respond to kindness right now. I wanted to touch him so bad. It was the only real way I knew how to console someone. In my family, physical contact was the ultimate form of affection, but...

"A hug?" I swiped another tear off his cheek. "Or you could hit me. I'm a fighter. I can take a punch or five."

Charles' eyes slid over me at that, taking stock of my broad shoulders, the thick muscles padding my frame, and probably all the tattoos and old scars that he could see since I was standing there with no shirt on. When that gaze returned to my face, there was a slight difference. An acknowledgement that he was really seeing me, and even if he hated it, he liked what he saw. That look, that change in the temperature around two men who had noticed each other, was what had first tipped me off that I wasn't exclusively attracted to women.

I stepped closer as my body responded to his awareness. "You could use me," I said quietly. "Stress release. Ragey rebound fuck. Whatever you wanna call it."

His lip curled, but his body shifted. I wondered if it was instinctual. He was looking at me like he wanted to hit me even as he widened his stance so I could press him against the sink.

"You must really think you're something," he whispered. "But at least I now see why you're being so nice."

"It's not like that."

"Sure."

There was contempt in Charles' voice, but he was breathing faster. It was him who shifted just enough for my crotch to press against his own. He might have hated me, but his body was interested.

"I'm good at three things." I pressed against him lightly and nearly melted when he released a liquid sounding groan. "Fighting, dancing, and fucking. Right now, I think you have more use for the first and last." If I shared that my dancing skills were usually used for stripping and burlesque, he might have more interest, but we didn't need to go there right now. "You wanna swing on me to get one back? I can take it. But if you want me to fuck you until you forget that douchebag's name? I can do that too. Just tell me how you want me."

A shiver tore through Charles' lanky body. He arched against me, hands reaching up to dig into my shoulders, but I didn't move another inch. He was still sneering even as his face flushed and his eyes dilated, and I knew went to wait for my move.

"I want you..." He licked his lips, heart pounding against my chest. "To get the fuck out of my apartment."

I backed up instantly. His fingers slid along my shoulders before falling away.

"I can do that too."

There was a flash of something in his face that might have been regret, or disappointment, but I didn't know him well enough to read him. All I knew was that I'd been given the "hands off" notice, and that was all I needed to know.

"Take care of yourself, man. That piece of shit doesn't deserve you." I backed out of the bathroom. "And I still might get you those cookies."

"Fuck your cookies."

"I'd rather fuck you. I wish I'd met you first." He stared at me, and I crinkled my fingers in a wave. "See you around."

When he didn't respond, I turned, grabbed my shirt, and strode to the door. In the living room, I caught sight of the porcelain figurine he'd referenced on the floor. Because I was a major sucker for a pretty face and tears, I scooped up the pieces in my T-shirt and took it with me. Gluing porcelain dancers was about to become another one of my skills.

I closed the door behind me after flipping the automatic lock, and headed downstairs. It wasn't until I was unlocking my own door, the door that stood directly next to his, that I realized I hadn't warned him that I lived downstairs in the same two-family house.

CHAPTER THREE
CHARLES

The doorbell yanked me out of nightmares that had teeth. No matter how deeply I slept, how much I drank to put myself into an even deeper sleep, the nightmares stalked me.

Dreams of Landon yelling at me, me begging Landon to come back, me deteriorating into a dark place I hadn't been in for about five years now, and nightmares about being trapped on that goddamn cruise ship again. Being trapped on it with Landon. Landon trying to throw me off the boat. Us both being arrested for brawling in the ship's ballroom.

Yeah, my dreams weren't welcoming. At all. I had no idea why I kept trying to succumb to a sleep more awful than my reality, but I couldn't stop. Two days since my flight had landed at JFK, and I hadn't even left my apartment to restock the barren refrigerator or go to the Verizon store. I'd drank the last of the vodka, ate Lunchables, and slept.

Until now. Because now someone was ringing the bell.

Groaning, I dragged myself up from the bed and staggered to the front door. My feet crunched over the random broken objects that still lay all over the hardwood floors, but I ignored them. At least it wasn't glass. I couldn't handle any further injuries. Not because I was super wounded—the cuts on my hands were already healing—but because it would remind me too much of... him.

The man with the tattoos.

Scowling, I stumbled down the stairs, opened the door leading to the foyer, but hesitated before opening the door separating the foyer from the rest of the world. What if it was Landon? I'd made sure to keep his keys. But...

"Charles? Is that you? I can see your hair."

Caleb's concerned voice was like a warm soothing blanket thrown all over my anxiety and fear. Pathetically, I felt myself coming undone all over again. When I yanked the door open, I practically jumped on him and proceeded to cry all over his soft polo shirt.

"What's happened?" Caleb demanded, holding me gently to his chest. "Your phone's been going to voice mail for two days, and I started to get paranoid. Did he hurt you?"

I shook my head, realized I was making a mess of him, and took a step back. "Um... not physically?"

Caleb looked me over carefully, those steady gray eyes searching for signs of abuse, before he sighed, a low angry sound. With pursed lips and clipped movements, he shut the outer door to the house. "Is he here?"

Caleb only sounded angry when he talked about Landon. It was something that used to make me feel guilty because part of me, even the parts that had been hurt, had always felt obligated to make excuses for Landon. To defend him. Now... Caleb's regal voice lowering with quiet rage comforted me.

"I kicked him out," I said, throay scratchy and raw from two days of sobbing and sleeping and not speaking. "It was bad. I made a huge scene. You would have been embarrassed."

"I'm sure he deserved whatever crippling humiliation you bestowed upon him," Caleb said reassuringly. He smiled, putting his big hands on my shoulders, and squeezed. "Why don't we—"

A loud creak emanated from behind the door next to mine, and I jumped. I put a hand over my heart, glancing back at the door, then at Caleb. "Let's go upstairs. My neighbors don't need to hear all this shit."

Caleb nodded, sliding his hands into the pockets of his khaki shorts, and followed me inside. "They didn't hear it when it was happening?" he asked quietly, ever conscious of people noticing *drama*.

"If they did, they didn't say anything. Although... I've been gone so long, the two sisters who stayed on the first floor could have moved out by now. Some of the houses on this block are like revolving doors."

"Strange. This neighborhood has good rent."

Of course he would know that. He'd probably researched it two years ago after learning I'd be moving to the city's forgotten borough. I didn't blame him. Before moving across the Verrazano, I'd never even stepped foot on Staten Island. The entire island had seemed like a strange bastard step child that people tried not to notice or talk about. I'd cringed at the idea of moving because it was so defined by the reputation of being strangely suburban, conservative, and full of people who acted like they'd escaped the set of Jersey Shore, but the cheap rent and larger square footage had won out. And, in the end, I loved my neighborhood and my beautiful apartment with never-before-seen square footage.

I halted in the upstairs doorway, and cringed at the idea of him seeing the mess of the apartment I've been so proud of. He'd never visited because of Landon, and now he'd be seeing it a total wreck. It was mortifying with a capital mort. I braced my hands on each side of the doorframe, but Caleb was a little taller than me and easily saw over my head.

"Oh, Charles…"

"I did it myself," I said defensively. "It's not like we brawled."

"Not this time?"

I pressed my lips together even as potential responses filled my ammo box of defensive retorts.

Caleb sighed, deep in his chest, and stepped around me to scrutinize everything. With his hands on his hips and tucked in shirt, his light brown and silver hair combed back behind his ears, he looked like a disapproving landlord. Or my super preppy older brother who'd gone to law school while I'd fucked my way across Europe before retiring to Staten Island to become a broke ass failure dancer of a hipster.

I wrinkled my nose. No Caleb as older brother analogies. Gross.

"Do you want me to not ask, Charles?"

Shrugging, I shut the door and locked each lock, including the deadbolt. "Honestly, boo? There's not much of a story. I came home unexpectedly, found out he was cheating on me and had a fucking meltdown. A meltdown that led to me throwing his shit out the window and mindlessly destroying some of my own." I turned, leaning against the door, and flashing a manic grin. "Classic Charles."

Caleb nodded, but he'd gone back to scrutinizing me instead of making fun of my theatrics. Not that Caleb ever made fun of me. He was one of the few people, maybe one of the only people, who didn't dismiss my highs and lows, or my frequent overreactive emotional responses, as "drama".

"What happened to your hands?"

"Hazzard of smashing stuff?"

His shoulders relaxed, and he went from platonically eyeballing my exposed skin to once again surveying my apartment. "Well," he said with a sigh. "Why don't you go shower, and I'll start cleaning?"

"Caleb—"

"Or, I could hire a cleaning crew while we go out for lunch? Oli says there's an amazing seafood restaurant in Totten—"

"*No.*" I put up my hands, waving them in front of me. "No crews. No outside."

"Then cleaning and delivered pizza?" Caleb nodded towards the bathroom. "You shower."

"Does that mean I smell bad?"

"Unfortunately, sweetheart, yes."

It was the least flattering thing to be told, probably ever, but his smile was so sweet and so... *Caleb* that warmth filled me. When everything was terrible, I could always count on him to be my rock. Sometimes it made me wonder what he got out of our friendship. He was always rescuing me, and I was just the person who forced him to attend boozy brunches and recommended fun new sex toys for he and Oli to try.

"Oli's lucky." It was out of my mouth before I could stop it. His smile turned a little apprehensive, and I forced an awkward laugh. "I'm just saying... You're so fucking good, Caleb. The actual best person I know. Not because you're reliable, but because you genuinely fucking care about people and expect nothing in return, and that's so rare. You're rare."

Awkwardness piled on top of his apprehension. "Ah, well, that is..."

"I used to have these fucked up fantasies about you telling me you were in love with me, and I'd leave Landon for you." Actual horror was blossoming over Caleb's face, and I started waving my hands as word vomit poured out of my gullet. "No, no, no, this was before Oli. I would never—I know, uh, I heard you guys are engaged now. I would never... secretly hope for anything bad to happen. I'm just—I was just trying to say, that... um. I wish I'd had someone like you instead of someone like Landon."

"Sweetheart, Landon is actual trash. If I was the sort to hire hitmen, or to know how to hire hitmen, I'd have had him killed the first time you came to my house with bruises."

I wanted to laugh and cry at the same time. How had I ever thought I was fooling him? What an idiot.

"I'm gonna go shower."

"I'll order pizza," he said. "Favorite place?"

"Brothe—" I cringed, remembering *that man* all over again. "Brothers. You can have it delivered with UberEats."

"On it."

I backed away, watching him furrow his brow at his phone. "Caleb?" He looked up. "Congratulations on your engagement. You better fucking make me your best man."

Caleb's smile was wide and beautiful and so full of relief that I wanted to hug him all over again. Instead, I scurried to the bathroom and stood under the too-cold-for-comfort water so the grime and sweat from two days of drinking and sleeping in a hot bedroom could drain away. I hoped my depression and self-loathing would go with it, but no go. As soon as I was alone, my thoughts flew back to Landon. Then they rewound to the past few years of our lives together.

How had I ever been so stupid? So desperate? I'd *known* he was cheating on me. My friends had warned me that they suspected him of being unfaithful while I was on the cruise. So, why was I so shocked? Why hadn't I left him before? Why hadn't I mentally prepared?

There was a small ugly part of me that wondered whether everyone was right about me. Did I live for drama, and that was why I'd stayed around? Had I found something exciting in the game of *gotcha* I'd been trying to play with Landon for years? The possibility made me sick, especially since everything else about our relationship had soured years ago.

How could I have been enjoying a game when I'd been too miserable to get anything else out of being together? The only reason as to why I'd stayed was that... I hadn't known how to leave him until he'd given me no choice. Somewhere along the line, I'd conditioned myself into thinking our combative relationship was normal. Or like there was something romantic about wild fights followed by intense passion, as if we were in an Eminem video.

I stepped foot out of the shower and wrapped myself in my favorite black and pink sugar-skull robe. I faced the mirror, preparing to cringe at my likely haggard face, but was instead hit with the memory of me on the sink and Luis' muscular body between my thighs.

The thought of him sexy and strong and propositioning me with pity and guilt in his eyes was enough to turn me on and make me want to break shit at the same time. The worst part was that I'd almost gone along with his little proposition. I'd pictured it so clearly—him fucking me until I saw stars instead of Landon's awful indifferent face—even before Luis had made his offer to let me use him.

Use him.

A shudder went through me. I told myself it was bone-chilling hatred for a man arrogant enough to try to fuck me after nearly fucking my boy—ex-boyfriend, and not another supersonic burst of lust. I could not be basic enough to regret that pathetic of a hookup. Pity sex was not, and would never be, something I stooped to. Especially not with that asshole.

Skipping an up-and-close-and-personal with my reflection, I walked out to the kitchen with water still dripping from my legs and hair. On autopilot, I popped the cork on a bottle of wine, and poured it in a glass for Caleb while sticking with a chipped I Can't Adult Today mug for myself.

He'd already cleared the living room and dance space of debris, and was in the process of using a microfiber rag to wipe down my bookshelf.

"Caleb, dusting isn't the issue."

"It should be. This bookshelf is outrageous."

Snorting out a laugh, I handed him his wine and flopped down on the purple velvet chaise lounge in the living room. He sat on a bright yellow arm chair, crossed his legs at the knee, and watched me over the rim of his glass.

"Are you waiting for me to tell you what happened in detail?"

"Yes," he said. "But I won't push if you don't want to talk about it. But I'll say this—if you admit he's put his hands on you again, I'm going to insist you go to the police."

"Caleb..."

"No, Charles, it's wrong. The fact that I haven't said it before now—" Caleb shook his head, eyes closing briefly. "He's an animal."

"Caleb, it's not like he beats me—"

"He hits you, and then you defend yourself, and you fight." Caleb's voice rose again, sharper this time. "How would you respond if it were Meredith and a boyfriend? Or Stephanie?"

"I'd kill the guy," I said without pause. "But it's—"

"No, it's not different, Charles!" Caleb put his wine glass down on a side table and sat on the edge of the chair. "Darling, abuse is abuse. That you're two men doesn't make it any less abusive. That you two tend to fuck after you fight doesn't make it any less abusive. It's not kink or rough sex. It's him *hitting you out of anger* and you *defending yourself.* So, if he comes around here again, if he threatens you or tries to intimidate you, you need to go to the police. You should also consider a restraining—"

"Stop. Just... stop."

My heart had begun to thrum in my chest as fear washed over me, a cold wave that lapped at my feet even after the initial shock retreated. The police? Fucking Christ. Landon would— I didn't want to think about what Landon would do if I ever called the cops on him, which meant Caleb was right.

"I should have left him a long time ago," I said finally. "But I was caught up in this fucked up... viewpoint that I had to make it all worth it. I had to stick it out because if I didn't, I'd gone through all the bullshit for no reason. I'd wasted the good years of my life... for nothing."

"The good years?"

I laughed dryly. "Before I met any of you, I was a fucking mess. *More* of a mess. Despite my relationship with Landon, the last couple of years have been the best since I was eighteen or nineteen."

"In what way? You never talk about your past except to call yourself a failed dancer."

"Because failed dancer was my primary identity," I said dryly.

"When I was younger, I had big dreams about being a famous dancer. In my mind, going to LaGuardia High School and getting into Julliard had proved that my success was fucking inevitable because I was talented and hot and everyone said I had the 'it' factor or whatever." Shaking my head, I looked into the depths of my mug and saw a random piece of lint floating in it. Nice. "I remember when I got into Julliard... God, I thought it meant I was guaranteed to be a professional dancer. Seven percent of applicants get into the dance program there, and I was one of them."

Caleb nodded, sympathy pouring out of him as he waited for me to explain how those dreams had stayed dreams. For most people, accepting the fact that your big dreams are unattainable is a part of life. It's a part of growing up. For me? It had crushed my soul. Realizing I'd have to endure a lifetime of mediocrity and unfulfilled potential had made my life seem... not worth living at all.

"I'd paid for school with financial aid and inheritance money from my grandparents. Well, the inheritance ran out faster than I was ready for because no one had ever told me how to manage money, and I realized I'd squandered like over a hundred-grand trying to become something that had never been fucking inevitable. So instead of trying to be a famous dancer, I quit and worked odd jobs and drank myself to sleep every night until I met Landon."

Caleb's shocked face drew a tiny smile out of me. I drank my lint dusted wine.

"Yeah, he was a friend of a friend who was letting me rent her couch. Landon suggested we get a place together since he also needed a roommate but had no credit to get an apartment in his name, and the rest is history."

"History?" Caleb asked scathingly. "You mean how he gas lit you into isolating yourself then convinced you to never get another job in entertainment? How he convinced you that you were pathetically holding onto a stupid dream, and how he made fun of the Carnival offer—"

"Caleb, I get it. I was there."

"I'm sorry," he said, exhaling slowly. "So, I'll ask outright. What finally caused you to throw him out?"

"I told you—I walked in and found him begging to be fucked by some guy. On *my* bed."

Caleb's jaw dropped, and I recounted every detail of what had transpired two days ago. Well, every detail that I could remember. There were parts that were blurry—especially after I'd started throwing shit out the window—but I painted a vivid picture complete with wild hand gestures and reenactments. By the time I was done, and had collapsed onto the chaise lounge again, I felt tired all over again. I'd been going for funny, but... no. I wasn't ready to look back on this and laugh just yet. It felt too much like I was the thing that needed laughing at. I was the joke.

"Who was the guy?" Caleb asked, seemingly bewildered. "A friend of his?"

"No. Fucking. Clue." I stood, my robe sliding down my shoulder as I strode to the kitchen to refill my mug. Caleb didn't follow, knowing my voice would reach across the apartment. "He was... just this guy. This tattooed, jacked up, super fucking hot guy named Luis. I'm assuming he lives nearby somewhere because he claimed he didn't know I existed and had never seen me around since he moved in."

"Were they dating?" Caleb asked once I'd returned to the living room with my mug and the bottle. "Was he also—"

"No, he wasn't upset," I said darkly, flopping down. "Well, he wasn't upset the way I was upset. He was distressed that... that he'd caused *me* to be upset."

Caleb blinked. "What?"

"Ugh. Caleb. He was all guilty looking and sad eyed and fucking *tended to my wounds* after Landon left. And I sat there and cried like an idiot while the guy who'd just been making out with my boyfriend bandaged me. It's pathetic."

"It's not pathetic," Caleb protested. "He doesn't sound terrible at least. It's not like he knew Landon had a boyfriend."

"Oh, fuck that. He offered to let me ride his dick for a little revenge sex. Not exactly a noble gentleman."

Caleb cradled the mug between his long fingers, weighing responses. Judging from the way his face flushed, I was going to guess they were responses relating to sexual relations.

"Perhaps you should at least consider rebound dating?"

"Babe. No. There is no rebound good enough to elevate me from the funk of that relationship."

"Well, no, but... maybe a distraction could help?" Caleb spread his hands, smiling a little hopelessly. "When David and I ended things, I fixated on him. Our relationship. Then all the things that were wrong with me. It wasn't until Oli came along did I stop constantly thinking about the past."

"Right, but Luis is not Oli."

"I didn't mean him."

Ah, right. Funny that my thoughts had automatically shifted back to Luis and his tattoos and thick biceps and thicker cock. The fact that my attraction tended to run hottest for men who were bad for me had to be a symptom of something terrible. The same terrible thing that had prevented me from ever seriously pursuing my past feelings for Caleb. Instead of making a move back when he'd been single, I'd stayed with Landon.

"Just consider leaving the apartment," he said. "Maybe not today or even for the rest of this week, but you can't hide forever, sweetheart."

"Wanna bet? That shitty job helped me save a nice little nest egg. I could probably hide in here for months."

"I'm sure you could, but..." Caleb tilted his head, watching me with so much worry that I felt guilty for causing him stress. "I know you, Charles. Being around people makes you happy. The longer you isolate yourself, the more you'll ruminate about what happened, and it will be harder to pull yourself out of this place."

"Ugh."

"Start small," he suggested. "Tomorrow, maybe go to the store? The next day, go to get a new phone."

"At that rate, I won't be rebound dating until Halloween," I joked.

"Maybe not, and that's okay. What's not okay is you blaming yourself for that bastard." Caleb practically spat the word, his handsome face twisting whenever he referenced Landon. "And hiding your light from the world because you're convinced you brought this situation on yourself."

"Didn't I?" I asked, laughing humorlessly. "Didn't I stay even after all my suspicions? After we started fighting? After everything? Didn't I fucking defend him and argue with you and Meredith whenever you dared to insult him?"

"Yes, you did those things, but that's because you kept fighting for a relationship that you thought you had to salvage." Caleb moved from the arm chair to sit beside me on the velvet lounge. "You and Landon were nothing like me and David, but I understand that instinct so specifically. I understand how you can twist yourself into a pretzel trying to tell yourself to force things to justify all the tears and the fighting and the wasted time."

His voice wobbled, and I pulled him into a hug. He squeezed me, and I closed my eyes, relishing in his nearness. In not being alone in this apartment anymore.

"It's not supposed to be like that when you love someone," Caleb went on, voice hushed. "There should be no doubt, no question, that your person is the person for you. The one who makes you happiest and who makes you feel most wanted. Who knows what you need even when you yourself aren't sure. The one who, despite ups and downs, will always have your back."

"I don't think I'll ever have that, Caleb. I'm too fucking jaded. Too wary. I feel like Landon ruined me for everyone."

Caleb shook his head, rubbing my back as tears welled in my eyes again. "It's not true. He's just a dark cloud that's been hovering and hiding your light for far too long."

"Maybe," I said. "Or maybe I'll just die alone with my trunk of sex toys."

Caleb released a startled laugh, and I pulled away, laughing too. I lifted the wine bottle, affected a big smile, and tried not to think about the fact that I had not been joking at all.

CHAPTER FOUR
LUIS

"**W**hen are you gonna fight again?"

"Aw, come on, Duffy," I groaned. "Can't you just make my food without causing me to have an existential crisis at ten in the morning?"

The man behind the counter puffed out his barrel chest with a scowl. "Save your big words for my daughter, bud. Just give me the info on your next fight so I can root for you in person."

"Duff, I'm literally done competing. I've found other things to do with my time."

"Uh-huh, yeah, sure, so how come you haven't started doing your personal trainer thing yet?"

I rolled my eyes up at the ceiling and sighed with exasperation, but I was smiling the whole time. If anyone ever would have suggested one of the first people on Staten Island to befriend me would be a fifty-something Irish American good ole' boy who owned a bagel shop, I'd have said they were nuts. But here we were.

I tended to pop into Hot Bagels after rush hour, so I was used to Big Duff's brand of prying during the mid-morning lull. Bagel shop owner, coffee connoisseur, and boxing fanatic—the dude was into all my favorite things. He even had a bisexual son, which he'd been quick to share because, apparently, word of my "scandal" had made the rounds in online boxing forums.

"I just haven't gotten around to it," I said, looking over the counter to watch him put the finishing touches—salt, pepper, and ketchup—on my breakfast sandwich. "I'm making good money doing what I'm doing right now, and having fun for the first fucking time ever, sooo..."

"Yeah, having fun shaking your ass like Magic Mike down at Male

Revue." Duffy shook his head, scowling, and folded my sandwich up neatly with wax paper and foil. "Or wearing funny costumes with that burlesque crap—"

"Hey! No dissing the boylesque. The troupe makes me way happier than my homophobic ass boxing team did, man. C'mon. Let me live."

Duffy's face softened at that, and he heaved another big sigh as he trudged over to the register. "All right, fine. But I sure hope you're saving the tips and dollar bills to open your gym, kiddo."

"That's the plan."

The plan would be a lot easier if I had a roommate to split costs with so I could afford to rent a studio or private gym to start training. I'd already had tons of followers on social media from boxing, and many of those people had reached out to ask about training and prices after my Instagram had transitioned from pictures and videos of me fighting to me working out. Unfortunately, the idea of giving up my first solo apartment and the beauty of privacy was rough.

Besides, dancing was fun, even though my stripping had been one of many things that had finally sealed the deal on rumors about me liking dick. My good mood dampened at the thought of the shitstorm that had rained down on me at my old boxing club in the Bronx, and the way social media had very briefly been a nightmare of constant homophobic backlash. There wasn't much that could get me shook, but having people I'd grown up with suddenly turn on me, drag me, and threaten me had been fucking traumatic.

The bell above the door jingled, signaling another customer to distract Duffy from his interrogation. Relieved, I went up to the counter to pay for my sandwich and coffee. His daughter greeted me with a smile even as she texted.

"What's up Adr—"

The words died on my tongue when I realized it was Charles who had entered. I stared at him like he was a mirage—a tall, long limbed, sinewy mirage with a cloud of dark curls, huge eyes, and the kind of style that was as abrasive as the expression on his face. His stonewash jeans were so full of gaping holes he was showing more skin than denim, and he had on a white tank top with a plunging neckline and arm holes that was embroidered with a rainbow-colored marijuana leaf.

He stopped in his tracks after catching sight of me, lips curling down. I wished I could see his eyes, but they were hidden beneath huge sunglasses.

"Hey baby," I said, grinning.

Charles cringed with his entire body and marched over to the bagel counter without giving me a second glance. It was an indicator to leave the man the fuck alone, but I wasn't too good at directions or taking cues even when I understood them, so I glanced back at him. Those skintight jeans were encasing his ass, and my God that culo was a thing of beauty. I wanted to see him naked more than I wanted my breakfast sandwich. I wanted to eat *him*. I'd feast on that ass of his all day long.

"Eight bucks," Adriana said from behind the register.

I ripped my gaze off Charles, who was standing tensely and growling out an order that Duffy had to lean forward to hear, and peeled a bunch of singles off a ridiculously thick wad. Adriana smirked knowingly.

"So, what's that my dad said about Male Revue…?"

"Twenty-one and older to get in," I said with a wink. "Meaning—Duffy's kid isn't allowed."

"Too bad. I could bring my boyfriend. He'd find it hilarious."

"How is the boyfriend?" I tried not to glance back at Charles even though my body was fully tuned into his presence. Somehow, I knew he'd already ordered. And I knew he was hanging back and waiting for me to leave before he could pay for whatever he'd ordered. "Still at MIT?"

"Yep. He just finished finals, and I'm picking him up next week."

"Nice little road trip for you two." After she nodded and looked back at her phone, I collected my brown paper bag and coffee. "I'll see you later. Tell your pops I said bye. And…" I leaned forward, lowering my voice and shoving another wad of bills at her. "I'm paying for the dude behind me."

"Um."

I was flashing a deuce and walking out of the bagel shop before Adriana could protest or ask her father how much to charge me for Charles' order. Something told me to haul ass, so I speed walked across the street and walked even faster up the hill. I'd made it nearly halfway back to the house before I heard a voice yell after me. A voice that was yelling something that vaguely sounded like, *get your ass back here, motherfucker.*

I didn't stop, but I slowed down to a leisurely stroll as Charles' long legs allowed him to catch up with me in only a few seconds.

"What the fuck is your problem?"

"Problem?" I cocked my head. "It's a beautiful day, I have a bagel sandwich and a cup of coffee—what would be the problem?"

"What's your problem with me, dickhead? Are you trying to piss me off on purpose?"

It was so absurd that I snorted out a laugh. His hand slammed down on my shoulder and dragged me to a stop three houses down from the one we shared. Not that he knew he was my upstairs neighbor just yet.

I let him spin me around, mostly because I liked the feel of his big hand clenching on my shoulder, and smiled. It was hard *not* to smile. Even while holding a greasy paper bag and an iced coffee, he was a beautifully enraged force of nature. Anger rolled off him and washed up against me in a way that would usually feel like a challenge. But instead of making me buck up defensively like I would have to just about anyone else, I struggled not to blatantly stare him down.

"I bought you breakfast. That's what makes you mad?"

"No, jerkoff, the guy who was fucking my boyfriend trying to pay his way to a guilt free conscience makes me mad," he snapped, voice echoing up and down the block. "I don't give a fuck about how bad you feel—"

"Ah-ah." I wagged my finger at him. "My conscience is as smooth and clear as my skin. I didn't know he had a man, and it's that simple. Every time I meet someone on Grindr, I ask them outright if they're involved. He lied. Not my fault."

Charles' face flushed, but he didn't deny it. "And that means I'm supposed to be your fucking friend? Because fuck that all the way to Tottenville."

"Nah, I don't want to be your friend."

"Oh that's right." Charles forced his voice to go higher into a mocking falsetto before jerking right back down to his typically deep register. "You were just so kindly going to let me ride or suck your cock."

"I could suck yours if it would make you feel better."

"I wouldn't let you touch me even if you were trying to save my life. I don't need your help or your dick or your *fucking* money."

Charles' jaw clenched so tight I could probably use it to cut glass.

His anger was no joke. It wasn't a flirtatious challenge. If I smiled again, he was going to physically assault me. I could feel it the way I could feel a coming punch in the ring. There was a lot of energy building inside of him that needed to release *somewhere*, and I had a feeling he wanted it to release in my face with a closed fist.

I'd never expected a pretty hipster dude to be so quick to throw hands, but he had the same simmer of aggression as some of the guys I'd known at the gym. Guys who'd started going to the gym so they'd figure out how to channel it. And of course, there were the other guys who didn't want to channel it, and who unleashed their rage on street corners and parks.

I wondered how Charles released all of that pent-up energy. How he worked it out. Was it fighting, fucking, or maybe dancing? Whatever it was—he needed that physical therapy. STAT.

It took me a minute to realize we'd been staring each other down in silence. He exhaled loudly and squeezed the iced coffee tight enough for the plastic to make a crinkling sound.

"Take the money," he rasped. "And leave me alone."

"Afraid I can't do that."

Charles shoved his sunglasses up to his forehead. He glared at me with such genuine hostility that I felt myself squaring my shoulders a bit, tilting my chin up, and waiting for him to do something silly. What a weird fucking situation to be in. He was taking all his Landon shit out on me, and it was ridiculous. Unfair even. I could verbally shred him if I wanted. Stun him with a list of reasons why he was throwing repeated tantrums at the wrong asshole. But I didn't because attraction aside, something about him was a little too familiar, and it drew me in. He reminded me of about a dozen angry young men I'd grown up with, who had zero control of their home lives and spent all their time taking out that frustration on the nearest target.

"Why the fuck is that?" he demanded, growing more belligerent and rough with each F bomb he dropped. "Are you a masochist? You want me to tell you how much I hate you on a regular basis?"

"Maybe. Maybe it turns me on." When he kept glaring at me with those flashing dark eyes, I jerked my chin at the house and the Dominican flag hanging at the bottom of the big picture window on the first floor. "And sorry to be the bearer of bad news, but... I live downstairs from you. Moved in around the holidays."

Charles turned to stone before me, an eerie calm falling over him before all that fury came roaring back. He fumbled in his pockets with jerky movements, face flushed even redder by the time he yanked out a handful of balled up bills and change.

"Take the fucking money."

"I don't need it."

"Take it!"

His shout echoed on the quiet street and, this time, I couldn't help it. I laughed.

Charles' nostrils flared, his lip curling. "Then take the fucking drink."

It didn't click until his arm jerked back and then forward, splashing iced coffee all over the front of my white T-shirt. I was so stunned that I could do nothing but stand there and stare silently as he turned on his heel and fled to the house. When he jerked the door open, I rallied.

"I see you kept that bagel, though!"

"*Fuck you.*"

Charles threw one last furious look at me, shoved his sunglasses back into place, and stormed inside. He slammed the door shut, and I was left wondering why I was so into someone who was so not into me. But that tended to be my curse. Whether I was fantasizing about a guy at the boxing club, or Ashton fucking Townsend, I tended to want people who would never actually give me the time of day.

Pointless crushes were so much easier than dedicated relationships and real dating, though. Or, that's what I'd always told myself. I'd come up blowing random dudes in stairwells and rooftops of the Butler Housing Projects, so I knew a lot about pointless crushes. Every guy I'd hooked up with for the past decade had ranged from straight-acting guys who would never come out and be with me for real since they were either secretly married or had a girl, or feared getting their fucking asses whooped by other people in the neighborhood. It had always been quick and dirty sex at random in the shadows where no one would ever see.

Having an actual boyfriend had seemed as impossible and pointless as waking up straight. I'd never known any other guy who was openly gay or bi except my former boxing rival Valdrin Leka, and even he'd never copped to it until his Hollywood boyfriend had come along. So, meeting Charles, who was out and proud and fucking loud, combined with his hot temper and quick tongue, was... different. Really different. It just made me want to know more about him.

I looked down at my shirt and pondered the lightness of the coffee and Charles' over usage of creamer. There were a number of innuendos I could have made about that had I been quicker with the wits and less focused on the heated staring.

A cackle exploded from across the street. Mrs. Hernandez was standing there in one of the neon sweatsuits she wore to go jogging in Willowbrook Park, and she was grinning from ear-to-ear.

I jerked a thumb at the mess. "This amuses you, vieja?"

She nodded, still dimpling at me from across the street. "You should have stayed away from that boy."

That smelled like information that needed to make it to my open ears, so I crossed the street as if I wasn't a mess, and casually sipped my own coffee as if I wasn't covered with somebody else's. "I'm an innocent in this. I didn't know he existed let alone that he was a boyfriend."

"Oh, so innocent." She snorted at me. Up close, she wasn't much of a vieja after all—even though she acted like a grumpy old person, she looked my mom's age. Mid-forties at the latest. She also had dyed blond hair like my mom. "You've had boys in and out of your apartment since you moved in, plus the loud music every night."

"You have me all wrong, mami. Swear to God. Seventy-five percent of those guys are guys from my dance troupe. And that music? Me practicing." She eyeballed me suspiciously, and I grinned. "Besides, what do you care?"

"I don't," she said bluntly. "But messing with those two was stupid. Everyone on the block could have told you they fight nonstop.

Everyone hears. A couple of times, I nearly called the cops because it sounded violent."

I looked back at the house and up to the windows in Charles' sun room. "No one did anything?"

"What were we supposed to do?" Mrs. Hernandez twisted her mouth skeptically, one eyebrow shooting up. "The one time my son tried, it was because the other one chased the gay one—"

"Mami, they're both gay."

She waved her hand. "The stupid asshole who got his clothes thrown out chased that one—" she pointed one fingernail up to the apartment. "—down the street while screaming at him about how often he goes out. They had it out right there by the light."

"Had it out as in they came to blows?" My voice rose at the very thought, and adrenaline pumped through me as if there was anything I could do about it now. "That motherfucker."

Mrs. Hernandez looked at me sideways for a moment, her mouth quirking up. "No, they didn't fight, but the other one was trying to force the one with the hair back into the house. My son went and broke them up, and he nearly got into it with that asshole. I'm glad he's gone."

"Yeah, me too. Fuck him."

Thinking back to the day he'd jumped in his Uber, I regretted not saying or doing more. Hindsight was twenty-twenty and all that, but in hindsight I should have kicked his ass. Not that Charles wanted me to be his hero. He didn't even want me to buy him coffee or look in his direction.

"From an objective point of view," I said to Mrs. Hernandez while looking up at those windows again. "How likely is it that the one with the hair will ever be cool with me?"

"He's more likely to set your ass on fire."

She was not wrong.

CHAPTER FIVE
CHARLES

The dancing boy figurine was sitting outside my door in the middle of the landing.

At first, I thought it had to be a hallucination. Or maybe it wasn't the same figurine. I'd accidentally smashed it to bits while spinning out of control in my wildest meltdown to date, and had assumed Caleb swept the pieces away. The delicate porcelain statue being gone had hurt me almost as badly as Landon.

Not only was it beautiful, but it symbolized so much in my life. The dancer was androgynous with long hair tied in a bun and slender limbs, wearing a tutu and leotard, and flawless makeup, but he was a boy. As a young person, I had been awed that an artist had spent time creating something that meant so much to me, as if they'd created it with me in mind. But even more so, it'd meant everything that my grandmother had found it and gifted it to me. Her acceptance, in a sea of turned faces and shame, had meant the world.

I gingerly picked it up, examining it closely, and realized someone had glued it back together. There were some pieces missing—the tiny length of a finger and an ear—but my dancing boy was in one piece. I could not imagine the time and patience it must have taken to recreate the figurine. I equally couldn't imagine who would have done it.

I backtracked into the apartment, cupping the tiny porcelain statue before returning it to its place on the bookshelf. As I dragged the pad of my finger along the carefully pushed together pieces, signs of someone hunching over this pastel chunk of my childhood and waiting for glue to dry, I smiled for the first time in days.

A sudden blast of reggaeton filled the apartment through the floorboards, and I froze with my finger pressed to the dancing boy's torso.

Could it have been...

No. There was no way. It had to be someone else.

Maybe Caleb? But no, I'd never discussed the dancing boy with him. And he'd have knocked on my door to return it before checking in about why I'd yet to go buy a new phone.

Landon would have known what the figurine meant, but I'd broken it after he'd left. And besides that, he would have never spent so much time on something so tedious. Something that was only important to me. He hadn't even bothered to water my plants while I was gone.

The only other person who'd been in the apartment, who I'd discussed the figurine with, had been Luis. Luis, with his warm brown eyes, wise guy smirk, muscles, and tattoos. Luis, who had paid for my coffee before having it thrown all over his crisp white T-shirt.

Fuck.

The brief moment of happiness faded, and my spirits sunk to my faded motorcycle boots. I'd been dressed to pound the pavement and start applying for new jobs, maybe even at bars in the area, but weariness filled me. Why did being depressed have to make me so fucking tired? Even simple tasks seemed impossible these days. Brushing my teeth, showering, tending to my increasingly wild curls, and eating. I'd cook, enjoy the smell, and lose my appetite almost as soon as it was on my plate. The act of chewing and swallowing seemed monumental. Washing dishes? An impossibility. Going to the grocery store was a nightmare.

This morning had been my first spark of motivation in two weeks. I'd planned to go to the mall, get a new phone, and apply to some jobs along the way. But now? After realizing I'd thrown a fit that had resulted in me throwing coffee all over the guy who'd saved my dancing boy? I wanted to go right back to bed.

Groaning, I slid to the floor and slumped down in a child's pose, arms stretched forward and head pressed to the floor. It helped with the tension and tightness in my back, but did nothing to spark enough energy to deal with the outside world. It didn't help that it was gray and drizzling. It didn't help that a voice in the back of my head was whispering that I'd probably piss off someone else while at the mall.

Or get in another argument with a salesman because I refused to go back to iPhones. It happened every single time I went phone shopping.

I took a deep breath, and another, and let Luis' blasting music wash over me. The floors and walls in the house were paper thin, so I could hear the beat clearly. It was music to move to. Honestly, it was music to fuck to. Not slow or sensual, but aggressive and challenging. A tempo that was so off the chain it dared you to try to keep pace with your steps. With my eyes shut, and my brain disengaged from everything else, I found myself choreographing an entire sequence of steps. When the sound of feet slamming against a floor began to match the music, I had a moment of profound concern that I was hallucinating. Then I realized the sounds were coming from below me.

Luis was dancing.

It took all of five seconds for me to press my ear to the floor like a complete freak. For several seconds, I could hear nothing but the music but then, half a beat later, the unmistakable sound of sneakers hitting the wooden floors. I could easily picture him dancing to this, shirtless and sweaty with his tattoos glistening.

The music stopped abruptly, the house lapsing into silence, and I realized what a fool I was being—laying on the floor and eavesdropping. But then the song restarted, and the faint sound of him dancing caught my ear again.

He wasn't just dancing. He was practicing. My breath caught, and a half smile crept over my face. My own practice sessions on the cruise had been incredibly dull. Dull music for older guests who wanted pre-Johnny shows instead of faster beats with dirtier dancing. I'd wanted to drown myself on a regular basis, even more so because the other dancers hadn't minded. There was something to be said about commiserating for comradery, and being the only creative on the boat to notice that the passion was non-existent had been awful.

I sat up, hands pressed to the floor, and looked up at my dancing boy again.

What would Luis be practicing for? A sexy video? Posting something on Instagram or Snapchat? Just perfecting his dance moves for a night out or a party? I had no idea, but I suddenly wanted to know. I was addicted to performance, and endlessly intrigued by other performers. Even ones who made me want to crawl out of my skin from discomfort, embarrassment, and shame.

I got up and found a piece of paper and a pen in the kitchen's junk drawer. After a moment of staring, and listening to the music, I jotted down a note.

Thanks for fixing my dancing boy. I don't know what you think this is going to do, but okay.

It was as nice as I could manage, which really said something about my state of mind. Even so, I didn't change the note, and stalled. I checked the weather—thunderstorms looming, the time the bus was said to arrive down the block—five minutes, and randomly decided to take out the trash all before heading downstairs.

The music was still blaring, but the song had changed. It got louder the closer I got to the entryway, and was honestly the perfect distraction for me to shove the paper beneath his door. But I still punked out. Shoved the note in my pocket and rushed outside with the bag of garbage in my hand.

Saying thank you in an incredibly shitty way was nothing to be hesitant over. Yet I *was* hesitant. Not just to acknowledge the time he'd spent on his newest version of "I'm sorry", but to let my guard down even a little. He'd already seen me at my absolutely lowest point and had witnessed epic explosions of rage. I made it a point to never show that side of myself to anyone other than Landon, who had inspired it. Ashton, Mere, Steph and Jace had never seen me lose my shit. Not even Caleb. But Luis? He'd seen it all. And then some.

Cursing myself, I jogged down the stairs, cursing more when thunder boomed in the distance. It was an omen for leaving the house. Had to be.

I jerked up my hood just as it started to drizzle, and went to the side of the house to toss the garbage into the can. It put me level with one of the picture windows in Luis' living room, and because I had no self-control, I looked up.

He wasn't just twerking along to music with his phone docked somewhere and recording. He was *really fucking dancing*. The drizzle turned into a full-on downpour but I stood there as rain pelted me, and watched as Luis stood facing away from me in the middle of a room that had been cleared of furniture. He was using it as a dance studio—the same way I did with my dining room.

Inside, Luis was shirtless and wearing a pair of tight grey sweatpants, slicked with sweat just as I'd imagined, and performing an obviously choreographed dance. The professional part of me, the creative part, wanted to memorize the moves so I could try it myself. I analyzed the timing as he twisted from one side to the other, spun before arching forward with his entire body, and jumped into a spin before landing with a mesmerizing gyration of his hips. But the slut part of me that wanted to lick the sweat from his back could only focus on the motion of his hips and ass. Someone that good at thrusting and writhing against the air had to be an amazing fuck.

I stood in the rain as the song drew to the end, but just before it did, Luis flipped backwards into a handstand. With his crotch level with the window, and my face, he pumped the air with his hips. There was nothing hiding his dick print. Regret ripped through me because, honestly? I could have had that dick in me if I'd taken him up on his offer. And I hadn't been fucked in over six months.

Thunder cracked again, and I glanced up at the sky. Ominous clouds were ominous. It was time to stop thirsting and go. I backed away and snuck a look at the window again just in time for the song to end and Luis to flip to his feet. He was dripping sweat and breathing hard, and his eyes immediately met my own.

Fuck.

Luis' eyebrows shot up, and the fucker started laughing.

God, I hated him. Repaired dancing boy figurine be damned, I could not stand this cocky bastard.

I flipped him off and spun on my heel, stomping away from the house in the rain.

"Finally, motherfucker," Stephanie said, after picking up on the second ring. "I thought you were dead."

I snorted and trudged up the hill from the bus stop, holding a black bag from the Verizon store and a shopping bag from Express. Express was usually the kind of evil I stayed away from, but a pair of tight black joggers with leather knee patches and zippers called to me in a way that I had to answer.

"I'm not on social media for two weeks, and you thought I died?"

"No, asshole. You vanished right after coming back to the city. I figured you were either dead or trying to fit six months' worth of sex into two weeks."

"Ha. Well, awkwardly enough, that won't be happening since I'm now single." When she didn't say anything, I scoffed. "So, I take it everyone knows."

"Yeah, he kind of had a Snapchat meltdown."

My stomach twisted and bile rose in my throat. I knew, deep down, that nothing he said would affect my friends' opinion of me, but... what if it did? It was enough to feel exposed and caught out there in my own corner of the city even without every single one of my associates bearing witness to it as well.

"And?" I asked, voice dropping lower as the rain once again began to pound against me. I clutched my umbrella and walked faster. "What did he say?"

"It was incoherent, to be honest. But it alluded to the fact that you destroyed all his belongings because you caught him with another guy, and yet he knows you were fucking everyone on the cruise ship."

Okay, not what I'd expected. "That's stupid. I'm a flirt, but I would never cheat on him."

"Yeah, everyone told him he was a fucking idiot. You were faithful to him even when he was trying to fuck anything with a pulse. We dragged him, and he deleted it like an hour later."

I nodded even though she couldn't see me. The idea of my friends, and maybe even my mutual friends with Landon, having my back should have calmed me, but it didn't. I knew Landon. Being shut down and publicly humiliated would have enraged him, and even though I had not been involved with the shit show, he was surely blaming me.

It was only a matter of time before he went on a full campaign to smear me and show his own innocence. To make me look like a master manipulator who convinced my friends he was the bad guy, meanwhile he was misunderstood and mistreated. That was his game. To keep me isolated and wary that my own friends would turn against me. To have me believe I couldn't trust anyone.

Another jolt of thunder boomed in the sky, and I jumped. I'd hung around the mall so long, telling myself wandering was the equivalent of peopling even if I spoke to no one, that it was now dark as hell. Normally that wouldn't affect me. Now, I kept wondering if Landon would pop up, grab my arm, and demand to know where I'd been.

"Hey babe, let me call you back, okay? It's pouring."

"Okay, papi. Please call me. I want to talk to you."

"I will. Promise."

"Okay," she said, sounding skeptical. "Love you."

"Love you too."

I shoved my new phone into my pocket and jogged the rest of the way to the house, eyes darting around the streets and corners. Landon had never leapt out at me in the dark before, but he had loitered around bus stops waiting for me to return home. His plan had always been to catch me before I was prepared for one of his interrogations, but I'd never had anything to hide. Because, as Stephanie had said, I'd been unwaveringly faithful.

Luis' apartment was still and dark when I approached the house, which twisted my guts a little more. Sometimes I wondered what would happen if Landon showed up to confront me instead of manipulating me from afar, and I wasn't prepared for that. We'd had fights before, but only over petty stuff that had spiraled. Never over something like this.

The skittish feeling didn't fade even after I was in the house and dropping my bags. I went through each room of the apartment, opening closets and the bathroom, making sure no one was lurking, and only then did I calm. Which is when thunder exploded loudly, indicating a lightning strike nearby, and the power went out.

"Fuck," I hissed. "Really?"

I squeezed my eyes shut, counted to ten, and waited for my heart to slow before heading outside again. The good thing about the house was that the landlord had converted the basement to a laundry room, so tenants had access to it and the circuit breaker. I was hoping it was just the circuit breaker that had been tripped, anyway. Sitting in the dark for hours on end in my current state sounded fucking horrendous.

The rain drenched me as I jogged down the front steps and around the side of the house to the basement door. I found it unlocked, and stumbled my way down the narrow stairs in the pitch black. My boots slipped once I reached the bottom step. I flailed wildly, spinning as I grasped for something to hold onto. The wall was the only thing I managed to press my hand against, but a presence behind me sent me scrambling again. A hand brushed my shoulder and a chest pressed against my wet jacket, bumping me against the wall.

I slammed my elbow back, hitting a solid chest, and stomped my booted foot on the man's instep. A grunt exploded in my ear.

"Hijo de la gran puta—"

The words didn't process in my ear because all I felt was panic and a need to escape. I shoved my back against his chest, trying to get away. When that failed to work, I wildly tried to aim my elbow for his solar plexus. That snapped my attacker out of his lull, because he grabbed my hands with a powerful grip and slammed them both up against the wall.

"Let me fucking—"

"Oye lindo, it's just me."

Things clicked into place. Spanish. Broad muscular chest. The smell of cologne. Unlocked door.

Luis.

Not Landon.

Luis, who lived here and who would have gone down to flip the breakers.

Not Landon.

My breath gusted out of me in heavy pants, but I didn't move. Everything felt surreal, and my heart was beating so fast it felt close to bursting through my chest. I closed my eyes, inhaling deeply, and let him pin me against the wall.

"You good?"

I scoffed at the absurdity of the question. No, I wanted to say. I'm not fucking good. I'm a mess. I'm terrified of my own shadow. I'm ashamed of having stayed with Landon for so long. I hate myself for various good reasons. I want to hate you for various irrational ones.

"Hey..." Luis released my hands but wrapped a strong arm around my chest. He felt so warm against me, so solid, that I didn't pull away. "Tell me you're okay if you're okay. You got me worried."

"I don't need you to worry about me."

"But I am, anyway. I wasn't trying to scare you." His fingers ghosted over my face and dragged along my forehead. He probably meant the gentle touch to calm me, but it had the opposite effect, and my stomach flipped. "I was trying to help you not crack your fucking head open on the radiator like I almost did when I came down."

"I don't need you trying to save my life either."

His fingers slid through my wet hair, smoothing it away from my face. My breathing hitched, and the sound was regretfully loud in the quiet basement. His hand dropped to my chest, brushing along one hard nipple, and I felt his dick twitch against my ass. I inhaled again, and the following exhale bordered on a groan. Without thinking, I pressed back on his crotch. His hips canted against me. It was an abrupt movement, like he hadn't planned it, but I went from embarrassed and scared to absurdly turned on.

Fuck, why was I like this?

We were both breathing heavily now, and it got worse when he planted his hands against the wall on either side of me. My wet hair was all in his face, so he smoothed it away again. This time, his calloused fingers grazed my parted lips. His dick got harder against me. I fucking loved that I could feel every inch of him responding to my body. It had been so long since someone had wanted me.

Luis pressed his mouth to my ear. "Is there anything you need from me?"

"No," I croaked. "Just the lights on."

There was a pause where I wondered if he would push. Maybe reach around and grab the bulge straining against my jeans. Or yank my face to the side and take my mouth in a forceful demanding kiss. Rip my jeans down, even if I protested a little, and show me what else those muscles were good for besides fighting. And dancing.

But he didn't.

He stepped away without a word and left me panting against the wall. I squeezed my eyes shut, tried to catch my breath, and tried not to think about the erection raging in my jeans. I turned so my back was to the wall and listened to him move around in the dark. There were some thumps, a mumbled swear, and then I heard the clank of the metallic circuit box.

I heard a couple of snapping sounds before the small bulb above the washing machine and dryer lit up. I'd been waiting for lights but now with one dangling above me, I felt exposed. I was drenched, hair a mess, pale, and honestly not looking my best in general after two weeks of hiding in my apartment with little grooming. But Luis? Everything from his haircut, to his carefully trimmed facial hair, to his body was perfection.

Cringing, I turned away and hurried for the door. He was right behind me, walking a little too close but not speaking. When he paused to lock the basement, I tried to force myself to sprint around the house and into my apartment, but I paused in the much lighter rainfall. Drops fell on his shoulder, and the light on the side of the house illuminated their slow slide down the muscular stretch of his back.

He turned to me and looked surprised that I was still there. "I didn't mean to scare you."

"I know." I cleared my throat, and flicked my gaze around to avoid meeting his dark eyes. "Look, Luis, I just wanted to say..."

"You're sorry for beating me up?"

I snorted. "Yeah, right. I thought you said you could take it because you're a fighter."

"Yeah," he agreed, nodding slowly as his gaze slowly scanned me. "I said some other shit too."

God, why was *he* like this? Shameless unrelenting fucking flirt. And he was filthy about it too. Not coy. Not teasing. Not going for charming or sweet. Everything from the way he ran his eyes all over me to the way he bit the side of his lip made it clear that he wanted to fuck. He wanted to fuck badly. Probably over and over again.

I cleared my throat and focused on the street. "Thanks. By the way. For fixing my figurine."

"Don't worry about it. It was my fault."

My lips mashed together, and I concentrated really hard on not correcting him. It wasn't his fault. As much as I wanted to blame him, to dislike him, to take every ounce of my rage out on the nearest and easiest target, none of it'd had anything to do with him.

"And," I said haltingly. "About earlier." From the corner of my eye, I saw those shapely lips of his forming into another rakish smile. Ugh. Cocky motherfucker. "I wasn't spying on you, you conceited prick. I was just surprised about the dancing."

"Yeah?" His tone of voice was so smug and humoring. As if he thought I was full of shit. "Why's that?"

"Because I'm a dancer too," I snapped. "That's why I was gone for six months. I was on a Carnival cruise as a dancer in cabaret shows."

Luis dropped the arrogant smirk and his eyes opened a bit wider. "Yeah? How'd you get a gig like that?"

His response gave me pause. I could smell the interest on him. The excitement at the prospect of dancing leading to a real job. It was exactly the way I'd reacted after hearing about an opening eight months ago.

"It was awful," I said flatly. "You would never get to do the type of dancing you were doing in your living room. It's country club bullshit with safe performances and no creativity whatsoever. I was surrounded by stone cold suckers."

"Damn, baby," Luis said, laughing. "Tell me how you really feel."

"I'm just saying. You wouldn't like it. I can tell." When Luis opened his mouth to ask me more, I turned away. This was not a conversation I was going to have with him. I'd rather talk about the size of his dick than the artistic connection I could already feel forming between us. "Anyway, thank you for fixing my dancing boy. And I'm sorry for throwing coffee all over you."

"Not a problem," he called after me as I headed for the front steps. "It was barely coffee, anyway. I can tell you like a lot of cream."

I tripped on the bottom step and grit my teeth when the sound of his laugh floated from around the side of the house.

CHAPTER SIX
CHARLES

I couldn't decide if my lack of desire to travel outside of Staten Island was yet another insidious part of my depression or a sign that I was over the bar scene in Williamsburg and the Lower East Side. For a car-less person, living in Staten Island was like residing on the moon. People knew it existed, saw signs of it every time they got on the R train or spied the giant orange ferry crossing the East River, but they weren't sure what people actually *did* there.

Once upon a time—okay, like two years ago—I was one of those people. I enjoyed the cheap rent and the access to delicious bagels, but I turned my nose up about just every other aspect of the borough. I'd spent a solid twenty hours a week just getting back and forth to my apartment in my first year of living on the island. Now? I couldn't bring myself to make the trek across the river. And I certainly wasn't set up to spend over a hundred bucks one way in an Uber or Lyft, draining the tiny nest egg in my bank account, when the job hunt wasn't going well.

After hours of pouring over job listings on LinkedIn and Craigslist, my will to leave the apartment shrank further. It was strange to consider how experienced I felt, and how competent I knew I could be, only for the Internet to make me feel like I was worth nothing. I'd briefly looked at administrative jobs because—why not? Maybe putting myself in a nine-to-five scenario with actual benefits for the first time in my life would ground me.

But no.

Apparently, I was not experienced enough for administrative work. I also did not have a college degree in anything that meant something to people outside of the entertainment industry. Two years

SANTINO HASSELL

at Julliard apparently meant shit if you wanted a job as a receptionist. Same if you wanted to be a personal assistant—which I actually thought I'd be good at but had zero experience in.

The failures in those sections had led to me slinking back to listings for service jobs—bartender, waiter, host. Those were things I had the most experience in. Those were jobs I *knew* I was good at. And they were jobs I fucking hated with every fiber of my being.

If I was honest with myself, I'd been suffering from a continuous low-grade depression since leaving Julliard. So having to *always* be around people while wearing a big fake smile, having to be *on* in order to get the tips I needed to survive? It was soul sucking. And exhausting. It had been that way before the cruise, so now that my state of mind and general mood had deteriorated further? Impossible.

With office and service jobs on my do-not-want and cannot-have lists, I girded my loins and navigated my way to backstage.com. The website was basically a trap because it exclusively listed performance-based casting calls and jobs, but every creative in the Tri-state area flocked to it. There had been so many times when I'd shown up for a call for dancers in a show, or a music video, or a tour, only to end up on a line with hundreds of other people. And the times I *had* scored a gig, my pay had been along the lines of five or six hundred bucks a week.

Unless I made it big, it wasn't a livable wage. I couldn't figure out *how* to make it a livable wage. At the end of the day, I wasn't good at figuring out how to exist in this city as a creative person with no desire for a "normal job". I wasn't like Ashton or Meredith or Jace. I didn't have the luxury of wealth to back up my passion projects. I had to hustle to exist in New York, and to try to match their lifestyles, and I was frankly... exhausted by it. I was exhausted by living in a city meant for rich people with rich friends who would never understand why the fuck I was so disgusted with my life.

I was even exhausted by having to explain my depression to non-rich friends who didn't understand my rants about not being able to follow my passions. It wasn't their fault. I knew it wasn't. They'd found their niches and were happy there. But my only niche was dancing, and it was hard to accept a life of mediocrity when I knew I had so much more potential.

Bleakness settled over me, and my throat constricted. Here came

50

the tears. It was almost a month since I'd returned to the five boroughs, and I couldn't think of a day that hadn't led to me crying at least once.

"Fuck," I whispered, pushing myself to my feet. "Enough already, Charles."

I abandoned my laptop on the floor where I'd been sprawled, ignored the phone I had still yet to fill with social media apps, and went into self-care mode. Survival instincts for me led to me sitting in the papasan in my sunroom in my underwear with my feet propped up on the window sill as I smoked a perfectly rolled joint and drank a glass of wine.

It was sunny outside for what felt like the first time in days. I set my phone to play a random list of my favorite song, closed my eyes while absorbing the delicious Vitamin D, and inhaled deeply. I was pretty sure I was smoking Landon's stash, but the asshole had yet to contact me or attempt to return to it, so I figured it was safe. And he hated wine, so my collection had sat untouched for months.

The combination of my favorite things eased the stress from my body and turned me into a languid mass. While slightly baked, I could console myself with the knowledge that I had at least three or four months before I completely ran out of money for rent and bills. Finding a job *right now* was not urgent. If anything, maybe I could get spend a couple of months getting a handle on my depression—maybe even seeing a doctor—before venturing out into the world again. Maybe I could just hide out in Staten Island and learn how to be a version of Charles who didn't always need to be surrounded by friends and parties and events.

The daydream of a fresh new me lulled me into a daze, but the sound of a deep voice speaking Spanish snapped me right out of it. My neighborhood was a solid mix of just about every ethnicity, leaning more heavily towards Latinx, so it could have been anyone's voice. But I knew it wasn't. My awareness of Luis had fucking quadrupled since our little moment in the basement.

Because my apartment was usually so quiet, and we both kept our windows open, I heard every random thing he did. When he woke up and hummed to himself, when he spoke loudly on the phone in rapid-fire Spanish, when he watched TV, and especially when he played music and danced. It was a struggle to *not* find reasons to spy on him again, but... I wanted to see.

It didn't help that we'd started playing weird games. The other day, we'd both been at Hot Bagels yet again but this time *I'd* paid for *his* breakfast before leaving in a rush and hopping on the bus. He'd followed up by ringing my bell and leaving a pink drink from Starbucks in front of my door. How he'd known I was a whore for pink drinks was beyond me, but I suspected my downstairs neighbor had found my Instagram where I'd done near weekly posts of me holding the beverage.

I'd slipped a handwritten 'thank you, creep' note under his door. Then he'd started leaving a neat stack of my mail by my door since the mailperson jumbled it all together and shoved it in our joint box. I returned the favor by leaving Landon's unopened Species protein powder in front of his, because I wanted nothing to do with that shit and it was expensive as hell.

We were like, silently courting each other, but when we crossed paths? No words spoken. Just a nod, an eyefuck, and we went on our ways. This was not normal. It was even less normal that I went out of my way to avoid him but then moments like now, when he was walking down the street, I peered down like a freak of nature.

"Yo no voy pa'alla mami. Por Dios que no. Si tu quieres verme, ven a Staten Island. No estoy por buscar problemas con Bronson y su gente.."

I was only able to pick out bits of his words to translate, but it seemed like he didn't want to go back to the Bronx to avoid getting in a fight with someone named Bronson. Also, he was talking to his mother. Which was cute.

I watched him stride up to the house, wearing sagging jeans with a studded belt and a tight black T-shirt, and admired what I could see of his body. When he disappeared from view, I sat back in the papasan and finished my joint. I was buzzed enough to ponder my sudden interest in Luis without residual feelings of embarrassment or shame. Except, I was *so* buzzed that my pondering mostly revolved around me thinking about how good he'd looked while dancing.

My dick hardened and without thinking, I reached down to grip it through my underwear. I closed my eyes, sighing, and stroked myself slowly. It was only the sound of Mrs. Hernandez across the street, yelling at her son, that broke my hazy almost-jerkoff session. With the spell broken, irritation swamped me. I was really jerking off and thinking about Luis now? That's what it had come to?

Maybe Caleb was right. I did need to get out there and get laid.

Groaning, I left the sun room. Time to distract myself from jobs and guys and the fact that I hadn't had sex in months. I needed to do something menial. Like laundry.

I gathered all the dirty clothes I'd accumulated in the past month, as well as the stuff that had been sitting in my bags since the cruise, and slapped on a pair of galaxy patterned leggings and a tank top. At the last minute, I also grabbed a spoon and container of Ben & Jerry's from the freezer before heading down to the basement. The plan was simple—gorge on milk and cookies ice cream while watching dance videos on YouTube as my clothes washed nearby, but that plan was thwarted as soon as I loaded the washer.

I'd just perched on top of the dryer with one leg tucked under me and the other bent at the side, my phone propped up, when I heard the basement door open. I nearly dropped a spoon full of ice cream when Luis came downstairs. He was holding a mesh bag of laundry, barefoot, and only wearing a tiny fucking pair of cotton shorts. Good Lord. I stared at those shorts with the spoon halfway to my mouth, eyes glued to the outline of his cock and the way those shorts only hit his upper thighs. Upper thighs which were thick and muscular and juicy...

"Well, well," he said, dropping his bag onto the floor. "Finally, we cross paths."

I nodded and shoved the spoon into my mouth.

Luis smirked, looking me over, then flicking his gaze to the washing machine. The display read that I had twenty-five minutes to go on my wash.

"Mind if I wait?"

"Do what you want."

I focused on my phone and did not meet his steady gaze. Part of me wondered if he knew how dramatically my body reacted to his presence. It went into high alert, every sense tuned into him so I could categorize everything about him. His cologne, the way he leaned against the wide wooden table I used as a folding station, and the faint music I could hear from the large headphones hanging around his neck. I noticed all these things, sneaking glances from the corner of my eye, but I kept my mouth shut.

We sat silently for a while, him absently moving his head and shoulders to his music while staring at me, and me slowly eating my ice cream and pretending not to stare back. I wished he would at least pretend to not be checking me out. My plan in life was to pretend I was unaffected by his presence, but with his attention so fixated, I found myself playing into it.

I arched my back in a stretch and let my leg fall open a little more so my own muscular thighs and crotch were on display. There were reasons I didn't normally wear leggings with a shirt this short in public, and me not necessarily wanting every thirsty closeted married fuck staring at my ass and dick were two of them. But Luis wasn't a thirsty closeted fuck. He was hot, and dirty, and mouthwatering.

The feel of his gaze on me, unshifting and obvious, was turning me on. Which only made me want to turn him on in return. I dragged my spoon through the softening ice cream just enough for it to coat the outside, then sucked the thin liquidy layer off. Then I did it again, slower, and dragged my tongue along for good measure. I looked his way, unable to stop myself from seeking a reaction, and found his eyes hooded. A glance downward gave me a good look at his dick poking through the thin fabric of his shorts.

I scooped another spoonful, eating it while we looked at each other. After I licked it clean, he asked, "What're you eating?"

"Ben and Jerry's." Another spoonful. Another slow lick. "Milk and cookies flavor."

Luis nodded slowly. "Never tried it."

"Want some?"

My mouth was a traitor. My dick even more of one. Where had that offer even come from? I willed him to say no, to call me out for being a weirdo, to do *something* to bring me back to reality, but he was Luis... so he didn't. He pushed away from the table and sauntered over to me, doing nothing to hide the iron rod in his shorts. He draped himself against the dryer where I was perched, angled towards me so my leg brushed his back with his hand was only a few inches from my bulge.

I waited for him to ask for a bite, but he just arched an eyebrow—the one with the scar running through it—and opened his mouth. My dick didn't just pulse. It throbbed with such intensity that my balls ached. In a lust-drenched state, where the basement wasn't part of the real world and what we did down here had no consequences, I scooped up more ice cream and slid the spoon into his mouth. I watched his lips close around it, his deep brown eyes slide shut, and listened to the low *mmm*.

That moan fucked me up. My own mouth fell open, and I listed forward. I wanted to lick the traces of ice cream off his fucking mouth. To suck it off his tongue. Too late, I realized what I was doing and jerked backwards just as he opened his eyes. I pulled the spoon away too quickly and dropped it. We both watched it bounce off the dryer and fall onto the floor.

"Whoops," I said, trying to go for flat instead of breathless. "So much for that."

"I dunno," he said. "That's pretty fucking good ice cream. Be a shame to waste it."

"Then you can use the floor-spoon." I nudged the container towards him but left it in front of my crotch. "I'm done."

"You sure?"

He was up to something. I knew he was. A something that would further stretch the tension between us, maybe even to the breaking point. I knew this, but I still nodded, shrugging my shoulders like I didn't give a fuck what he did. It was a good time to shove the container at him and watch YouTube again, but I didn't.

I watched him take his index finger and drag it through the ice cream before popping it into his mouth. I watched the way he sucked it off that long digit, his cheeks hollowing, before he drew it out. Then he did it again, and I kept watching because at this point there was no such thing as shame. There was only him, me, the ice cream, and an unfulfilled desire to fuck each other. Or not fuck and instead drive each other to the edge of sanity.

He scooped up ice cream with two fingers this time, his index and middle, and slowly sucked them clean. His eyes fell to half-mast, dilated and darkened, as the tension between us snapped taut. He knew I wanted him. Could probably feel it soaking into his body. My lust, my need, my desperation to touch him and have him touch me, but we both kept playing the game.

"You sure?" he asked quietly. "Just as good as a spoon."

Was he asking me to suck ice cream off his fingers? Because no fucking way. I would come. Right now. But the idea lit me up like a Christmas tree, and suddenly I was sitting up straight with my legs spread wide and dangling off either side of the dryer. We were closer now, with him standing between my thighs and only the ice cream and my spandex covered dick between us.

"Be a shame to waste it all—" Luis graced me with another mega invasive eyefuck. "—when it tastes so fucking good."

If I spoke, he'd hear the desire in voice. So instead, I followed his example and shoved my fingers into the container. It was a mess. I was a mess. And I made a mess sucking it off the three fingers I'd covered. I had ice cream all over my lips and in my stubble, but I didn't give a damn. All that mattered was that Luis was panting for me now, his eyes dilated and trained on the white sticky residue smeared on my face.

Yeah, I thought as I deliriously scooped up some more. *Pretend this is your cum.* I dragged the flat of my tongue along my fingers before plunging them in my mouth. *Pretend you have me fucking covered.*

"You're a mess," Luis said, voice a growl. "It's all over your face."

I took all three fingers into my mouth, sucking obscenely, then dragged them down. "Am I?"

"Yeah, you are." Luis stepped in closer until his thighs hit the dryer. He lifted his hand, causing me to freeze in place. He braced my jaw with his big hand while I panted like a beast. Then he jerked me forward a bit, just enough to make my pulse race before running the rough pad of his thumb over my mouth. "You got it all over these big fucking lips of yours."

I let him drag my lips apart, leaning into him and panting audibly now, but I didn't say anything to encourage him. He didn't need it. He slid his thumb over my lower lip and half into my mouth, wiping it of ice cream, and then sucked it into his own. My hand twitched with the need to grab my dick and ease some of the pressure, but I kept them pressed against the dryer. I didn't move them even when he smoothed his saliva covered thumb along the bottom of my mouth, which was also sticky. I held it together until he leaned in and dragged his tongue over my chin.

A moan tore out of me. A louder one followed after he yanked my hair back to angle my face up for him to bathe with his tongue. The wet velvet slide against the roughness of my stubble caused me to tremble. When his tongue grazed my lower lip, I groaned so loud it was fucking obscene.

He pulled away, lips parted and breath coming out in great gusts. He stared at me from beneath his eyelashes, so intense it was almost frightening. His hand was still bracing my face, fingers tight and caught in my hair. He yanked my head back again, just a little, and I let him. And when he leaned in to tongue at my jaw and the side of my mouth, licking at the rest of the ice cream, I let him do that too.

I put a hand on one of his big shoulders and groaned again. The power in his body was incredible. I wanted him to unleash it on me, to shove me to my knees and force me to take his dick in my mouth. Fuck my mouth wide open until it was his cum all over my chin and jaw and mouth.

There was a moment when Luis just stood in front of me, clutching me and staring, and I thought he would step away. That he'd brought me to the brink of me begging him to just use *me*, then he'd walk away. But he didn't. He yanked me into the wettest, most sensual kiss I'd ever had laid on me. He covered my mouth with his own, his soft lower lip dragging against my sticky skin, and swept his tongue into my mouth.

He made that *mmm* sound again, drew back so our lips smacked loudly, then went in for another wet kiss. His tongue was everywhere— tracing over my lips, delving in to drag along the inside of my cheek, then sliding out again to tease at my chin. That's when I realized he wasn't kissing me. He was literally licking every smidge of ice cream off my flesh and from the inside of my mouth. I didn't care. I sat there and let him treat me like a delicious dessert he wanted to savor, and a fog fell over me. In the haze, nothing mattered but his mouth and taste and his hands.

Luis leaned away again, just slightly. I narrowed my eyes at him and hoped it looked like a challenge, but I probably looked as hungry as I felt. The next time he drew me in, our lips pressed together, and it was a real kiss.

Our tongues coiled in a wet dance that I couldn't get enough of. I needed more of his touch, those strong fingers digging into me, and more of the wet heat inside his mouth. I grabbed the back of his neck and held him in place. No escape. No backing away to take the measure of me. I needed him to fuck my mouth with his tongue until I couldn't breathe. Until I couldn't think.

Luis reached between us to move the container of ice cream out of the way. I immediately slid to the edge of the dryer and yanked him against me. His dick pressed against my own, but instead of grinding against him the way I wanted to, I just held him there. The pressure was delicious enough combined with the thorough way he was exploring my mouth, and it was dizzying. My head was spinning. I was falling down a rabbit hole, and I couldn't stop myself or bring myself to care.

The ding of the washing machine cut through our frantic kissing. I jumped and pulled away. The reality of the last several minutes crashed down around me. The basement spell broke with both of us staring at each other wide-eyed and flushed, and trying to calm erratic breathing.

Then, his phone rang.

Luis cringed with his whole body and briefly shut his eyes in annoyance.

"Let me move my shit," I said quickly.

He didn't say anything, so I slid off the dryer and turned to the washing machine. My dick was trying to punch a hole through my leggings. It was so hard it hurt. I subtly adjusted as I yanked out my belongings in a giant wet ball, and shoved them into the dryer. My hands were still shaky as I fumbled with the dials, probably choosing all the wrong options. Meanwhile, his fucking phone just kept ringing. Over and over while he stood behind me without speaking.

I inhaled deeply after the dryer was going loud enough to cover the sound. Once my heartrate steadied a bit, I turned and found Luis looking down at his phone. It was great timing for me to haul ass out of there but, for some reason, it annoyed the shit out of me. Here I was having a panic attack over having had his tongue in my mouth, and he was texting.

"All yours," I said, and hurried by him.

Luis caught my upper arm. "Wait."

"What?"

He forced me to face him, using all that delicious strength to his advantage. And God help me, I instantly started fantasizing about him holding me down and fucking my brains out again. Or holding my head and jaw while he shoved his thick cock down my throat.

I met his eyes again and found them wild. Blazing. He was as turned on as me.

"We good?"

"We're the same as we were before," I grit out.

Luis' lips pursed, and it seemed like he wanted to say more. I hesitated for just long enough for his phone to start ringing again. He swore in Spanish and glared down at it.

I took the opportunity to hurry up the stairs.

CHAPTER SEVEN
CHARLES

The sound of the doorbell once again startled me awake. I needed to figure out how to disable the fucking thing. It had become a real obstacle to me sleeping in while hungover and miserable.

Groaning, I yanked my raggedy quilt over me, shifted around, and realized I'd fallen asleep in the sunroom after getting blazed. I'd also killed another bottle of wine, but that was a minor detail except for the way my head was spinning.

The doorbell rang again. This time my unwanted visitor leaned on it until it rang continuously. The only people who would dare to be this obnoxious were my friends or...

I bolted upright, heart pounding.

"Charles, open your fuckin' door!"

Jace's accent always came out strongest if he was yelling or speaking too fast, and now wasn't an exception. The sound of it calmed me enough to stand on wobbly legs and peer down at the sidewalk. The sunlight was brutal for my headache, but a smile stole over my face.

The sight of my squad standing near the curb while staring up at my windows drowned my Landon-related fears. Ashton was looking more leggy than usual in a short black romper that barely hit mid-thigh, and Mere stood beside him in the tallest spiked heels I'd ever seen and some gauzy Fashion Week monstrosity, and Jace wore skintight white pants and a flowy dark blue poet's shirt. Stephanie was the only one who didn't look like she'd just come in from a MET gala but was gorgeous as ever in a plain black sundress. They looked so hilarious standing together in this blue-collar Staten Island neighborhood, that I wished I'd had my phone charged and handy to take a picture.

I shoved up the screen and leaned halfway out the window. "You look like an aesthetically pleasing band who has no idea how to play your instruments," I called down to them.

Jace flipped me off. "I'm *really* good at playing with instruments, boo thang. Just ask—"

Stephanie covered his mouth, laughing. "Don't scandalize the neighbors with your dick talk."

"Let us in!" Jace demanded after turning his face away from her hand. "Or I'll describe what Chris and Aiden did to me last night really fucking loudly."

"Okay, I actually want to hear this up close and personal, so I'll be right down."

The little cloud that had been hovering over my apartment for days shifted away, just a little, and was replaced by genuine excitement. I hadn't seen my friends in so long that I'd started telling myself that maybe I was better off alone. With just my misery to keep me company, my fucked up head had convinced me that seeing them would only make me feel worse. I tried to be a good person and a supportive friend, but I couldn't deny that I was sometimes jealous of their lifestyles. I equally couldn't deny that I'd felt abandoned after learning that every single one of them had found lovers while I was away. The icing on the cake had been Caleb getting engaged.

So I'd stayed away. Avoided social media and happy couple, or throuple, pictures, and holed up in my apartment while allowing my phone to die for days at a time. But now that they were here? I was speeding through brushing my teeth and washing my face, left my hair as the wild mass of curls it was, and jerked on a pair of oversized sweatpants in my effort to get downstairs.

I went through a list of questions for each of them as I hurried down, but my thoughts scattered once I stepped into the entryway. There was a spoon sitting in the middle of the mat by my door. The spoon from last night's ice cream makeout session.

The sight of it transported me back to the basement and the memory of our demanding, hungry kisses. We'd been desperate for each other even while pretending the mutual want was just teasing or a stupid game. Even after fleeing to my apartment, I'd pretended that all night long while refusing to jerk off to the thought of him.

My continuous hard-on was why I'd once again decided to get super high. It was only in the light of day could I admit to myself that I'd have let him do me right there in the laundry room had we not been interrupted.

"Charles!"

I grabbed the spoon and yanked the door open, letting in a flood of sunlight and my ridiculously loveable friends. Stephanie instantly pulled me into a big hug, squeezing me tight, before Ashton and Mere did the same. Jace hung back and pointed at the spoon.

"Are you doing heroin or something?"

"Jace!" Stephanie protested, laughing. "What the fuck?"

He shrugged. "I'm just saying."

I shoved the spoon into my pocket. "No heroin. And, uh, I'll explain. Upstairs."

Away from Luis' prying ears, assuming he was home or tracked my movements the way I'd been tracking his. For all I knew, he looked at me as nothing more than a fun little challenge and had a slew of people sending him dirty Snaps and trying to hookup every night. I had noticed that he went out and came home at all hours.

Yeah, I was paying way too much attention to someone I was supposed to be resenting until the end of time.

"I don't have anything to offer you guys," I said once they'd settled their gorgeous selves around the living room. "The food and drink situation is so dire that I had Rosé and peanut butter with saltines for dinner last night."

"Rosé?" Stephanie shook her head sadly. "Really, Charles?"

"I know, right? But it was that or going into the world, and I'm not prepared to walk the ten minutes down Forest Avenue to hit up the liquor store just yet."

The four of them exchanged worried glances before Ashton held up a shopping bag with one of his big sunny smiles. "Luckily, we brought refreshments." He removed a gold wrapped bottle. "Champagne." He wrestled a package from the bottom. "A charcuterie platter."

"And me and Steph ordered a bunch of Fresh Direct for you, which should be arriving tomorrow," Jace said with a winning smile. "Can't have your skinny ass getting any skinnier, can we?"

"Oh, you should talk," I scoffed. "You tiny little bastard."

"Hey, I literally do not get any bigger. Caleb said you had lost weight when he saw you, and now you're looking really underfed, lovely boy." Jace was smiling at me, but his dark eyes were serious and he was giving me that critical once over. The one I could never escape from. If there was anyone who could identify the signs of me sinking into the cloud of my depression, it was Jace. "Friends take care of friends. Don't make me fight you about it."

"Spoiler," Steph chimed up. "Jace will win. I've seen him do an arm bar on Chris when they were watching the fights, and it wasn't pretty."

Jace pretended to dust dirt off his shoulders, and I couldn't help but smile at them. I also felt like the ultimate shithead. I'd been outright avoiding them for over a month, which I was sure they knew, and yet they were here with snacks and champagne while trying to distract me.

"Do I get to grill you all on your new relationships yet?" I asked once I was folded into an armchair with a stomach full of meat, cheese, and champagne. "Now that you've spent thirty minutes criticizing Staten Island commuting."

"Hey, we took a city bus for you," Mere said, pointing a tiny knife. "Not even an Express bus. We looked like freaks."

"You are freaks," I informed her. "Now tell me—how freaky are you getting with Tonya Maldonado? Is she good at eating pussy? Because I imagine she basically lives for it. You're a walking meal prep service."

Stephanie choked on her champagne, and Jace obnoxiously pounded her back.

"Oh she's more than good," Mere purred, grinning wickedly. "Morning sex is basically out of the question since she leaves me a wreck."

"You don't even have a job, so I fail to see what you have to get up for anyways," Stephanie pointed out. "Just sayin'."

Mere flipped her off. "Hey, I work! I've been doing way more event planning and hosting for QFindr lately. And... I'm still trying to get these dicks to start a fashion line with me."

My eyebrows flew up. "Okay, tell me more."

Meredith went off on a spiel about starting a fashion line created and modeled by queer people, and I could not help but be engaged by her passion for the dream. To me, it really did sound pipe, but I knew she could make it happen. So could Ashton. They had tons of connections in the fashion industry, so it could likely come to fruition pretty quickly. It was that realization that settled a new stone in my gut even after I'd just felt so uplifted and free.

I hated the bitter pills I constantly found myself swallowing around my friends, but it happened no matter how hard I tried to smile and encourage. But, at the end of the day, it was a bitter reminder of how much easier my life would have been if I'd been born into their status. Maybe I would have been able to continue studying at Julliard. Or maybe I would have been able to slide into dancing roles without Julliard. Maybe I'd be teaching lessons at an exclusive studio somewhere. There were so many maybes and no guarantees that it helped ease my resentment, but I was still left melancholy.

Their discussion about various styles devolved into a serious discussion about pricing, and I tuned out. A lot of people assumed I was a slave to fashion because of my often-outrageous clothing choices, but I got most of my shit from thrift stores. And, apparently, me tuning them out meant me once again keeping an ear out for Luis. I sat up straight as soon as the sound of his deep voice speaking Spanish floated up through the window.

Stephanie noticed me craning my neck to look out the window and smirked. "Who was that?"

"Just my neighbor."

"You're trying to break your neck to creep on that guy," Ashton noted around his glass of champagne. "That's less *just* and more *thirsty.*"

"Ugh. Shut up." Groaning, I flopped back in the chair with my legs splayed out in front of me. I looked between them slowly before throwing my arm dramatically over my face. "I'm going to run through this quickly, so keep up and do not ask me to repeat myself because I fucking won't. Seriously. It's mortifying."

Ashton knee crawled forward to refill my glass. I accepted it gladly and took a deep drink.

"So, the guy I walked in on with Landon? It was my downstairs neighbor. Luis." Sensing a million and one questions about to bombard me, I raised a warning finger. "Apparently, he'd had no idea I existed since he moved in after I went on the cruise, which I can't deny. Landon has been cheating on me for years probably, and now he had a free house for like six months. But Landon aside, Luis has been..."

How has he been? Relentless? Flirtatious? Delicious? A fucking temptation?

"He felt really bad and has spent *weeks* trying to make it up to me. I think he can't stand the idea of me hating him for something that isn't his fault."

"And your stubborn ass has held out?" Stephanie guessed.

"Uh. Yeah. Mostly." I took another drink. "Except for the parts where we've wound up in compromising positions in the basement during a blackout and when we were both down there doing laundry. We shared ice cream, silently, right before he licked it off my fucking face." Oh God, it sounded even more absurd when said out loud. I was ridiculous with a capital Dic. Rolling my eyes, I held up the spoon. "That's why he left this for me outside my door. Returning my property but also reminding me of what happened last night."

"Wait, wait, wait, time out." Stephanie made the time-out symbol with her hands. "He licked ice cream. Off. Your face."

I slid down the arm chair, nodding. "I know."

"Is he fine?" she demanded.

"So fine," I groaned. "And I haven't had sex in over six months, so I have very limited will power against a walking Instagram thirst trap."

"Does he have an Instagram?" Ashton asked, perking up. "I want to see this for myself."

"Ohhh yes! Good call." Mere whipped out her phone. "Spill it."

I slid off the chair and onto the floor with my face pressed against the wood. "Guys, I haven't even redownloaded any apps. Plus, I've been trying to cope with my obvious desperation since I am fiending for a man who was two minutes away from plowing my disgusting ex-boyfriend. Can we focus on that and *not* encourage me?"

Ashton gave me a sideways look. "If I can forgive Valdrin for secretly being my bodyguard for years, you can forgive a sexy and endearing man who nearly slept with some douche he thought was single."

"How do you know he's endearing?" I demanded.

"Because he's been trying to earn your forgiveness for *weeks*?" Ashton sniffed and tossed his long blond hair over one shoulder. "I would have quit after the first rebuff."

I made a face, pretending to mimic him.

"So, is he not endearing?" Jace pressed. "Maybe he just wants to get in your butt."

"He definitely wants in my butt. Although..." Sighing tragically, I flung a hand vaguely towards the bookcase in my makeshift dance space. "He may be a filthy horn dog, but he's a filthy horn dog who must have spent hours gluing my porcelain dancing boy figurine back together after I destroyed it in my blind rage. He left it outside my door."

Jace and Ashton made swoony faces. Even Stephanie made an *aww* noise. Mere was the holdout with a skeptical eyebrow arch. I high fived her.

"But enough about me and my weird neighbor. I'm not done interrogating you people about your love lives."

There were questions practically brimming in each of them but, by some miracle, they allowed me to shift the topic away from my bizarre infatuation with Luis the sexy neighbor. The last thing I needed was them making a case for me caving to my basic desire to bend over for someone who probably made it a habit of charming eager bottoms. Considering he'd had Landon begging to be banged, I was willing to wager Luis' behavior towards me wasn't exactly exclusive to me. The boy had game. And I wasn't going to be anyone else's toy.

LUIS

I was supposed to have the evening off from Male Revue to practice my routine for my ongoing gig with the burlesque troupe, but two dancers had bailed. Now, I was called in with promises of two bachelorette parties plus a queer bachelor party having been booked for the night. Which meant a packed house and a lot of dollar bills being shoved into my underwear.

Did I need to rehearse? You damn right I did. My choreography was on point, but there were still moments when I forgot a step or a twist. That was fine when I was stripping at Male Revue, but when I was performing on stage with other people? And being scrutinized by the other dancers? Actual dancers with talent and experience? It wasn't okay.

Unfortunately, I also needed money, and I rarely got scheduled to work these big money nights with bachelorette parties. Those were usually better kept for the favorite dancers and the ones with a way longer tenure than I had. It usually didn't bother me, but I was starting to be desperate for cash to save.

As much as I loved the dance troupe with every fiber of my being, especially considering how the other dancers had helped draw me up out of the slump I'd been in after quitting boxing... it paid barely anything. And it was pretty painful to admit the thing you love would never make you any money. So, I needed to get raunchy at SI Male Revue and hope I had time to practice later.

My mood was so foul that I was oblivious to people standing in the vestibule of the house until I jerked my door open and stepped outside. My eyes focused on them—well, mostly on Charles. I could tell he'd probably been wasting away in his apartment all day again, but he was fucking stunning in his silky robe with his curly hair and long elegant limbs.

I didn't miss the way he automatically ran a hand through his hair and couldn't help a half-smile. Looking at his bedhead just made me thinking about waking up next to him after—

"*Luis?*" A tall lanky blond walked to the front of the group and gaped. "Oh my God. *You're* his weird neighbor?"

My jaw dropped. A booming laugh popped out of me as recognition set in. The long legs, all-black ensemble, ridiculously long platinum hair, and androgynous features... What in the hell was Ashton Townsend, otherwise known as the celebutante A-Town, doing in my house?

"Holy fuck. Hollywood!" I stepped forward to drag him into a quick hug. Normally, I'd squeeze the hell out of him, but... something told me to keep my mitts off. And that *something* was the half confused, half wary expression on Charles' face. "What are you doing here? You and my boy Charles are friends?"

Charles' gaze flew between me and Ashton, as did the eyes of his other friends. A short guy with long black hair, a blond in high heels, and a fly looking Latinx chick.

"I'm not his boy," Charles grumbled. "What is going on?"

Ashton shook his head slowly, his expression a study in shock as he stared at me. "Charles and I are close friends, actually. But... I can't believe I'm seeing you." A big smile stole over his face. "I never thought I'd see you again after the night of the fight. I know Val has been talking to you on Instagram now that he actually uses it, but—"

"Wait," Charles said, frowning. "For real. How the fuck do you two know each other?"

I crossed my arms over my chest, unable to hide a smug grin, as Ashton explained. "Luis trains at Valdrin's old boxing gym. They were... kind of friends? Sorta?" He scrunched up his face. "They were set to fight at a tournament, and during their match, this total asshole started harassing me. Valdrin noticed and lost, and later... Luis gave up the title because he knew Valdrin had been distracted."

The blonde woman nodded approvingly.

"I don't fight at Cadet's anymore," I said. "That same asshole, Bronson, and his fucking friends made life miserable for me for a while. So I quit."

"You quit the gym?" Ashton frowned. "Or... you quit boxing?"

"Both."

"But—" Ashton stopped after catching my cautioning glare. "I'll just make Val demand the information from you and then tell me."

"Or you could just ask me yourself," I said dryly. "I'm not trying to talk about it in front of strangers, but you can hit me up just as quickly as your man. I'm on Instagram just as much as you, Hollywood. And while we're on the topic, I'd appreciate some regramms so your rich friends will eventually become clients when I get into personal training."

Ashton bounced in place, clapping excitedly. "If you train me, I can post pictures as your first client!"

The words blew me away. I hadn't even expected him to agree about the regramms let alone offering to be a client. We hadn't exactly been close. Me and Valdrin hadn't even been close. We'd been somewhat rivals for years at the gym, although it had mostly been me wanting to beat the dude everyone had claimed would be the first champ the gym would spit out in years. I'd even come onto Ashton a couple of times after seeing him wonder around the neighborhood, so this excitement and support? It wasn't what I expected. Especially considering the lack of it I'd been getting from everyone but my mother since I'd come out.

I cleared my throat, looked over the group, and then at Charles. He was studying me closely, his plump lips pursed as he tried to read the situation.

"Thanks, Hollywood," I said, rubbing the back of my head. "If you're really interested, I'll hit you up once I have my shit together. It might not be for a long time, though. Renting studio space won't be cheap, and it's hard to save money since I moved out of the Bronx."

"Please let me know what I can do to help," Ashton all but pleaded. "We could even do a fundraiser—"

"Nope." I shake my head, laughing. "I got this, A-Town. Trust me. This apartment is cheap as hell since me and Charles' landlord is never around and lets repairs lapse for fucking weeks, and I've been making decent money dancing. It will just take a little while to save."

"Dancing?" Charles immediately made a face, as though he hadn't been planning to speak.

"Yup," I drawled. "I dance at Male Revue, and do some shows on the side with a traveling dance troupe."

"Male Revue?" the tiny long-haired guy demanded. "Sounds like a strip club."

"That's because it is one." I hefted my duffel bag on my shoulder and looked at Charles once again. His face was priceless. Lips parted, brows lifted, and those chocolatey eyes narrowed. I hoped he was imagining something amazing. Like everything he'd seen when he was peeping through my window. "It's not a new development. I've been stripping for years. I always liked dancing, and I made no money from boxing, so it made sense to put this body to good use."

Ashton nodded seriously. "Totally true. I support this. Completely."

"I do too," the short guy said, smiling widely. "And Charles. I can tell."

Charles sent him a glare full of daggers. "Shut up, Jace."

It wasn't hard to figure out that Charles had told them a lot more about me than me being the "weird neighbor". And because I was a master at pushing boundaries, and my luck, I rooted around in my duffel bag for one of the glossy postcards from the club. It was promo I was supposed to drop at random places, and this set had my picture on it—me with boxing gloves, a fake title belt, and a g-string, with flames behind me. Cheesy as fuck, but it amused me. It also amused the hell out of my mother.

"Here," I said, handing it to Jace. "I'm dancing pretty much all night tonight if y'all wanna come through. It will be crowded, but I can get you a table at the front. Not for nothing, but if I say A-Town is coming with his rich friends, you'll be treated like kings. Also, honestly, it might make me look pretty good to the owner. The place has politics just like any other job, and anything I can do to stay in that dude's good graces is pretty dope. Turnover is high, and I need the cash."

"Can we bring friends?" The Latinx woman asked, grinning wickedly. "Like... five or six more friends?"

"You can bring whoever the hell you want." I hesitated then frowned. "Except Valdrin. That's just weird."

"Oh, he would never come," Ashton reassured me, laughing. "I still have to tell him I'm going, though."

"Wait—" Charles stepped forward. That one simple motion was all it took to captivate me. He had such control over his body that it was hard not to appreciate every inch of it. That, and the way his robe slid down slightly to show the delicious curve of his collarbone. "You're going?"

"*We* are going," Ashton said. "To support a friend. So go get dressed."

Charles flushed as he appeared to swallow whatever protests he had, but ultimately inclined his head. He turned on his heel to head upstairs to his own apartment, but not before shooting me a quick glance. I don't know that I was supposed to catch him looking so openly intrigued by me, but I did. And that covert sign of interest? It was all I needed to stop backing off.

CHAPTER EIGHT

CHARLES

Nothing says *I don't give a fuck* like going to a male strip club on Staten Island's south shore wearing thirty-seven layers under a green army jacket, a scarf, and a beanie. But spring in New York City meant a heatwave one day and sixty degrees the next, so I could get away with covering every inch of myself. The fact that I needed multiple protective layers in order to deal with the fact that I was about to see Luis naked and gyrating on stage was something I needed to work out.

Instead, I researched Male Revue while my obnoxious and overbearing friends waited for the rest of our crew to arrive at the bar up the strip from Luis' club. It was marketed as a gay strip club with drag nights alternating with dance nights, but there was also a section on the website for bachelorette parties and the such. The most shocking thing to me was that there was an openly gay club in one of the most conservative parts of Staten Island. Although, most of Staten Island was conservative.

By the time Chris and Tonya showed up—Raymond and David had unshockingly declined the invitation, and Aiden had gone to watch some sports shit with Angel—I was a brimming bundle of nerves. The others were so excited that they mostly missed my quiet tenseness, except for Stephanie.

She slid her arm around my shoulders and drew me in, walking side-by-side as Ashton led us to Male Revue. It was in a nondescript building on Arthur Kill Road, and looked just as seedy as every other club on Staten Island that I'd ever been to, but the door man received us as if we were royalty. Obviously, Luis had informed them that A-Town and an entourage would be showing up, and they'd planned accordingly.

The inside was way nicer than I'd expected, although the neighborhood definitely was on the upper end of the borough's social scale. The club consisted of one large room with a wood paneled bar at the end, several clusters of leather seats dotted around with the occasional larger table for groups, and a single stage in the center. It had a staircase on either side and was surrounded by leather captain's chairs.

The host led us to the chairs surrounding the stage, and I nearly passed out.

"Calm down, papi," Stephanie said in my ear. "He's just a man."

"I know." When she arched an eyebrow at my sharp town, I sighed. "Sorry. I'm just... I can't explain it."

"Try to explain," she suggested. "Do you not like that you're attracted to him? Because, hate to say it, the tension between you two was thick enough to karate chop. You stared him down, sweetie. And he did the same to you."

"I know," I groaned, sinking lower in my chair. "I'm so fucking attracted to him. It's not fair."

"Why isn't it fair? Because of the way you met?"

"Yes! It's ridiculous. I should hate him."

A guy walked over, tall and muscular and lean, wearing nothing but a pair of Andrew Christian underwear and boots. He was carrying a shots tray and trying to entice our group into buying some. Because Ashton was Ashton, he immediately bought the whole tray and proceeded to ask for bottle service. I couldn't help a smile. He clearly had no interest in the dancers or the scantily clad waiters, and was here for the sole purpose of making Luis look good to his managers.

Stephanie threw back her shot, cringing, then turned to me again. "Okay, real talk."

"Ugh."

"Don't *ugh* at me, Carlito," she scolded, using the Spanish version of my name. "If anything gets under my skin, it's someone who blames the *other person* in a cheating situation. Especially someone who had no idea the person they'd been involved with wasn't single. I've had so many friends who would start an entire harassment or shit talking campaign directed at the third party instead of the person who deserves it—the guy who cheated on them. There is no one to blame but Landon for his actions."

"I know. It's just—"

The first dancer came out from behind the stage wearing a kilt and some kind of leather strap across his chest. I couldn't help a smile at the shrill wolf whistle Jace let out. A quick glance his way showed he was also halfway sitting in Chris' lap. They were so absurdly cute together. I wished I could see them with Aiden. I would have already if I'd ever stopped hiding in my apartment.

Sighing, I turned back to Stephanie. "It's just... I don't know if I'm so hungry for him because he's hot and accessible and I've not been..." I struggled with the next part, feeling myself flush as the pieces came together in my mind. "Ever since I kicked Landon out, I've been thinking about the past two years and have realized things changed between us long ago. In the past, our dynamic was always explosive and volatile but there was this passion I used to justify all the bad shit." I cringed at the description, but Stephanie just nodded in agreement. "But a couple of years ago the passion wasn't even there. It was just us fighting, badly, and me running to my friends. Hiding from him. Avoiding him. And him avoiding me. He stopped showing interest in me sexually, and there were times when I was relieved. But then I'd feel... so fucking empty?"

A quick glance at the stage showed the dude sliding down the pole and doing the splits once he hit the floor. He vaulted up into a squat and started twerking.

"Why empty?" Stephanie pressed, drawing my attention again.

"Because as much as I hate to admit it, my entire adolescence and adulthood has been me feeling shitty about myself and needing validation from others to shove all of that self-loathing to the side. It's partially how I'd ended up with Landon in the first place." More bitter pills slid down my throat as I realized I'd never really wanted him. Just how he'd initially made me feel. "And sex and affection somehow became these things I used for validation, which I fucking hate. You have no idea how much I hate it. I want to change it. So this thing with Luis? Him being so obviously into me and wanting to fuck me? I keep feeling like me being drawn in is just me desperately seeking that same validation. Especially because I haven't felt desired by anyone in so long."

Stephanie made a sympathetic sound and slid her hand over mine. She paid no mind to the dancer or our friends, even when Jace loudly noted that Chris should dance because of how delicious his dick would look in tiny underwear.

"I understand more than you think," she said. "But for me, I thought of relationships the way you think of sex. As a thing people used to validate their existences, so I rejected them all. I had to reconsider a lot of things before me and Angel could be together, and I realized I was willing to put aside that baggage and that whole thought process if I didn't want to lose him."

"But that makes sense! You and him have been in this tug-of-war forever. I just met Luis."

"Oh, I'm right there with you. And he could just want to fuck you. You have no idea what his motives are." She reached over and grabbed my hand, bringing it to her lips. "But what I would say is maybe if your interest doesn't go away, you could let yourself get to know him before you decide to write him off for good. You don't have to hold yourself back only out of fear of making a mistake."

It was exactly what I was doing. The ridiculous thing was, I was blowing it all out of proportion. I knew Luis probably just wanted to fuck me, and there was nothing wrong with that. I wanted to fuck him too. But even without the extra Landon baggage, I had no idea if I casual sex was something I was capable of anymore. I couldn't even find a guy attractive without sniping at him viciously. Who knew how I'd act if we touched dicks?

"Ugh, I need a drink," I moaned. "Did Ashton get a bottle yet?"

Stephanie patted my shoulder again and stood to find out about the bottle situation. While she was gone, I cast a look around and realized I was the only freak hunched in my chair wearing a jacket with my hood up. The place had somehow become packed in the ten minutes since we'd settled in. There were to large clusters of women wearing bride and bridesmaids gear and another table with a group of dudes in similar outfits.

Other than them, the clientele seemed to consist mostly of guys—seventy-five percent of them were older guys. And about fifty percent of the older guys reminded me of Duffy Costigan from Hot Bagels.

The good ole Staten Island boys with the old school deze-and-doze accent. It really was another world from the clubs I'd been to in the gayborhoods of Brooklyn and Manhattan.

As I studied the people around us, the first dancer pulled one of the brides-to-be on the stage and sat her in a chair in the center. She honestly looked terrified, and I wondered whether she'd paid for this extra or whether her bridesmaids had put her up to it. Either way, I didn't know whether to laugh or cringe as he did a whole Ginuwine pony thing behind her before stripping his pants off and gyrating in her face.

"That would not be me," Mere said loudly from the other side of the stage. "Seriously."

Tonya pinched her side. "Yeah, 'cause we're never getting married."

Mere surprisingly made an affronted face, which led to Tonya winking and pulling her in for a kiss. It was cute. Sickeningly cute. And I wondered whether all of my friends would be married by the end of the year. They'd be settled down with their jobs and significant others while I continued hustling my way across the city angsting every time I found a guy attractive. Ugh. What a mess.

The bride-to-be finally left the stage, looking a little shell shocked even as she laughed, and the man with the kilt left after collecting the money that littering the stage. He'd made a killing, and I could see why this would be a lucrative part-time or even full-time job for someone with a good following.

There was a brief lull in activity and during that time, several of the younger people came up to take pictures with Ashton. He loudly told them to tag the club on their social media pages and to mention his friend Lou, a dancer at the club. I smiled behind my drink. He was not subtle about his aims. I had a moment of wondering whether "Lou" was really Luis' stripper name, but that was solved when a voice boomed out of the speakers to announce he was next.

Nerves soared through me. I downed my drink and frantically asked Mere to pour me another. My voice was hushed, and she looked at me like I'd lost my only remaining wit, but I didn't care. This whole thing had me on edge. I felt so much fucking safer beneath my scarf and jacket. It was hot as hell in the club, but it was basically armor.

I was on the edge of my seat until Luis stepped out onto the stage with a pair of boxing gloves tied at the back and hanging around his neck, and wearing a pair of low slung sweatpants and a skintight T-shirt that said Cadet's. The idea of him wearing his old boxing gym's gear during his strip routine struck me as the height of passive aggression, and I loved every minute of it. There was no way he'd left that club on good terms judging by the way he'd acted when Ashton had inquired. For some reason, that minor act of rebellion soothed me just enough for me to turn and watch his act.

Stephanie refilled my glass as Luis took his place in the center of the stage, arms up to hold onto the gloves and head down. Wolf whistles exploded all over the room, and I wondered whether he would also give a show to one of the brides, or grooms, to be. I instantly didn't want it to be so, and what a red flag *that* was.

When the music started, I immediately recognized it as the same reggaetón song that had been blasting the day I'd watched him practice. My nervousness went out the window, and excitement soared through me. The last quarter of his routine had been pure fire. I'd spent days wondering about the rest of the routine and mentally trying to write my own choreography, but nothing had felt right. Now, I could see for myself. And when Luis started moving, I almost forgot that he would be stripping. He wasn't just shaking his ass and getting naked, it was fucking dancing.

He started low key, one hand thrust out in front of him as he moved his hips the music, causing those oversized sweatpants to already slide down his hips. Someone from the groom-to-be's table screamed, and I shot a glare over my shoulder. Like, could he shut the fuck up and let me study these moves? For fuck's sake.

Luis had twisted to the side so his back was to the audience, and he was winding low, hips thrusting and pants dipping low to tease the jockstrap he was wearing beneath. If I said my dick didn't throb at the sight of the curve of his ass cheeks, I'd be a liar. But the sight of him suddenly launching backwards into a backflip as the beat picked up was more exhilarating than seeing his ass.

He transitioned into a series of steps that I tried to ingrain in my mind. Every twist, lunge, and moment of him grinding against the air before dragging his hands down his chest with a naughty grin. He took a surprisingly long time to derobe, but the gloves came off first.

He danced his way over to Ashton, writhing and grinning knowingly as Ashton cat called, then whipped off the gloves to drape around Ashton's neck. There was literally nothing sexy about it, but Ashton fanned himself as if he was going to die, and promptly took a selfie. The boy knew hot to promo.

The stage was covered in dollar bills before Luis took off his shirt, so when he did in the middle of a complicated series of steps that I needed to record to study, everyone went wild. I'd already seen his shirtless, ripped, and tattooed self so at first I continued to focus on his footwork. But once the hip thrusting began without a flap of fabric to cover his crotch, my body was aflame. His dick was clearly outlined in his sweatpants. The combination of the size and his deliciously tantalizing hip movements? I was finished.

I finally let my gaze wander up to his face and further died due to his unabashed naughtiness. The groom-to-be had been hauled to the side of the stage in the hopes of getting the full treatment, but Luis wagged his finger no while smiling his filthiest smile. The smile I wanted aimed at me, and not some desperate getting married fuckboy. I watched with hatred as Luis threaded his fingers behind his head and gave the guy the pleasure of sliding those sweatpants off Luis' hips. When they caught at his knees, the guy yanked them down further... with his teeth.

"Thirsty bitch," I muttered.

Stephanie choked on her drink and fell to pieces from laughing. Her loud infectious giggle drew Luis' attention, and then I was caught. His grin widened even further at the sight of my likely exasperated expression. Once he was free of his sweatpants, and had a couple of hundreds tucked into his jockstrap, Luis danced over to me.

Stephanie did the sign of the cross, probably in case I died of my own lust, but there was no lap dance to be had. Instead of grinding his balls in my face like the other guy had done to the bride-to-be, Luis launched the last part of his dance. The one I'd caught him practicing and had creepily watched through his window.

I was entranced by the sequence of steps, the way he lunged to each side while raunching it up by humping the air, and that teasing smile he wore the entire time. He could have been half the dancer and still put on a helluva show just based on his charm.

Luis ended his dance with a back flip and, just like in his living room, he balanced on his hands while thrusting his hips in that poor almost-married bastard's face. The guy looked ready to pass out, or touch the merchandise, but Luis slid into a split that left him facing me again.

He arched an eyebrow. "You like it?" he asked over the music.

I swear to God, everyone's head whipped over to me in my giant knitted scarf and army jacket. Blushing should not have been a thing I was capable of, but I felt one warming my face. Even so, I raised my chin and said, "I'd like it better if you taught me."

Luis' eyes widened, and the smile that crossed his face far outshone any that he'd thrown at his audience.

CHAPTER NINE

LUIS

"**Y**ou were great tonight!"

The exclamation from a man who was usually as expressive as a Key Food coupon caught me off guard. I looked over my shoulder in the dressing room, half-in and half-out of my costume, as I hurriedly shoved everything in my duffel bag.

Riley was standing right behind me, a big smile on his face. He looked like he'd just seen Jesus in the whipped cream of his latte.

"Thanks," I said, forcing a grin. "For the compliment and for calling me in tonight. I've never been here for the party bookings."

"I knew you could handle it."

It was some bullshit, but I grinned wider. He had his favorites who he scheduled for party days, most of whom were straight dudes who'd been working at the club for years. Basically, before the owner had decided to switch tactics and begin marketing to the queer population as well as the straight women wanting a show.

My main issue with that was that a lot of those dudes couldn't dance worth a damn, and usually just did the shove my crotch-in-faces routine instead of putting on a real show. Apparently, straight men had it in their heads that a person about to get married really needed some sweaty balls all up in their nose right before the big day. Meanwhile, me and the few other queer dudes who made the effort to entertain were often scheduled on days without a real peak. Why? Because we were new. And not straight.

In Riley's mind, it was okay to take money from gay dudes but he didn't want other gay or bi dudes benefitting from that paper. I'd be pissed about it if it wasn't so typical. But I wasn't trying to work at Male Revue for long, so I wasn't about to march in and try to change the order of things. Riley could kiss my big ass.

"Does that mean I'll get scheduled for another bachelorette party?" I winked, turning the question into a tease just in case I came off too assertive and frightened him back to his faves.

"If you keep bringing celebrities in, you will."

Yeah, fat chance of that. Hollywood coming through had been a total random accident. If I asked Ashton another favor, it would be to take him up on his offer to be my first client. Or to pimp my gym on his social media if I ever opened it.

"I guess we'll see," I said vaguely. "But... I also had an idea about another event since you said you were considering taking one of the dance nights off the schedule due to low numbers?"

Riley's eyes immediately glazed over. He wanted me naked and doing salsatón, not thinking and having big ideas. "Oh?"

"Yeah. I was thinking you could offer dance lessons with some of us on the night you were planning to close." I yanked my T-shirt over my head. "You'd be surprised by how many people in these wedding parties comment on how they wish I could teach them or whatever. If anything, people would sign up just to get lessons by hot sweaty dudes."

Riley nodded slowly, but nothing about his body language or expression gave away a vibe that he was interested in my suggestion. I had no time for ignorant pendejos with no biz savvy, so I threw my duffel bag over my shoulder and glanced at my watch. My shift was over, and I was hoping to catch Charles before he took off with his friends.

"All right, well I'm taking off," I said, nodding at Riley. "Take it easy, man. I'll see you on Friday."

He was just dying to ask me if I had any more famous friends, I could tell, so I speed walked out of the dank locker room. I'd made a ton of fucking money tonight so I didn't want to burn the bridge with him, but there was only so much irritating conversation I could take. It would be different if I could bullshit a little better, but I had too much of my mother in me to face off with a fake person with a smile.

I jogged up the stairs from the basement, taking them two at a time, but Charles was already gone by the time I got to the main floor. Disappointment hit me hard, and my heart sunk. My own dramatic reaction irritated me a little, because I really needed to dead this infatuation, but I couldn't help it. Even though I logically knew I was starting to look pathetic for chasing a boy who was more hot-and-cold than the shower in our busted house, I wanted him. Badly. And not just for fucking.

I dragged my feet on my way out of the club, sulking my way down the block. A number of guests waved to me or reached out to me as I left, but I ducked them all and thought about the way Charles had watched me dance. His attention had flicked all over me, yeah, but I could tell he'd been fascinated by the choreography. Did I want him to be attracted to me? Yes. Had I been hoping he'd been overcome by lust after seeing my sexy ass half naked and gyrating? Fuck yes. But was it his obsession with performance and the unconscious way he'd moved his shoulders and head to the beat what had made my heart pound? Yup.

I loved how exciting dancing was. And Charles got it. It wasn't the dancer who was necessarily beautiful or thrilling—it was the dance itself. The rhythm, the movement, the way a dancer's body flowed seamlessly with a song... that was the best part of a performance. Not many people got it. Even my cousins and my friends who'd known about my love of dance, and my stripping, back in the Bronx hadn't gotten it. So many times I'd sent them a YouTube clip of one of Yoandy Villaurrutia's dance classes, excited about what I planned to practice, and they'd hit me back with "he's hot as fuck".

Not. The. Point.

With bummed out not beginning to describe my state of mind, I waited forever to catch the 74 bus to Richmond Avenue, where I then waited for the 44 to the North Shore of the island. Traveling at night in Staten Island usually wasn't a problem, but the commute always made me a little tense. Maybe it was because the bus stops were so deserted at the hour I got out of work, or because I was leery of cops stopping me for some bullshit reason, but I usually needed a beer by the time I got home. Now wasn't any different. Between my disappointment in not getting to talk to Charles—who was probably gonna go back to ignoring me like a punk—and my leeriness, I was on edge by the time I got off the bus and walked up the hill to the house.

Times like these, I replayed my mother's worried and somewhat dramatic yelling about my decision to move to Staten Island. She'd said it wasn't like the Bronx, and I would be surrounded by racist conservatives and shady cops who would fuck with me. Of course, I'd pointed out the shady cops who literally roved our neighborhood along with the shady ass homophobes wanting to whoop my ass, and had sold it to her with acknowledgement that the rent was cheap. And it was a fresh start.

Still, she'd worried. And nights like these, when I was on my guard and feeling discouraged, I thought she was right. It wasn't just the wariness I felt about working down on Arthur Kill in a largely white neighborhood, it was how isolated I felt in general. Besides Duffy Costigan, and the handful of dancers I'd loosely befriended and who came over to practice sometimes, I was isolated here. It was nothing like the concentrated bunch of family I'd grown up with near the Grand Concourse. Not having my people nearby was so fucking *odd*. People always asked me if I misseded boxing, but it was my family and friends that I missed. Too bad, except for my mother and handful of cousins, they weren't missing me in return.

"Why so serious?"

I jumped, putting a hand on my heart, and looked up from the sidewalk to find Charles sprawled on the front steps. All my morose brooding melting away as I took him in. There was something about how Charles carried himself that was gorgeous. His face was striking, and I would never stop wanting to play with that hair, but seeing is long elegant body gracefully sprawled or arranged was what stirred me.

The first word that came to mind was dancer. The other? Flexible.

Clearing my throat, I walked to the edge of the stairs. "What are you doing down here, papa?"

Charles shifted from his lazy sprawl to hunch forward, hands shoved into his pockets. "It's a nice night."

I snorted. "Yeah right."

He glared at me. "Fine. I was waiting for you."

"What for?"

Charles gave me another of those distrustful glares. The guy was always ready for a fight. Even when we were being low key nice to each other (or obviously horny), there was something grudging about how he graced me with his attention. It was that, more than anything else, that had been one of my indicators to consider backing off if we couldn't find a way to functionally get along. My plan for post-show conversation had been to test the waters for the last tme."

"I wanted to know who did your choreography," he admitted. "It was amazing."

The grin I aimed his way was probably bright enough to light up our block despite the flickering street lights. People used to say my grin was "infectious", and Charles proved that little tidbit by smiling in return. It was still reserved, just a tiny flicker at the sides of his mouth, but it was there. I was claiming that tiny bit of happiness or amusement, damn it. That smile was for me.

"I did it," I said. "It took a lot of practice and watching YouTube videos, but it paid off, no?"

"It paid off a fuck ton. You have more talent in your left foot than in the entire entertainment crew on the cruise I was working on." Charles' voice was blunt and flat, but it was still a goddamn compliment. And the way his eyes ran over me as he spoke made it even better one. "Which videos did you watch?"

"A lot of them," I admitted. "It's mostly borrowed moves put together into a new thing."

Charles rolled his eyes. "That's what all dancing is so you don't have to act like you're some fraud. Just tell me which videos. I want to watch them."

I ran my hand over the strap to my duffel bag, toying with responses and wondering why the hell I was being shy. I'd never been shy. Even as a little kid, I'd been kind of entitled and demanding. A product of my mother treating me like a little prince up until the teenage years when she'd realized I needed a lot of sense slapped into me. I was better at it now, but until Charles I'd never skirted what I wanted for fear of rejection. But he was a fucking wild card. One I really wanted to keep in my back pocket.

"Why don't you come in and I'll show you?"

Charles crossed his arms over his chest, shutting me out with that one simple movement. I held up a hand to caution him that I wouldn't press, but he surprised me by saying: "Sounds good."

CHARLES

His apartment was nicer than mine. It shouldn't have bothered me, but it did. I'd put a lot of effort into finding bits and pieces on Craigslist and various apps people used to hawk their old furniture, but it was still sparse. Mostly because Landon had considered my attempts at decorating the place to be a waste of time and money. Money that he'd never contributed to.

Luis, on the other hand, seemed to live for knick knacks. His front door opened to his makeshift dance studio the same way mine did, but he'd had the wooden floors polished to a shine. There was a Dominican flag in one of the big picture windows, and long sheer dark blue curtains hung around it. Besides those two items, and an enormous television spanning one wall, the room was empty. However, from what I could see of the living room beyond, it was decorated in rich earthy colors with random pops of color, little figurines and statues in a giant bookcase, and an entire wall of vivid island art.

"Wow."

Luis dumped his duffel bag in a closet by the door. "Wow what?"

"Your place is..." I couldn't help walking deeper into the house so I could get a better view of the artwork. They all looked like originals and were on a variety of canvases. "I'm impressed."

"You should be impressed with my mom," Luis said with a fond smile. "She collected a ton of art over the years on various trips to DR. She's all about supporting local artists."

He came to stand beside me. I knew he was surveying the paintings, but I couldn't help but notice how close we were. I could smell his cologne, and it brought me right back to the basement. His body pressed against mine in the dark. Then his tongue swiping across my face. My dick stirred, and I cursed myself.

"It's beautiful," I said quietly. "Your affection for your heritage is really apparent."

Luis winked. "Because my heritage is fucking amazing."

After finding myself smiling at him again, I quickly turned back to the dance space. "So, the videos?"

"All business, huh?" Luis tsk tsk'd at me but returned to the studio and faced the television. He controlled it with his phone, using it as a remote control. "I'll cast them from YouTube to the TV, but do you really want to see them all? I told you—I've been watching a ton for years. That act was a mix of like twenty videos plus just me growing up dancing to bachata and salsa."

I unzipped my jacket, then my hoody, and sat on the spotless floor facing the screen. "I'm just curious. I haven't..." A twinge hit me, but I knuckled past it. "I haven't done my own choreography since school."

"School?" Luis swiped at his phone, still standing. "Were you on a dance team or something?"

"I uh... I went to a performance arts college called Julliard. It was part of my—"

Luis looked back so fast he probably had whip lash. "You went to fucking Julliard?"

Heat flooded my face and my body. It was a struggle not to zip my jacket up and hide behind my scarf again. "Yes," I said with an edge. "I know it sounds ridiculous since I—"

"My man, you're basically professionally trained. Why are you making me play myself by showing you my bootleg-ass way of learning shit?"

It was the last thing I'd expected him to say. His somewhat embarrassed expression was also the last thing I'd expected. The combination of his bunched brows and him shoving his phone in his pocket jerked me out of the defensive conclusions I'd jumped.

"No, no, don't say that." I sat up on my knees and waved my hands in front of me. "Please show me? I just spent six months on a cruise being forced to do stilted cabaret for audiences who only attended because it was free."

"Okay and?" Luis still wasn't buying it. He'd shoved his phone in his pocket again and was still looking embarrassed. "How is this gonna ruin that weak ass memory?"

"Because I haven't felt this excited about dancing in a long time. I avoided it for years after dropping out of Julliard, then I did *that*, and started to forget why I fucking love it. I was starting to feel like an idiot for missing it so much." I sat back on my heels. "But watching you dance tonight, like, breathed the fucking life back into me. You were amazing. And knowing it's all-natural talent? God. I'm obsessed."

The sly expression returned to Luis' beautiful face. "With me?"

"No, stupid. With your choreography."

He sighed tragically but pulled his phone out again. "Fine. But if we're gonna watch YouTube videos together, you need to take off your jacket and shoes. I don't play that shoes-in-the-house bullshit."

It reminded me so much of Stephanie and Jace that I laughed again. And this time, I didn't try to hide it. Or the way I smiled wider in the face of his dazzling grin.

The little knot I'd carried in my chest for the past several weeks loosened. Once my shoes were off, my layers discarded, and I was sitting in the middle of his studio with music flowing around me, I almost felt at home.

CHAPTER TEN
CHARLES

I t hadn't taken long for watching to turn into dancing. Charles seemed to experience performance with his entire body. He didn't just watch or listen, he moved to the music seemingly unconsciously while analyzing each video and absently moving his feet as if mimicking the steps. I could tell he was itching to try them out. When I suggested he do so, he showed zero hesitation.

In nothing more than his bare feet, leggings, and a tank top that looked more like a shredded rag, Charles threw himself into it. I expected some degree of self-consciousness because it was obvious dancing to salsatón and reggaetón was new to him, but once he started moving I saw nothing but confidence. And that confidence drew me in.

By the time he'd upgraded from slowly following the steps and rewinding the video to perfect each part, to working up a sweat, I was dying to join him. I drummed my hands on the floor to the beat, nodding my head and grinning as my boy lost himself in the beat. Within an hour, he had every hip thrust, turn and twist, and step almost down to a science.

The only thing missing was...

"Muéve ese culo, papi."

Charles looked back at me with his hair wet and sticking to the sides of his face. He stopped dancing, breathing hard, and nodded at me. "Can you show me?"

"You sure?" I teased, wiggling my eyebrows. "You're the big shot Julliard grad."

Charles rolled his eyes. "And you're the one who actually dances professionally."

"Professionally," I drawled, getting to my feet and pulling off my shirt. I did not miss the way those big brown eyes absently took in my torso and tats. "You're probably the first person to describe stripping that way to me."

"Because most people are dumb fucks. Pole dancing is legit hard. I wouldn't even have the leg strength or strength in my core to do it now."

"I rarely pole dance," I admitted. "But I'd love to watch you do it some time."

Charles' mouth twitched at the side. "Let's focus on this for now."

"Yeah we can." I winked. "For now."

We replayed the video again, and this time I danced while he watched me. We went through it multiple times, pausing in some sections, with me demonstrating in slow motion how he needed to move his ass, before he did the same. I guided his hips at times, then stood behind him with our bodies pinned so he could feel the motion of my hips and follow through with his own. He got it just like I knew he would, but I didn't sit down again.

Him practicing, and me teaching, evolved into us dancing together. Side-by-side and then modifying the dance as if we were partners showing off for each other. We let my playlist cycle through videos, dancing to each one. By the time we collapsed to the floor for a break, it was three in the morning, and I was drenched from sweat and exhausted.

"So hungry," Charles moaned. His arms were flung out dramatically as he sucked in breaths, still recovering from a routine we'd bungled multiple times before getting somewhat right. "And I have nothing upstairs but champagne and cheese."

"Fancy."

He snorted. "Yeah, Ashton and my other friends brought it for me. *They* are fancy."

There was a little edge in his voice when he said it, which hooked me in. I'd wondered about his lifestyle—how he managed to seemingly not work and stay home all day while I busted my ass to afford the apartment. After seeing him with Hollywood, I'd kind of assumed he was rich. Now? That seemed doubtful.

I rolled onto my stomach, leaning on my forearms, and ran my eyes over him. I deserved a fucking award for not getting wood while grinding all up on his ass the way I had while we were dancing. My body knew this was a precarious situation. Hitting on him was still uncertain territory. But us connecting through dance? That was a go.

"You can eat something here," I said after a while. "Raid the fridge."

"Really?" Charles rolled over to look at me. "Because I'm dying."

I snorted and squeezed his chin. "Get whatever you want, lindo. If you don't mind sharing that champagne."

Charles' lips curled up. "Go get it while I scavenge. Apartment's unlocked."

"Bet." I bit my lower lip, still holding his gaze, then kissed his cheek. "I'll be right back."

I was on my feet and leaving my apartment before he could make a thing about the kiss. There was a chance he wouldn't flip while lapsed in this post-dance euphoria that had his face rosy and eyes alight, but he was unpredictable. Leaving well enough alone was the right thing to do when it came to Charles. Letting this angry complicated man work things out on his own was the best plan—I knew that with every brain cell I had. But I also knew that his body called to mine and made it absolutely impossible to create the distance we probably needed.

"Luis, you stupid asshole," I muttered to myself after letting myself in through the battered wooden door leading to his place. "Coño. Yo tengo que dejar de pensar con el ripio."

His apartment was a big improvement from when I'd last visited. Besides the mess of his angry destruction, Landon had kept the place a mess. Now, even with the evidence of Charles having been in hermit-mode with one too many bottles of wine, the place was tidy and eclectic. There were paintings on the walls that I hadn't noticed before—abstracts and water colors all themed with dance or performance. I wondered if Landon's trifling ass had taken them down to further the impression that he'd lived alone.

Fucking scumbag.

Shaking my head, I found an unopened bottle of champagne in his completely empty fridge, and headed back downstairs. The music blasting through my door put a smile on my face. He'd switched from dance videos to stream a Princess Nokia album, and the sound of her old school hip-hop beats filling my apartment immediately uplifted me.

I padded to my kitchen all ready to tease him about raiding my playlists, but stopped in my tracks. He'd skinned out of his sweaty leggings and was standing in front of my fridge in nothing more than a pair of tight black briefs and his tank top. The refrigerator door half-hid the front of his body, but I drank in the miles of long legs, muscular thighs, and that tight round ass. His tank top was hanging off one shoulder, and his hair was wilder than usual as he half leaned over and studied the contents of my fridge.

Someone being that fine should be illegal. The fact that he looked fine while more than halfway naked and standing in my kitchen like he belonged here? That was just straight-up hacking.

"You haven't found nothing yet?" I asked, setting the bottle on the counter. "Because there's a bunch of—"

"Oh shit." Charles leaned down, sticking out that big ass of his, and popped back up cradling several foil containers with plastic tops. "Please fucking tell me this is what I think it is and that I can have some?"

"Dominican food from R.A. Deli?"

Charles bounced on his toes. "Oh my fucking God. Please share?"

I burst out laughing, legit charmed by him being all bright-eyed and excited about DR cooking that tasted like my mom had come down from the Bronx to put it together. The place was a total hole in the wall on Forest Avenue, but someone's abuelos were in the kitchen putting in serious work.

"Please, Luis?"

"Mmm. How can I resist you saying my name like that?"

"You can't," he said, arching a brow that disappeared into his halo of messy hair. "So gimme the food."

"Heat that shit up then. I don't fuck with cold food."

Charles grinned again, so big it lit up his entire face, and began raiding my cabinets for plastic containers. I literally had none because I tended to heat up everything on the stove, so he settled for making two huge plates of food as I popped the bottle. With Princess Nokia rapping about New York, the smell of food filling the kitchen, and Charles sitting on the edge of my counter with his long legs dangling, all remnants of my earlier bad mood were totally gone.

Once both plates were hot, we sat in the middle of my dance studio with the lights dim and the music lowered. I drank from the bottle of champagne and watched him bite into a platano maduro.

"Mmmmm," he moaned, closing his eyes and shivering. "So fucking good."

"Is that why you took them all?" I teased. "Greedy."

Charles' mouth turned up again at the side. He was so stingy with his smiles. "I only took one more than you."

"Still greedy."

"Split one?" he asked hopefully. "I'm desperate for good food. This is dire."

"Oh, well since it's *dire*...." I leaned in. "Gimme a bite and we'll call it even."

He chewed slowly, eyelids lowered as he studied me. It was only after I parted my lips did he hold the remaining platano to my mouth. My lips brushed against his finger as I ate the second half, so I licked the sweet greasiness from his fingertips.

I chewed and swallowed, mindful of his gaze on my throat and my mouth. Before he could catch himself, I pushed forward and kissed him. It was brief, just a slight press of marginally parted lips, but he sighed against me. Emboldened, I kissed him harder, slicked my tongue against the seam of his mouth, and groaned when he let me inside.

There always seemed to be a high chance of me never getting to kiss him again, so I poured myself into it. Closed my eyes to the dim gold lighting, and the food and the bottle, while the music syncopated and everything faded but the taste of Charles' mouth. The feel of his hand on my shoulder. His tongue sliding against my own. The way he sighed against me and slanted his mouth so I could taste even more of him.

He released a raw moan as my lips moved over his, and my dick throbbed in response. I slid my hand into all of that hair and curled my fingers into a fist, jerking him against me. He liked that. God, but he fucking liked that. He showed it by moaning again, louder this time, and attacked my mouth with the same hunger he'd showed for those tin takeout containers.

My entire body was burning, and I knew it was time to back off before I pushed the envelope a little too far, but he started sucking on my tongue. Yeah, he was as desperate for this as I was.

With my breathing already erratic, and my heart racing, I decided to give myself a heart attack by brushing my hand against Charles' dick. He was rock hard and poking through his underwear. I dragged my fingers against the length, and he pulled away with a long throaty groan.

It was my cue, and I instantly took it. I sat back on the floor, still sucking in hectic gulps of air, and stared at the food. Thankfully, it still looked delicious even when juxtaposed by the magic of kissing Charles. Instead of saying some wack shit that would ruin the chill vibe we'd had going all night, I leaned down to shovel moro de guandules into my mouth.

"I need to learn how to cook," I said around the food. "My mom isn't trying to drive down here to feed me every weekend anymore."

Charles took another deep breath, then grabbed another platano. "Did she when you first moved in?"

"Yup. She was paranoid about me living so far away."

"You're from the Bronx?"

"Yup. Val and Ashton live not too far from where I used stay at, although now they're in some gentrified condo thing." I leaned against the wall and balanced my plate on my lap. "Me and Val grew up talking shit to each other like every night at the boxing gym. We had different trainers who were both determined to make each of us the next motherfucker with the big name who would shine a spotlight on Cadet's. Then he matured, and I kept messing with him just for the fun of it. And because I had a feeling dude wasn't exactly hetero."

Charles watched me for a second, then shifted so he was sitting beside me with his back to the wall. He relaxed visibly, shoulders dipping down as he tucked into his plate. "Why didn't you try to bond with him instead of fucking with him then?"

"Psh. Because if I was wrong, and I went up to him all *hey guy, I'm pansexual, and you are?* There was a high chance of me getting my fucking ass whooped when he blabbed to everyone. Even when I kinda hinted at it while flirting with Ashton, I couldn't bring myself to just come right out and say I wasn't straight. I made it out like I'd make an exception for him."

Charles' chewing slowed. "You tried to fuck Ashton?"

Uh-oh. There was some fire brewing in that gaze of his, which was just so fascinating. "Calm yourself. It was like almost a year ago, and he's pretty as fuck. Also, I liked making Val mad."

Charles rolled his eyes and changed the subject. "You were always closeted then?"

"Pretty much. I knew it wasn't gonna go down well with my friends and even my family. The only reason I knew my mom wasn't a hater is because she has a trans sister so was aware of LGBT issues when she was mad young. Every time we go to my grandparents' place, they say some shit about it and my mom is the lone one standing up to them. Yaneris, my aunt, just stays away."

"That sucks," Charles said. "I fucking hate people."

"Yeah, me too. That's why I'm on Shitty Island instead of in the BX where I belong."

I shoveled a healthy forkful of rice, peas, and pernil into my mouth. Comfort food and Charles' warm body so close to my own prevented me from clenching up the way I almost always did when thinking about home.

"Am I allowed to ask what happened at the gym?"

I swiped my tongue over my lower lip. "Yeah. But then do I get to ask about you?"

"What about me?"

"Everything. You're a mystery."

Charles scoffed. "Not really. Everyone on the block knows me and Landon used to fight like animals."

"I'm not talking about that," I said quickly, looking at him. "I want to know about *you*. Not you and that dick. He's not worth your time to even talk about in the retrospect."

Charles nodded slowly, his fork clutched in one hand. "I like that plan better."

"Good."

"And we don't have to talk about your stuff it it's upsetting," he said. "I don't... want to ruin this. For either of us."

"Ruin what?"

He set the fork down and tilted his head against the wall. "This night. Us hanging out? If I'm being honest with myself, this is probably the best fucking night I've had in a long time. Is that weird?"

"Nah. I'm pretty quality company."

Charles laughed, but this time he didn't try to cover it. "I swear to God, Luis. I'm supposed to hate you but you've been my defibrillator."

"Sexy." I smiled when he laughed again, and squeezed his shoulder. "What about with Ashton and that whole crew who came through the other day? They seem fun."

"They are. But…" Charles grabbed the bottle and guzzled champagne. "Even when I'm with them or my best friend, Caleb, there was always shit I was keeping to myself because I didn't want them to realize I was even more of a disaster than they already knew about. So, I hid most of the Landon thing. How… angry and depressed I get. That I'm super fucking jealous of all of them, and that I hate my life. It was always me being me but not entirely. Like acid-washed Charles. The trendy version that's kinda cheap and shitty."

"I get it."

He arched an eyebrow. "Do you really?"

"Yeah. You pretended to not hate people, and I pretended to be straight. Equally cheap and shitty versions of ourselves."

This time when Charles laughed, he was mid-sip of champagne and choked on it. I slapped his back, snickering, and grabbed the bottle before he spilled the last of it.

"Okay, but for real, I will tell you why I left boxing if you tell me what's up with you and dancing. Because…" I wagged my finger at him. "I can tell there's a thing there." He didn't deny it, or refuse, so I continued. "Basically, I've been stripping since I got this body. I love to dance, and I love having people look at me when I'm naked, so it seemed to make sense. The place I stripped at was this fucking hole in the wall farther up the Grand Concourse, so I didn't think anyone would find out except who I chose to tell. But… a guy from the block showed up one day and word got around."

"He admitted to being at a strip club with male dancers?" Charles asked incredulously. "Or he made up some shit?"

"Said he heard I was giving dudes lap dances and made up this whole dumbass story." I rolled my eyes. "No one believed him, to be honest. I mean people had jokes sometimes, but the way my friends reacted—trying to force me to fuck the dude up for making up supposed lies—pretty much showed me it was better off I stayed closeted. This kid Bronson basically wanted to go stomp the dude out. Like fucking kill the guy. He's a total maniac."

Charles drew his knees up to his chin and wrapped his arms around them. He looked vulnerable that way, as if he was trying to shield himself. "So, he thought this guy saying you might not be straight warranted him being... *murdered*?"

"Yeah, I mean he didn't say it outright, but I could tell he was ready to put the dude down. So, when I finally came out, no big surprise that Bronson threatened to put *me* down. He really can't handle being around queer people. That's why I tried to keep Val and Ashton the fuck away from him. It's why I'm here now. I can't deal with watching my back all the time, waiting for this dude to try to convince people to jump me since he's too chicken shit to fight me on his own."

"Jesus, Luis," Charles hissed. His hand shot out to cover mine, fingers tightening. "I'm sorry."

"Don't be." I squeezed his hand in return, loving that they were rough like mine. "Anyways, I only came out because of the shit with Valdrin. Word had gotten around about him and Ashton, so Bronson was harassing Ashton while me and Val were in the ring. I didn't realize it at the time, and knocked him out. I felt like shit after, and refused to accept the win. And I let them rile me up during an interview while they were pressing me on why I wouldn't accept, and I said he wasn't the only queer dude at Cadet's, and that people needed to stop acting like him and Ashton being together was the fucking distraction and not some piece of shit homophobe." I dragged my thumb against Charles' hand, thinking about that day and how the shit had gone viral in the amateur boxing community. "I get too hotheaded and run off at the mouth. I regretted it at first, but now I'm glad it's done."

"Even though you quit?"

"Yeah." I shrugged, like it didn't matter, even though it did. Not because I missed fighting but more because I hated that the choice had been taken out of my hands. "My trainer dropped me, and I knew no promoter would really be into me, so why the fuck should I get my face beat in while making no money to no end? It's bullshit. I was going to start up with a new trainer here, but by the time I moved the story had spread. I was done. You know? I'm not too good at taking shit and there was no way I was going to suck up the hate just so I could keep fighting."

"So you started dancing," Charles said. "And... planning to be a personal trainer?"

"If I can ever get the money together to start renting a space. Shit's not easy, you know? Money's hard to come by when you're on your own."

"Oh, I fucking know that." Charles whooshed out a disgusted breath. He didn't pull his hand away when I brought it to my lips and kissed the back of it. In fact, he shot me a tiny smile. "So, apparently we have more in common than dancing and living in this house. And Landon. My parents were super homophobes, and I haven't seen them in years. I really don't even care anymore. I was closest to my grandmother. She knew I was gay even before I knew, and would encourage me when it came to dancing and dressing how I wanted. Being me."

"She's the one who gave you that little statue?"

Charles nodded. "She also left me a fortune for school when she died. That's how I got into Julliar—"

"You got into Julliard because you're crazy talented. You paid with the money."

"Don't interrupt," he chastised even while smiling slightly. "Anyway, the money she left me only paid for two years, then I couldn't finish. And I didn't know what to do with myself. So, I panicked and started working random jobs to get by and let dancing get away from me. Then I met Landon, and... I was so desperate for validation from someone after being so down on myself that I sucked up every drop of attention he gave me. And back then, he gave me a lot. Toted me around like arm candy."

I shifted closer to him, protectively. He leaned against me, letting me put my arm around him.

"I used to think his possessiveness was a sign that he loved me. Didn't want to share me. After being lonely and miserable, the idea of someone wanting me that much was fucking gold. I was so hungry to have attention. But then he got controlling and started talking me out of everything I wanted to do, all while twisting it to make it seem like he was saving me from disappointment. He talked me out of auditioning for tons of roles until I gave up on dancing altogether. Then he'd try to... turn me against my friends by overanalyzing situations or things on social media to make me feel like people were subbing me or doing things without me."

Charles laughed dryly. "It seems so stupid now, but back then those things were so important. The idea of my dancing friends moving on and forgetting about me was a massive blow, and now I don't even know if it was true or if he just gaslit me into thinking it was true? Either way, he used that to alienate me from everyone until I started bartending and met some of my current friends. Michael Rodriguez, David Butler, Caleb Stone... Through them, I met everyone else. And without them, I don't know where I'd be."

Without thinking about it, I started rubbing his shoulders—digging my fingers in and trying to work the growing tension out of them. I should have known that he'd be unable to divorce talk of his past from Landon. And I should have known better than to push for more info about someone who was reluctant to show something as small as a smile.

"I don't even know where I am now," he said quietly. "Just... drifting. Wishing I could dance but knowing I only have a couple of months before I'm totally out of money. So I'll have to go back to juggling multiple jobs and hating my life and feeling worthless. And being dramatic about my failures in the process."

"Ey," I said, bopping his ear. "You didn't fail. Life just got in the way. Same for me and boxing, right? I didn't quit because I'm a failure. I quit because it wasn't the right time for me to fight. And now I've found something else I want to do."

"But I haven't. I thought I'd want to do the cruise, but it was awful. I honestly would rather not dance than dance with zero creativity or vision. I felt like they were collectively ruining everything that dance means to me." When I nodded, Charles glanced over at me, expression wry and smiling again. I was winning the jackpot here. "You have no idea how nice it is to be able to talk about this with someone who gets it."

"Same." I snuck a kiss to his cheek. "I appreciate you talking to me at all. And I hope that means we're past all of that shit that happened?"

"I am."

"You promise?" I asked warningly. "Because…"

"I promise," he said, rolling his eyes. "What do you want me to do? A fucking blood pact? Pinky swear?"

"Yup. Pinky swear." I held up my pinky, and he looked at me like I was an idiot. "Yo, this is serious shit. Pinky up."

Charles shook his head, but he held up his pinky and cinched it with mine. When I squeezed hard, he broke out in snickers.

"God, you are so weird."

"Yeah, the weird neighbor," I said through a yawn. "That's all you had to say about me?"

Charles lifted his eyebrows and flicked his gaze away. "I said some other stuff too."

The lower pitch of his voice stirred my interest. I traced his profile, the high cheekbones and shape of his wide lips, and had to stop myself from asking him whether he'd told them about how we'd ground our dicks together in the basement. How sloppy we'd kissed while clutching each other.

"I'm gonna go to sleep," he said, pushing his empty plate away. "It's like four in the morning."

"You could sleep here."

"If I stay here, we won't end up sleeping, Luis."

I just grinned up at him.

"No, boo. No." Charles got to his feet, and in the brief moment when he was in front of me, I saw he had a semi of his own. We were in total sync, and needed to fuck each other. Soon. "I want to leave things like this for now. It feels good." He paused, arms crossed over his chest. "It feels comfortable and safe."

And… there went any plan to seduce him into staying. I got to my feet, standing close to him but not all up in his space, and nodded. "I get it. But just so you know, I'm gonna be tight as fuck if you go back to ignoring me and pretending like… There's nothing going on here."

"I won't." He laughed sardonically. "I can't. I told you—you're my defibrillator. I said before I didn't know what I'd have done without my friends. And these past few weeks? I don't know how it would have played out if you hadn't been around."

I clutched my hand to my chest. "Stop. You're gonna kill me. Even more so when you come down the stairs tomorrow and play me by giving me all that attitude again."

Charles shoved my shoulder. "I won't!"

Grabbing his arm, I pulled him closer. "You swear?"

He searched my face with those dark eyes of his, then pulled me in for a kiss. Maybe it was supposed to be short and sweet, maybe not. Either way, it turned into us pressed against the wall while tonguing each other until we were breathless all over again. If I had one wish in that moment, when his fingers were digging into my shoulders and my hand was gripping one of his thick ass cheeks, it would be for him to realize we could stay safe even if we went to bed together. But I had no guarantee of that. No way to make it a real promise. And I had no desire to talk him into something he'd regret.

So, I pulled away from him, licked his taste off my lips and adjusted my dick, and nodded at the door. "Go to bed."

He exhaled slowly, a shuddering sound, then grabbed his leggings. "I'm taking the champagne. I need more alcohol."

No, he needed my dick in him, but we were not going to discuss such obvious things.

"See you later, lindo."

Charles snagged the last platano from my plate and wiggled his fingers. "Bye Luis."

CHAPTER ELEVEN
CHARLES

C atching glimpses of my downstairs neighbor had become one of my favorite activities in the past couple of days. My time basically consisted of me curling up in the sunroom while smoking pot and idly looking at inadequate job listings, or my rapidly shrinking bank account, and straining to see him out the window if I heard his voice. As much as I told myself that getting invested in the happy-feeling that expanded in my chest when I spent time with Luis, it didn't change that the feeling existed.

So, I chased it. Discreetly.

Luis was a busy boy, so I heard him coming and going a lot. To the store, the gym, to work... He was always on the move, unlike me. For some reason, I could still not bring myself to venture too far from the house. However, despite always going here or there, Luis didn't have many visitors.

That was probably why it stood out so much when a white sedan pulled up outside of the house, and a group of people got out. There were two women, and a guy who looked like an older but less muscular version of Luis. One of the women was carrying a large bag, and the other had a case of beer.

"Luis," one of the women called as she approached the stairs. "Open the door, papi!"

I leaned against the screen, trying to see more, but was thwarted quickly. The entire house creaked when Luis opened the front door, and everyone disappeared inside. If I had to guess by their appearances, and the fact that they were now downstairs excitedly speaking Spanish to each other, I would guess they were family. The man had definitely been his dad or an older brother.

This was usually the point in time when envy would put the whammy on me. Parental jealousy didn't happen often since most of my friends had equally disastrous relationships with their folks, but every now and again I turned into the green monster when someone got to bragging about their family. It had happened a lot with Landon, but now part of me was starting to wonder if he'd talked about his amazingly supportive parents to twist an invisible knife in my gut. He'd known my story, and had constantly compared it to his own. If I grew agitated by the conversation, he'd only lay it on thicker.

The thing about Landon was that he'd grown up super privileged. He'd come from a family of white preppy liberals who'd acted like their only son was a golden ticket to a special afterlife if they constantly paid him tribute. Shit you not—those people had ensured Landon would never need to work a steady job through high school or college, had paid for his apartment for a few years after college, and had continued to float him money until his late twenties roared in with the same freight train of entitlement. The terrible thing was that they'd been shocked at his blunt refusal to work a steady job even though they'd helped to create that monster.

After they'd pulled back, he'd often whined about them "cutting him off". That was the part that had always made me twitch. My parents had literally disowned me after realizing me liking makeup and tight clothes wasn't just a phase. What Landon meant by being "cut off" was that they still floated him cash, but had revoked his access to their credit cards.

What a hardship.

He'd started selling weed and pills on the side to keep his lifestyle going and, because I'd been so *in love*, I'd accepted his major flaws and picked up the slack. His whole family situation had been a different breed of screwed up than mine, but still I'd gritted my teeth and fumed whenever they sent him gifts or called. Three times a week without fail. They were always checking in.

My parents hadn't called me since they'd realized my grandmother had left her money only to me.

And now I was jealous and bitter all over again. I'd bet *anything* that Landon was at their house right now—the huge colonial in Connecticut not too far from Brown University. Maybe his dad, the professor, was once again wasting his brain cells trying to figure out how to get Landon back into college. As if he'd do anything but hawk his petty drugs to the students.

For a long moment, I stood in the middle of the sunroom and glared into space. The questions about where Landon was and what he was doing tripled in my head, so loud and demanding that they even managed to yell at me over the sound of Luis and his family downstairs. I tried to fight that desire to find out, because I knew what would happen.

I'd find out he was just fine after having moved on with his shitty selfish life, and I'd hate myself for still fixating on our past. On becoming a weird hermit who had started using pharmacy shampoo on my hair. I knew all of that would happen, and yet I still strode out of the sunroom to grab my phone from the charging dock by the door.

I sat on the floor in the middle of my dance studio as music and the loud tangle of voices floated from Luis' open windows. Focusing on them was the right thing to do, even it was weird and marginally pathetic to be comforted by my neighbor's voice. Again, I told myself to put the phone down, but... I didn't do it.

Within five minutes, I'd redownloaded all my social media apps.

Within ten, I'd scoured Landon's accounts and was promptly filled with humiliation so intense it was amazing I didn't burst into flames. On each account there was a steady mix of subs that had escalated to outright attacks... on me.

It had started right after our breakup. There were a series of vague posts about how "someone" had discarded him and abandoned him to find his own way, just like his parents had in the past. It led to dramatic posts implying he was living on the street despite the fact that the locations made it clear he was at his parent's house, and then a series of overt rants about how I'd broken up with him before going on the cruise and had agreed to remain roommates.

It was a blatant lie. But the worst part?

It's weird how the story changed when C failed... once again... at his dream, and needed someone to take it out on. We had an understanding, but when he once again gave up or quit, I became the whipping boy. He slept with the entire crew while on the cruise, but he found me hanging out with my neighbor and destroyed my belongings before kicking me into the street. *How is that fair? How is that SANE? Anyone else would have called the police.*

Once again... I let his tears and emotional manipulation guilt me into letting him off the hook. As usual... he had a meltdown that led to be being convinced *I* am the one who did wrong, even tho I know I didn't. But here I am... with nothing... while he plays the victim.

When does it end?

I reread the rant over and over again, unable to believe my eyes.

How could someone be so narcissistic that they thought they could blatantly lie and get away with it? How could he think *I* was the one who was manipulative? Or that he was the goddamn whipping boy?

The reversal in facts had my head spinning. When I expanded the comments below to see the response, betrayal joined my humiliation until I felt like throwing up. There was plenty of support for him from his friends, which I'd expected, but there were also several likes and comments from people who had been mutuals.

A girl we'd once befriended at the gym had sent him broken heart emojis and a message that simply said "good for you for getting out of that toxic shit."

One of our old neighbors, half of an older gay couple, commended him for finally walking away even if it would be hard for a while.

My old co-worker, the other bartender who I'd worked with for years, stated that everyone knew I'd never been faithful. *Pretty sure he was fucking his teacher friend. Always had the suspicion, but didn't know if it was my business to tell you...*

Then another former colleague—a waitress at the bar. *Um, yeah, he was probably fucking his rich friend too. [eyeroll emoji] Charles is good at playing victim, but eventually everyone will see the truth. Be strong.*

They were just words. I knew they were. They were bullshit words, and those assholes were bullshit people, and I'd known Landon would do this. I'd known he would pull this card, go on the offense, and turn me into the villain. Part of me didn't know if he did it to protect his status as a loveable pothead that his friends needed to take care of and protect, further extending his multiple gravy trains, or if he was just that deadset on punishing me.

He would have known how deep those betrayals cut. And he

would have known that even though he was lying, the conviction in his text and those quick cosigns from our mutual friends, would have led to me doubting myself.

And they did.

I hunched forward with my forehead pressing against the floor and reminded myself of the facts. He'd lied to me. He'd admitted to cheating on me for years. He'd blatantly stated that he'd been running around behind my back when I was at work or with friends. He'd wanted to hit me when I'd called him out. He'd hit me before. He knew my deepest fear was my friends, my found family, abandoning me the way my biological family had. He was exploiting that fear even now.

Those reminders ran through my head like a chant until I was able to unclench myself from the tense ball I'd curled into.

I looked at the post and comments again. This time, rage swept up instead of a sinking feeling of dread. It made me feel better. Being angry was so much better than feeling worthless and alone.

"Fuck you, Landon," I snarled at the screen. "Hope you swipe your fucking metro card straight to hell!"

My words were so loud in my quiet apartment that they projected out the window, and echoed in the damn walkway leading to the basement. The rapid Spanish-speaking below halted. I nearly slammed my head into the floor in embarrassment. Always making a scene.

"Who the hell is that?" someone's voice floated up from Luis' apartment. "Someone fighting?"

"Nah," Luis' deep voice said, amusement threading through his buoyant tone. "That's just my boo."

I had to put my hand over my mouth to muffle the bark of laughter that nearly popped out. Of course, it would be Luis to say something so random, so out of the way, that it was almost impossible for me to stay upset. Leave it to him to effortlessly light me up when I was feeling down.

Sighing softly, I shoved my phone to the side and rolled onto my back. Was it pathetic to be so comforted by Luis? By the sound of music and the smell of food floating up from his apartment? Maybe. But at the moment, his existence was giving me something to look forward to.

LUIS

"So, when are you coming to visit?"

Hours had passed without mention of the Bronx, so I'd started to hope we could get through the visit without the conversation. Apparently not.

My mother looked at me from her perch in the arm chair, one leg crossed over the other and a cup of coffee in her hand. My dad was in the kitchen cleaning up the remnants of our feast, and likely packing away leftovers for me to have for the next few days, so it was just me, Mami, and Yaneris.

"Mami," I groaned from my sprawl on the sofa. "Why do you have to go there?"

"It's not just Linda," Yaneris said, raising one perfectly crafted eyebrow. "I miss you coming by every weekend."

My mom nodded her agreement. "It's not the same without you. I miss our breakfasts and lunches, and cheering for you at the fights—"

I held up a hand. "Okay, hold it there. The fighting is over, and you know it. You know why."

My mother sighed into her coffee cup, but Yaneris nodded. "Yes, we know, but that's different. Coming to the Bronx is not the same as going to Cadet's. That boxing gym isn't the whole neighborhood."

"But the people who go to it are," I said sharply. "I have plans here. I'm happy here. I miss y'all, but I do not miss being harassed on a daily basis by Bronson and his boys."

To that, my mother couldn't argue. She set her cup down before folding her hands primly on her lap. "Do you want me to call my cousin?"

I snorted. "No. Isn't he in jail?"

"Just released," she said innocently. "I'm sure he has some time on his hands since he's again sitting in my mother's house waiting for the next felony. Might as well be on someone like Bronson."

Yaneris hooted, clapping her hands, but I rolled my eyes. "No, mami, I do not want your cousin to assault Bronson. I'll deal with that homophobe on my own."

"But when?" Mami demanded. "I want my baby home, not avoiding my house because of *that homophobe*. Why is it fair that he still gets to loiter outside of Rite Aid while you hide in this ugly red borough?"

"I'm gonna have to disagree on Staten Island being ugly," I muttered. "And besides that, there's some good things here. I like it."

"*Bullshit.*"

My mother inhaled deeply, then proceeded to release of mutters in Spanish that drew my father out of the kitchen. He hovered warily, looking between us, before backtracking while holding a stack of empty Tupperware.

"Wuss," I muttered in his direction.

He raised an eyebrow then fled.

"I don't know where you think you are going, Hector," my mother snapped at him. "We just had this same conversation on the way here."

"And I agreed with my son," my dad's voice floated inside.

I clutched my chest, nearly dying of shock.

Yaneris put a hand on my mother's arm. "Give it time. If he's happy here, we can keep visiting him here. He needs time to establish his new life, and feel good about it, before confronting the old one. It's not easy, mama. Don't be such an ass."

Only Yaneris could get away with calling my mother an ass, but it was still dicey. I waited in anticipation, wondering if my mother would cool out or if they'd burst into an argument loud enough to rival Charles' big mouth, but she sighed.

"Fine, fine."

We spent the next hour watching dance videos, with my father doing his best to mimic my moves while Yaneris cat called. It turned into the three of them dancing while I sang along with the music, and my heart could not have been fuller. There were people in the world, even other queer people, who really thought it was no big thing to come out to your parents these days. Television had convinced them that everyone was accepting. That you would be safe. I had generally assumed those people had never known anyone outside of their own culture.

Even knowing my mother had been an ally for queer people, I'd worried about telling her. I'd feared telling my dad. I'd feared the ally talk flipping as soon as it came to their own son—the boxer who was supposed to be the pinnacle of masculinity. But they hadn't. They'd gone above and beyond to support me, and I would never stop being grateful.

Maybe it was a problem that I *felt* grateful for my parents continuing to love me, but it could have all gone so differently.

Once they were walking out, and we were all in the vestibule, I took turns squeezing each of them so tight they gasped for breath.

"I love you," I said, burying my face in my mother's hair. "I'll come visit soon, okay Mami? I won't let that piece of shit keep me from my family, and my neighborhood."

She pulled back, instantly worried despite having lobbied for it all day. "Be sure. I know I'm impatience, but I want you happy. I want you safe."

I waved my hand, scoffing cockily. "I'll be fine."

Yaneris gave me a sharp-eyed glare, and murmured for me to be careful, before I herded them outside and into their car. It was once again starting to rain, and rush hour was going to be a bitch.

My mouth shouted her love for me out the window as they drove off. I stood there smiling, and waving, but my fondness turned to melancholy as soon as their taillights disappeared.

I missed them so much. They were always at the back of my mind, but it wasn't until they visited did I really feel the hole in my chest at being so far from my family. Sure, we were all in the five boroughs, but the trek from the Bronx to Staten Island was no joke. Especially when they all worked full-time, and I refused to make the trip their way.

My mom was right. It had to end. Even if going back to the Bronx ended with me getting my ass whooped, I had to face that possibility and stop hiding. I just didn't know when.

The door creaked open, and I looked over my shoulder to see Charles stepping out onto the steps. Almost instantly, my smile was back. This dude was seriously up there making an obvious show of checking the mail and not paying attention to me.

I crossed my arms over my chest and watched him pick through the mail, looking edible in a pair of shorts that barely covered his ass and a slouchy tank top that barely stayed on his shoulder. Only after I stared at him without speaking for a solid thirty seconds, did he glance over.

"What's wrong with you?" Charles frowned as if he hadn't meant to say that and shook his head. "I mean... why are you standing in the rain like a weirdo?"

"It's barely raining."

He made a face.

"I'm being emo and dramatic?" I tried again, moving closer. "My parents were here."

"Oh?" Charles was not good at lying. In fact, he was so bad at it that I was convinced he wasn't even trying. He probably just felt obligated to pretend he wasn't paying attention to me. "You miss them or some sappy shit?"

I jogged up the stairs and stepped into the vestibule with him just as the rain picked up. "Yeah. I don't go see them much in the Bronx, and I told you—they stopped visiting here as much. It's far."

Charles toed the door shut, still holding his mail. It was a single bright red envelope, which was interesting because I'd peeked inside earlier and had seen about a dozen envelopes with he or Landon's name. In the past, I'd assumed his mail was an old tenant. Now, of course, I knew that wasn't the case.

"Didn't you check your mail already today?"

Charles pressed his lips together. "No."

"Hmm. Weird, because you had stuff in there earlier, and I'm pretty sure that envelope is just addressed to any current resident."

"Oh, shut up." He rolled his eyes and threw the envelope at me. "Why don't you go see your parents?"

"Because I'm avoiding my problems. My problems being... the homophobes who live on my block. Y'know, the assholes I told you about before?"

Charles scowled. "Fuck them. Just stay here and join the avoidant hermit club."

"Does that mean you officially accept me as a member?"

He couldn't hide the hint of a smile. If I was being honest with myself, I knew he was kind of a hot mess. His hair was wilder than usual, his eyes bloodshot from either lack of smoke or marijuana, and his lips were wine-stained. Yet, none of that changed that he was sometimes straight-up ethereal. A long-legged pothead fairy with a sinful mouth.

Charles cleared his throat, and I realized I'd just been standing and staring at him. He ran a hand through his hair, then took the smallest possible step towards his door. "Gotta get back to my Shameless marathon, so..."

"See you around?" I asked, taking a step towards my own apartment.

"Obviously. We live five feet apart according to Grindr."

I snorted out a laugh. "Bye, lindo. Go eat something."

Charles mimicked me silently, and didn't protest when I drew him in for a kiss to his cheek. I'd planned to let him go, I really did, but my mouth instantly followed the peck with a firmer kiss on his lips.

"Mmm." Charles reached for his doorknob with one hand, but the other was on my waist. We were still all in each other's face, his gaze glued to my mouth. "See you."

"Okay."

I was addicted, so I followed my second goodbye with yet another kiss and told myself to move my goddamn feet. Get in your apartment, asshole! It was only a few steps away. I made the move, or at least I picked up my foot, but this time it was Charles who leaned in again. When I backed towards my door, it was because my ethereal pothead was pressing me against it with his tongue my mouth.

There was no telling whether it was a farewell or an invitation anymore, but we spent the next several minutes kissing. His body molded to mine with his dick hard against my thigh, and my fingers wound in those tangled curls while our tongues tangled wetly. Neither of us made a move to escalate it, and for some reason that made my heart pound harder. This wasn't about getting off. I wasn't actually sure what this was about, but I was in love with how it made me feel.

We parted only when both our breathing had grown erratic. It was also getting difficult not to dry hump him, but I kept it under control.

"You really going this time?" I asked.

"Shut up." Charles finally backed away from me. His erection looked obscene in his tiny shorts, but he just messed with his hair and acted like everything was cool. "You want to come up and watch Shameless with me?"

"Netflix and chill?"

He sneered. "Netflix and you share that food with me. I know you have some."

"How do you know, little spy?"

Charles turned to his door. "Whatevs. Come up or not. It's your life."

"As long as I don't come without food?"

"Exactly."

He disappeared into his apartment, but kept his door open. It was more of an invitation than the actual words he'd used to ask me up. Maybe I *was* hiding in Staten Island, but at least I had Charles to keep me company.

CHAPTER TWELVE
CHARLES

"I'm starting to like Staten Island."

I snorted at Stephanie as we walked along Forest Avenue with Jace and Meredith. They'd made the trek onto the island for our weekly (or what had been the weekly) super queer brunch since I was still in turtle mode and refusing to commute into the city. They'd surprised me with a Facebook invite, and the real surprise had been that brunch would be on my turf instead of theirs. Ashton had been unable to come due to a special event at Gateway—the youth center he volunteered at.

"You're just saying that because you lazy assholes had Jace's bodyguard drive you," I said with a snort. "No ferry or bus."

"Chester doesn't mind," Jace reassured, grinning from beneath a big purple fedora that only worked because he was beautiful and looked like some fae creature from a Holly Black novel. "He knows what a brat I am, and he still demanded to be my personal guard. Said Tonya would be spread too thin if she covered me, Chris, and Aiden."

"I still can't believe this is a thing," I said as we turned onto my block and started up the hill. "Like, is it safe for us to even be walking around the island like this? Is some fucking alt right bro going to jump out of the bushes? Because I will cut a bitch."

Mere looked around at the question, mouth curling into a frown, and I instantly felt like an asshole. Somehow, being so disconnected from the situation led to me forgetting how real this must have been for all of them, but especially her.

"The threats are constant," she said, irritation coloring her tone. "They come to our emails, they get mailed to the office, and even our home addresses. So far, we haven't been able to trace the physical mailings, but Clive has been working on the subpoenas for the cable and Internet providers attached to the IP addresses that stem from the social media stuff. There's so much that goes into it that we may not track everyone down for literally years."

"But the guy who started this all, QFindr's former IT manager, is already being hit with a lawsuit," Jace said. "That's something."

"Not enough," Stephanie said with a frown. "I just feel like this spread so far that you'll never get everyone until they get bored and move onto something else. And even then, do you want them focusing on someone else?"

"Exactly." Mere ran her hands through her butt-length blond curls and shook them out. "It's just a big mess. Every time I forget about it, and try to focus on everything that's going right, I'll get an email or an envelope, and... I don't know. It's just always *there*."

I didn't know what to say, and I felt like shit for being so helpless. It was so easy to lose myself in my own problems and my own drama that I'd forgotten how much heavy stuff my friends were going through on their own. My version of self-care meant pulling back and isolating myself to feel safe. But what would happen when I tried to rejoin their fold full-time only to find that I hadn't been there when they needed me?

I put an arm around Meredith and pulled her in for a half-hug. She wasn't much of a hugger, but she pressed against me with a tired smile.

"The good thing," Jace drawled, jumping up on the brick wall surrounding my neighbor's house and walking along it. "Is that Clive thinks if he totally crucifies ole IT fuckboy, everyone else will back off so they don't get the same treatment. And he plans to hit him with everything he has. He got all growly while talking about it."

"I think his growliness is making him think he's invincible," Mere muttered. "He's gotten more threats than us because he's the one going after them legally. Yet he refuses a bodyguard of his own."

Jace shrugged. "Can't force him. He can take care of himself. I mean, he lives in fucking Whitestone."

"Whitestone is mad racist," Stephanie said. "One of those Queens holdouts."

They all lapsed into a moody silence at that, Mere scowling at the ground, Stephanie watching her out of the corner of her eye, and Jace silently strolling along in his purple hat. If Ashton were here, he would have thought of a way to lighten the mood or find a bright spot through all the storm clouds, but that wasn't really my bag. I didn't have an array of strategies in my bag of social tricks to cheer people up when I spent ninety percent of my life pretending I wasn't in a bad mood. The best thing I could do was distract them, but I was at a total loss as to how.

"Where's my boy A-Town?"

I looked up to see Luis standing by the steps leading to our house wearing his usual around the house uniform of Nike slides, tight sweatpants, and a tank top. Usually this uniform meant he was about to either workout or practice in his dance studio or at the gym, and that meant I would be receiving an invitation to join him. Which I generally accepted.

The last couple of weeks had been... different. Very different.

As in, he and I wound up seeing each other every single day. Sometimes more than once a day. I'd go down to check the mail, and he'd randomly appear to do the same. Same with taking out the garbage or cleaning up the front of the house. Dinner or lunch time had turned into a texted question about whether one of us had cooked and if we wanted to share. And blasting music meant practice or workout time, which was more fun as a pair so I almost always found myself drifting down to his apartment to join him.

What made all of this so exceptional was that these random encounters usually started and ended with a kiss hello or goodbye. And sometimes, especially after an exceptionally enthusiastic dance session, his seemingly careless showers of affection caused a chaste kiss to escalate into a hungry make out session. We were like fucking teenagers.

It was honestly refreshing in a way I hadn't experienced... ever. Even as a teenager, all my relationships had been plagued with an intensity and urgency that things *had to work* since things had been so disastrous with my parents. I'd *needed* other people to be the right people because there had been so few of those around me. Ninety-nine percent of my friendships had been spent with me overcompensating just so my friends wouldn't abandon me. And it had been the same with Landon.

But my friendship with Luis? Everything had been aired and put out in the open right from the get go—my extreme anger, my messiness, my depression, my bitterness and how spiteful I could be. He knew everything, and yet he was still pursuing my friendship. Still pursing me.

It was why dancing and working out together had also turned into the dinners, the random kisses good morning. And of course us doing laundry together and lazily exploring each other's mouths while sitting on the washers and dryers like two teenagers sneaking out. And the way we parted ways with no muss or fuss? It was delightful.

"Ashton had a thing," I said as we stopped by the stairs. "And he hates being called A-Town."

"Oh yeah?" Luis casually dropped a kiss on my cheek before jerking his chin at the others as a greeting. Such a New Yorker. Such a tough guy. "I'll stick with Hollywood."

"Or you could call him Ashton," Stephanie suggested. "Since that's his name."

"Or I could wait until he tells me that and ignore you since I don't know you," Luis replied with a wink.

She rolled her eyes. "If you want him to sponsor your gym, you might try to be a little more respectful."

"Sponsor?" Luis made an affronted face. "Mamita, I don't need—"

"Fuck that mamita shit."

"You're pretty mean."

Stephanie shrugged, unapologetic, while Meredith did a poor job of covering her amusement. Jace seemed more interested in the pitiful flowers growing by the gate than the entire conversation. He was shaking his head mournfully, probably sad that no one had taken better care of something so fragile. My gentle-hearted friend had a way of making me feel guilty over ridiculously small things.

"You remind me of my friend Raymond," Stephanie said. "So, I feel obligated to give you a hard time."

"That's real nice of you." Luis looked at me for a support and laughed when I only shrugged one shoulder. "All right, well, I'm gonna assume you're busy."

"I am." I shot a quick glance at my friends, then back to him. "At the moment."

"Hit me up later?" he asked, not masking his hopefulness. "I want your opinion on something. It's semi important."

"Semi? I dunno. I only give my opinion on majorly important shit."

He scoffed. "Just come down."

I sighed tragically, like it was a hardship. "Fine."

"Bet."

Luis kissed me again, this time a slightly longer kiss on the mouth. Even with the audience of my friends, I couldn't help but respond. The flutter in my belly and in my chest wouldn't allow me to do anything else.

He pulled away, nodded at my friends as if everything was totally normal, and jogged up the stairs to return to his apartment. I could feel stares on my face burning like the heat from the sun, but I stayed shut as we entered the house and trooped up the staircase to my own apartment. By then, music was blasting in Luis' place, and I knew he'd needed my opinion on something dance related. That was another delight.

Although we'd been dancing together several nights a week for the past two weeks, and I felt like I was learning things from him I'd never learned in a formal class, he constantly asked for my feedback on his routines. For me, my time at Julliard was a giant reminder of my failure. To him, it meant I'd worked with professional dancers who'd taught me things he wanted to know. It was the first time in a long time I'd used that time in my life for something constructive.

"So..." Mere drawled once we were plopped onto my mismatched living room furniture and recovering from overstuffing ourselves at Staten Island Diner. "You and the weird neighbor are dating? And you failed to mention—"

"We're not dating," I said, laughing incredulously. "Not even close. We've become friends. That's it."

Stephanie side eyed. "Carlito. I do not kiss my friends that way."

"Yes you do," Jace said between fake coughs.

Meredith dissolved into giggles.

Stephanie flipped him off. "Okay, I don't *anymore*."

"Just keeping everyone honest," Jace said helpfully. "But I too want to know about that very couple-like series of smooches I just witnessed."

"Oh my God." I rolled my eyes and grabbed a throw pillow, pressing it to my face. "That's just how he is. Affectionate as fuck. He's always hugging and kissing on me."

"And you kissed him back. Sooo... hate to break it to you daddy, but that's how I greet my men not my pals," Jace said. "Don't be weak and in denial."

"You're making too much of this. For real." I threw the pillow wildly, uncaring where it landed, but was satisfied to see it knock Jace's hat off. "We have a lot of shit in common. For example—"

"Sucking dick?" Stephanie asked.

I looked around for another pillow. "Y'all are seriously some assholes today. You should be glad that I'm starting to be less of a miserable bitch, not hassling me about my new acquaintance."

"Now he's been downgraded to acquaintance?" Meredith waved her hand like it'd just been burned. "Yowch."

"Girl. Shut up. We barely know each other. It's not a diss, he's simply not on the same level of friendship as Caleb or you guys. He's just..." I waved my hands around, looking between them helplessly. "I don't know. Hanging out with him makes me forget about Landon and all that shit, which sounds nuts, but is undeniable. We have so much in common, like for real. We connected on this weird artsy level over dancing, and that hasn't happened with me in a long-ass time. Not since Julliard." A grin stole over my face as I listened to him flipping between songs or videos downstairs. "And he's so fucking talented, you guys. He has so much natural talent that I envy. We've been practicing some of his routines for the burlesque show he does. They've finally let him come up with his own choreography, and he's so dedicated. It's fucking adorable."

My gaze had drawn to the windows running alongside the house as I spoke, but now I returned it to my trio of friends. They were looking at me with varying degrees of relief and happiness. I knew they still had the wrong idea about what me and Luis were to each other, but them not worrying about me was a bonus of the misunderstanding.

So, I let them believe whatever the hell they wanted just so the topic could shift away.

The less they interrogated me about our friendship, the less likely I would be to analyze it. Over analyzing my relationships never led to anywhere good, and this weird connection was something I desperately wanted to hold onto.

LUIS

"You really think it's good?"

Charles squinted at me, hands on hips and sweating all over the wooden floors. "I already told you it's brilliant. What more do you want? A star sticker?"

"Yeah, right on my dick hole."

Charles rolled his eyes and grabbed the remote, pausing the song before it replayed again. "Hun, do you really think I have enough kindness in my foul black heart to bullshit you? Because I don't. If I thought it was shit, I wouldn't have wasted my time helping you to perfect it."

I peeled off my sweat rag of a T-shirt and tossed it in the corner. He was right, but I couldn't help going over things in my head repeatedly. The concept was cheesy but it had that mixture of outrageous and sexy that Marquis—the manager of Man-dated Attraction—loved. It wasn't exclusively a queer troupe, and so far he'd cast me in the role of Punch Drunk Louie—a character who was so obsessed with boxing that seduction attempts went over his head. We were adding a bit where my previously seemingly straight character was seduced by an out-and-proud queer guy who'd had "seduce an athlete" on his *queer agenda*.

The bit had been my idea, my last minor *fuck you* to the boxing world, so Marquis had agreed to give me a shot at the choreography, so I wanted it *perfect* before I drew it out and presented it to Marquis and my partner. If I screwed up at the debut of the bit, we'd take it out completely and he'd likely never trust me to choreograph anything again. Considering my asshole manager at Male Revue had gone right back to ignoring the shit out of me since I'd failed to bring a minor celeb along since that one night, it was nice to be recognized in the one thing I actually gave a damn about.

Well, beyond opening my gym. But that was nowhere near to becoming a reality. I had no idea when it would become one unless I randomly became independently wealthy and didn't have to use all my stripper cash to pay actual fucking rent.

"Let's go over it again," I said.

"Oh my fucking, God, Luis—" Charles spun around but stopped talking after he took one look at me. I knew how I looked—like a puppy covered in tattoos. It was my special gift. And it helped that I was chewing my lower lip and clenching up my fists as worry ate at my guts. "Oh boy. Fine, fine, fine."

I grinned and yanked him close. When he slumped against my sweaty chest, smirking coyly as I kissed both his cheeks, my heart thudded. "Gracias, lindo."

"Ugh. Your words mean nothing to me."

"Uh-huh, right." I smacked his ass then shoved him away. "Let's do this. I'll order dinner after."

Charles brightened considerably and grabbed the remote again. Food was definitely the way to his allegedly small dark heart. Even after getting groceries delivered to him, he'd gone through them all in under a week and had gone right back to holing up and refusing to go to the store. I compensated by cooking way too much food for myself—a product of growing up in a household of six—and forcing him to eat it. Since he knew I'd get tired of my own cooking and order in a day later, wasting what I'd cooked, he tended to not turn down an invitation.

He restarted the song, and I took my place to launch into the bit. On stage, it would start with me strutting my way into the center of the stage wearing my boxing trunks, gloves, and a fake belt. It would be full time swagger as I bragged through body language alone about defending my title, and beating someone's ass, before launching into a taunting solo dance. That was the easy part since it was what I'd actually done in the ring for years. Flex, strut, wear the Dominican flag all over the ring so people knew who the fuck was about to whoop their ass, and be as cocky as possible. The more arrogant I was, the more intimidated people became. The trick to psyching people out was pretending to be invincible. If you believed it, they would too.

The tricky part of the bit was when whoever my partner would be joined me on stage. Ideally, they would be dressed in the same ass bearing booty shorts as a ring girl. They would flash a big number card while bending over and showing off their goods while bragging to the audience about their agenda to seduce an athlete.

Charles was sinfully good at strutting those long legs of his and bending over to rub his round ass all over my crotch. He was so good at it that when I dramatically dropped to my knees in front of him and transitioned from Punch Drunk Louie in the boxing shorts to Queer Struck Louie who stripped down to tiny rainbow boxer briefs, it was barely an act. Covered in sweat, we launched into a teasing flirtatious dance that eventually went from him leading me, to us dirty dancing together.

It was a filthy routine. A lot of ass humping, grinding, and kissing, but interspersed with reggaetón dance moves that required was to move in perfect unison in the exact spot we needed to be in order to transition to the next round of seduction.

The whole routine was only six minutes long even though it felt like a eternity in my head, and we nailed it once again. We nailed it so hard that the last part, where we wound up crushed together with my hand in his hair and his hand twisting my underwear enough to show my ass cheeks to the crowd, heated my blood and hardened my dick.

There was nothing between our bodies but tight flesh and beads of sweat. I had no doubt that Charles could feel the way my body was responding to the earth-shaking sensuality of his post-dance exhilaration. I'd been with a lot of people in my life, but ever someone who looked close to an orgasm from the pure joy of dancing. Never someone who looked at me so smoldering, with dilated eyes and parted lips, because us performing together heated his blood as much as our combined sweat and energy warmed the room.

I held him against me, heart pounding and not wanting him to move away. Not when his lips were so close and his dick was as hard as mine, pulsing through his tights and straining against my own. "You're fucking gorgeous."

Those generous lips turned up in a sneer. "Shut up."

"Kiss me."

The sneer twitched into a smile he desperately tried to hide. He leaned in to brush our mouths together in the barest of kisses, like a ghost of a touch, and moved away again. I kept staring at his mouth, obsessed. I was dying to have those big lips drag all over my body and slide over my dick, but for now I'd settle for a real kiss. The guy he only seemed to let me have in the basement.

"Let me kiss you properly," I said, flashing my most devilish smile. "As a thank you for helping me practice."

"Oh, is that what it's all about?" Charles asked with a sassy eyebrow raise. "You thanking me?"

"Uh-huh. I mean, whoever my partner turns out to be probably won't be as fly as you, but I feel less like I'm gonna screw up when I demo it tomorrow."

Charles was nodding slowly, eyelids lowering as he studied me. He'd relaxed against my body, one arm around my waist and the other draped over my shoulder. "Why don't you know who your partner will be?"

"'Cause my usual partner is moving away." I kissed Charles again, this time at the corner of his mouth. "So, it could be anyone from a fat booty twink who is used to twerking at the club to someone who dances professionally. We get all kinds." I dragged his lower lip into my mouth and sucked for a moment before releasing it. His hips jutted against mine, and I groaned. "Too bad it's not you. You'd make me look so good up there."

"You look good on your own," he said, voice huskier than it'd been a moment ago. "Maybe you could just make it a solo dance. Punch Drunk Louie becoming Out and Proud Louie instead of it being a whole queer-for-you seduction dance."

"Because it's meant to be with a partner." I backed him against the wall, moving slow and careful, and giving him ample time to escape me. "Why? Don't want anyone else seducing me but you?"

Something flashed across his face as I pressed him to the wall. A brief narrowing of his eyes, and a hint of a frown that looked a little too much like dismay. Which, no. No no no. We weren't having that shit tonight. There were times when I realized I needed to watch my mouth when it came to Charles, or he'd haul ass away from me like I was on fire and he couldn't be assed to put me out. Now was one of those times. I could already feel him retreating.

"Let me thank you," I said again, pitching my voice lower. "Come on, papi."

His fingers clenched and released, over and over again before answering. "How?"

"However you want. No strings. No nothing." I grinned and held his serious gaze. "Just me showing you how I express my gratitude when someone comes through for me."

Charles' breath came faster, blowing across my sweaty face as his heart beat against my chest. "You're a good kisser for such a cocky asshole. We could leave it at that."

"But then my superior kissing skills will get you all worked up, and you'll go home with blue balls." I stuck out my lower lip, feigning a mournful expression. "Pobrecito..."

The remoteness fled his expression. Charles smiled with another of his big eyerolls. "You're an idiot," he said, turning away from me.

"But am I lying?" I pressed my front to his back and jerked his hips back against my crotch. "I love your mouth, but I can also get you off so you don't have to do it all by yourself every night."

Charles went still. "You...can..."

"Hear you?" Oh fuck, could I. It had been breezy and cool enough to leave the windows open after our heatwave, and since his bedroom was right above mine, the low sound of his urgent moans would sometimes float down and into my own bedroom. "Sometimes I get off to the sound of you coming. Is that creepy?"

"Um. No." Another thing I loved about Charles? He was so honest. "That's fucking hot."

"You sound fucking hot when you nut," I rumbled in his ear, hand stealing down to brush over his crotch. His dick was practically trying to burst through his tights. "Do you jerk off, baby? Or play with your ass?"

Charles moaned so loud it sounded closer to the way he cried out when he came. I practically growled in his ear, humping his ass with serious intent.

"You're evil," Charles gasped. "I thought we were both fine with the teasing and flirting?"

"I am, but tell me anyway," I pleaded. "I'm so fucking horny.

Throw a dude a bone."

He turned his face, probably to speak, but I licked at his mouth in a fit of keen desperation. Charles moaned again, and wound an arm back so he could grip my head and keep my face against his. We kissed with the same hungry swiping of tongues and clashing of lips and teeth as our first frantic make-out in the basement. There was no rhyme or reason to this kind of sloppy hunger, and there was no more thinking or talking or cajoling. There was only his ass grinding back on my dick, and then me jerking him through his tights.

"Oh God, yes." Charles' hesitance slid away, dripping down to the floor like the sweat we'd rained on it earlier. He was simultaneously licking at me frantically, grinding back on my cock, and wiggling his hips so I could get his tights down. "Grab it."

"Hell yeah." I trailed kisses down his cheek then widened my stance so I could support him with both hands dropped down to play with him. "Tell me what you want."

"Just touch me," he breathed. "It's been so long."

"How long?"

Charles shuddered as I gripped the base of his dick. He bucked into it, not doing a thing to tamp down on his dangerously sexy pleading sounds. "Like almost a year."

"Fuuuck..." I started jerking him in earnest. My gut coiled at the feel of his throbbing dick and the precum gathering at his tip. I'd give anything to suck him off. To watch him fall apart while he came down my throat. "You been missing this, baby? Having someone take good care of you?"

Charles nodded, but his eyes were closed and I doubted he even knew what the fuck I was saying. I was jerking him with purpose, not teasing or drawing it out. He needed to come to someone else's hand, and I was gonna give him that. Judging by his trembling knees and sharply keening cries, it was gonna happen really soon.

"What else do you miss?" I whispered in his ear.

"I don't know," he breathed.

"Since what?"

"Since..." Charles arched his back and shoved his hips against my hand. "Oh fuck, don't stop. I'm right there." His voice filled the apartment, probably spilling out the open windows like it usually did.

"Tell me," I urged, pumping him faster.

"It's been so long since someone fucked me who actually wanted me," he gasped.

My body went cold even as he went bowstring tight. He cried out, hoarse and surprised, right before he spilled all over my hand. He closed his eyes and laughed breathlessly, a dreamy smile on his face. I wondered how long it would last before he remembered what he'd just revealed to me.

CHAPTER THIRTEEN
CHARLES

Orgasms turned me to lead. It was the only explanation for the sluggishness I experienced after blowing my load. That sluggishness was the primary reason I wasn't squirming away from Luis and making a break for the door after my pathetic admission.

Maybe he hadn't noticed.

His hand slid away, fingers dragging along my length. Another shudder went through me, but I managed to stand up straight without a stagger. I told myself it was my amazing skills at performance arts that allowed me to keep the pleased smile on my face, but in reality it was desperation to keep this thing between us normal. And easy.

"Well..." I tossed my hair out of my eyes and turned to face him. Luis was still slumped against the wall, his head tilted back and dark brown eyes heavy lidded. "That was definitely one of the better shows of gratitude I've ever received. Congrats on you're A plus hand job skills."

Luis nodded slowly, still gazing at me from beneath the wreath of his lashes. His dick wasn't as hard as it had been only a moment ago, and for some reason his lack of arousal sent panic racing up my spine. Not only that, but the look on his face. Serious. So serious. And he was studying me like he was trying to figure me out. Since our first fucked up meeting, I'd never seen him still or eerily silent like this. Not even when I'd cursed him to hell after finding him in bed with Landon.

The urge to flee heightened. I needed to be away from the silence and that steadily watchful gaze. I took a step back, smile fading, but he snapped out a hand to grab my wrist. Defensiveness surged through me, and I yanked my arm away with a snarl. The fact that he snorted out a laugh was the only thing that kept my feet rooted to the floor.

"You the only motherfucker who can be two secs off decking me in the face while your jizz is still all over my hand."

I looked down and saw the evidence on his fingers. Forget his laugh. The absurdity of the entire situation grounded me in this reality and not the horror movie my fucked up brain was trying to produce over a flicker of an expression. My mouth twitched, and I couldn't fight the hysterical laugh welling in my own throat.

"I'm a fucking disaster, Luis."

"Nah, you're cool." Luis wiggled his eyebrows and proceeded to lick my cum off his fingers. "Taste good too."

"Ugh, you're so fucking dirty. It's like my kryptonite."

"Yeah?" He winked. "Then let me fuck you."

"Uh. No." He stuck his lower lip out in an exaggerated pout, and I yanked him in for a quick kiss. "I'm pretty cool with this weird time warp back to being a teenager who makes out in laundry rooms and gives random handjobs."

"You didn't give me shit," Luis reminded me. "You busted in my hand then tried to stab me."

Another laugh bubbled out of me. I pressed my face into his neck, trying to control myself, but laughed even harder. It didn't help that he started rubbing my back like he was soothing a baby.

"You're such a dumbass," I gasped. "God. I swear. Only your silly ass self can get me snapping back from a freakout with barely any effort at all."

"Part of my charm."

He kept rubbing my back, palm steady between my shoulders. I relaxed against him until our half-assed embrace turned to a full-on hug, with my arms wrapped around his neck and his around my waist. I almost forgot why I'd panicked. It all seemed ridiculous now. Why would my lack of self-esteem freak him out if seeing me screaming and crying and breaking my own shit hadn't?

"I'm sorry," I muttered. "Really. I ruined it and literally turned you off."

"Yeah," he agreed. "But I kinda expect that shit at this point."

I bit the side of his ear and smirked when he groaned softly. "Really, though. I'm just... Weird. I get freaked out easily, and I try to hide it so I don't scare everyone away. But shit just pisses me off, and

I want to run before people can tell I'm mad. As you know, it's not pretty once I lose my temper."

"I get you, but let me ask you a question." Luis tilted my chin up and gave me one of his adorably inquisitive sideways glances. "What made you mad?"

"The way you were looking at me."

Luis said nothing, and I bit the inside of my cheek. I sounded like a basketcase. He knew it, I knew it, and I kept expecting him to say it, but he didn't. He watched me and played with my hair, probably wondering why he was wasting time on some pain-in-the-ass like me when there was probably easy ass and pussy being thrown at him after every performance.

A sizzle of fire scorched through my veins, and I recognized that burn as jealousy.

"I got mad at myself," I said. "About admitting nobody has wanted me. I've been trying to keep this whole thing light and easy instead of dragging it back to my drama shit, but it's hard. Ninety percent of my brain is constantly focused on emo drama shit, and it's easy to say too much around you. So I got mad."

"At me?"

"No. Not really." I shrugged and eased away from him. "Go wash your hands, cum-fingers."

"I licked it off."

He laughed at my withering stare at pushed away from the wall to go to the bathroom. I followed, checking out the tattooed stretch of his back and the shape of his ass beneath his sweats.

"All right, well, now that it's established that it's okay for you to drop some random drama emo shit—your words, not mine—can I ask about what you meant?" Luis shut off the water after scrubbing his hands, and leaned against the sink. It reminded me of that first day we met, and the way he'd held me as I'd cried. "Were you talking about the cruise or even with Landon?"

"Even with Landon." Why was it so embarrassing to admit this? Because I'd known all along and stayed anyway? Another lingering sense of *I have to make this work. I've wasted so much time trying that it just has to*? "He'd been fucking other people for ages. I suspected it but never had proof. What first tipped me off is that he'd stopped wanting to touch me or be close to me unless we'd just had it out and the adrenaline had pumped blood into his dick."

Luis' head jerked back, and a sneer marred his face. "He didn't fuck you unless it was after a fight?"

"Correct."

"Yo. I'm just saying right now? If I ever catch that dude around here again, I'm fucking him up."

How messed up was is that his promise had me grinning? Pretty messed up, I bet. But still so goddamn pleasing. "No, you're not."

"Oh yes I fucking am."

"You're a professional box—"

"Former amateur boxer," Luis corrected. "My fists aren't registered as a threat to anything but your dick."

"Wow." I was laughing again, so loud the people down the block could probably hear my guffaw. "I swear to God, you're ridiculous."

"And you love it. But for real. He's getting fucked up. I've been pretty tight lipped about him because it's none of my business, and I didn't think you wanted to talk about it but..." Luis' gorgeous face became a hardened mask, dark brown eyes shooting sparks and mouth twisted down. I imagined this was what he'd looked like in the ring. It would have been intimidating if I didn't know how kind and sweet he was beneath the layers of tough guy arrogance. "Regardless of whether you gave as good as you got, he had no fucking business putting his hands on you. But I've met dudes like him before. Motherfuckers who think they can hit another guy and it doesn't count as abusive."

"Did someone..."

"Not me." Luis kissed my forehead. "But I've met more than one dancer who showed up bruised because of a jealous boyfriend who doesn't like them dancing."

"I bet those boyfriends don't mind spending the money, though," I said bitterly. "Landon was that way. He hated that I was barely home, but he never worked and spent all my money."

"He never worked?"

"Well... He did 'freelance' writing for random blogs, as if anyone needs his white boy hot takes on the Internet, and barely made any money. I'm all about pursuing your passions but if all the burden falls on one person while you're out chasing a dream, that's just selfish. I think he knew I felt that way, so he started selling pills on the side to make some pocket money but he still didn't contribute to the bills or rent."

"Why—" Luis shook his head. "No. Let me just stop."

"What? Just say it."

He exhaled through his nose. "I just keep wondering why you were with him. What you saw in him. But I don't want to sound patronizing."

"You're not. After everything, it makes sense to ask." I shook my head, full of scorn for myself, and stepped over the side of the tub so I could sit down. Luis glanced at the door, probably wondering what was wrong with the perfectly good living room or kitchen that possessed actual chairs, but wound up sitting in the tub across from me. "So, when I met Landon, he was a writer and I was a dancer, and I thought that meant we were both creatives who would understand each other. We were sexually compatible too, so it helped. And because I was desperate, I fell so fucking hard for him. That he was possessive as hell just... made me think he *really* loved me."

Luis put a hand on my knee and stroked it while watching me intently.

"Anyway, it took a while for me to realize that what I thought was love and him being protective, was him being controlling and manipulative. He didn't want me around anyone else, because I think he was worried I'd find someone who treats me better and leave him, which meant he lost his cash cow. Or that other people would see our relationship for what it was and like... advise me to leave him. Which is why he hated all my friends." I leaned against the cool tiles, extending my legs so they were up over his bent knees. When he slid his hands over my thighs, I closed my eyes and kept talking. "I didn't realize any of this shit until we were deep in it," I said quietly. "And even then I just... I don't know. I didn't want to believe yet another person didn't really give a fuck about me. Or that I as being used. I didn't want to believe I was stupid enough to let someone use me."

"You're not stupid. He's just a fucking snake."

"Yeah..."

Luis gripped my knees. "When did he first hit you?"

"The first time we fought, I hit him first." My sigh filled the bathroom, and I avoided looking at him. "We got into this horrible argument. He was telling me my friends only came to hang out at the bar with me so I could give them free drinks. Making me doubt them and myself. The usual. But he was being worse than usual about it, I think because he'd just met Michael in person for the first time, and he was super threatened by this gorgeous gay teacher who was kind to me. Like, Michael wasn't fucking into me. We were just friends, but it didn't matter to Landon. He needed me to distrust everyone but him, so he kept driving the point home that I was an idiot who doesn't see how people just use me. I started got angry and started crying, and he laughed at me."

Luis' breath hissed out. "I'd have flipped."

"I did," I said with a dark laugh. "I smacked him in the face, and he smacked me back hard enough to make me see stars. We tussled a little, and somehow wound up... fucking. Thinking back, it's really twisted. Like so twisted. And it kept happening. He'd try to trigger me into snapping because he *knew* how to push my buttons, or we'd argue and he thought he had free reign to grab me or shove me or whatever. But the first time we had a really bad fight was when me and Caleb got close."

"Who's Caleb?"

"He's um..." I bit the corner of my lip, suddenly shy. "He's a really good friend. This really sweet insecure guy who has the world at his fingertips but was really depressed and lonely. We got close after he had a bad breakup, and I'll be honest that I had feelings for him."

"I see." Luis kept dragging his fingers up and down my thighs. "What's he like?"

I shrugged, laughing a bit. "Nothing like me? He's sophisticated and intellectual and thinks casual clothing consists of button downs or polos."

"Huh. I think I saw him come visit you about a month ago." At my surprised glance, Luis made a face. "I wasn't stalking you, dummy. But my windows face the front door, so I can see who comes by if I'm dancing."

"Right..." I couldn't help but notice the way the pressure of Luis' hands had increased on me. The way his lips had pursed a little. "Anyway, I don't have feelings for him anymore. He's getting married."

Luis relaxed, and I bit back a tiny grin. We were seriously like two foolish teenagers. "But Landon was threatened. Like... he hated how I commented on Caleb's social media so much, always pointing out I Was the first one to like or comment. Meanwhile, it was because I wanted Caleb to keep posting and knew he wouldn't if no one responded." Social media had turned everything so absurd and awful. A like or a comment had suddenly become capable of invalidating someone's entire existence. Being disconnected was so fucking freeing. "Anyway, he saw some texts about how I'd taken Caleb to a speed dating thing, and we really got into it. It was the first time we had an all out fistfight. He fucked me up. And when he found out I ran to Caleb's house, he was enraged. I was scared to go back."

"Fuck, baby." Luis grabbed my arms and pulled me over so that I was laying against him. It was cramped and uncomfortable, but his arms being around me felt right. "I wish I'd known."

"Why?" I asked with a snort. "So you could hit him when you had the chance?"

"Fuck yeah."

Even while smiling against his chest, I shook my head. "Nah. I wouldn't want you to. He's a snake, and he'd get you arrested. Then I would end his fucking life."

Luis' hands on me tightened. He kissed the top of my head. "What happened next?"

"Things got bad. That's when the cheating stuff became really obvious, like he didn't care anymore if I suspected even though he never left any obvious evidence I could find. I wanted to leave him so bad, but... I don't know. There was part of me that still felt like I had to catch him. I needed proof. I have no idea why I was obsessed with any of this, or why the fighting wasn't a big enough reason, but it just led to constant humiliation. And all my friends knew."

"Is that why you took a job that would send you out into the middle of the ocean?"

"Yes. You're the first person to immediately get that, by the way."

"I'm pretty smart."

"You are." We lay there for a moment, silence all around us, as he stroked my back and hair. "What was your first impression of Landon?"

Luis scoffed. "That he was a wack fucking hypebeast who ran around wearing Jordans and designer hats like it made him cool, but he was obvious a corny-ass wannabee. I couldn't stand him."

I burst out laughing so loud my voice echoed off the tiles. "Oh my God. That is classic."

"Am I wrong?" Luis asked. "For real. And he'd sit out front on the steps smoking his vaporizer like a fucking idiot. It's a vaporizer... it leaves no odor. Take your bitch ass in the house."

I kept laughing against his chest, shoulders shaking. "God, I hated him and his vaping. He used to go on and on about the *best* brands and was totally obnoxious about anyone who smoked cigarettes."

"Yeah, he tried to pull that shit when I moved in. My mom smokes a lot and was talking to the lady across the street, and he made some comment about them being cancer fiends. I wanted to deadass punch him in the eyeball. He's lucky my cousin didn't hear."

"It sounds like you couldn't stand him."

"I couldn't. I always got bad vibes. But he was thirsty for my dick for months and finally I was desperate and gave in." Luis sounded uncomfortable, as if he should have known how bad Landon was. "If I'd known he was selling drugs on the side, or how he treated you—"

"How could you?"

"I don't fucking know, but I got bad vibes for him. So did my mother, and she is usually spot-on with that shit. It added on to her worrying about me living here. First impressions matter a lot to us."

"Yeah?" I looked up so I could see his face. He was so fucking sexy, even when angry and musing over something he couldn't control, I was obsessed with his stubble, his goatee, his mouth... "What was your first impression of me?"

That mouth twisted into a huge smile. "I thought you were amazing."

I rolled my eyes. "Okay, liar."

"I'm not lying! Do you even remember the first thing I said to you?"

"Of course."

"Okay, so you know. You were so fucking pissed, like enraged, and I half expected to get cut, but goddamn you were gorgeous. That had nothing to do with how bad I felt—"

"Uh-huh. Suuuure."

Luis smacked my ass. "For real. I mean, okay, maybe that's why I offered to let you have revenge sex with me... And why I was so tempted to kiss you. But it was also because I connected with you instantly. Now, don't get it twisted, I'm not saying the sight of you crying and upset turned me on, but what I'm saying is..." He seemed to struggle with his words as I waited on the edge of a cliff, wondering if I'd start falling depending on what he said. "There's times in life when I meet people and instantly get that vibe I was talking about before. My mother is the same way, and I get it from her I think. She'd basically say... me da mala espina. Basically, that someone is giving her a vibe of *okay, you're a bad person. I need to watch you.* I got it with that dude Bronson, but I kept him close so I can keep an eye out. But with you?" He shook his head slowly. "I wanted to be close to you, and I'm never like that with people. I'm never soft and compassionate. You could ask Ashton or Val—they'll tell you. I barely ever say that I'm sorry because I hate being wrong. But something about you was... straight up different."

I fell from that cliff headfirst.

He squeezed me. "You okay?"

"Yeah. Just." I shook my head. "Yes. I'm fine."

He chuckled, probably knowing I wasn't entirely fine. "But besides this spiritual connection and whatnot, I felt like a monster. I knew it wasn't my fault, but I felt like it was my fault. And part of that was *because* of that fucking connection. I knew I had to make it right with you. I just had to."

I was Alice, and I was flailing down that hole. I dug my fingers into him. "I'm sorry for taking it out on you. Like unbelievably sorry." I closed my eyes, amazed at how good it felt to simply lay against someone. To absorb the warmth from their skin and bask in affection that was rarely given. "I know this probably sounds like bullshit given how I treated you, but I'm grateful for meeting you, Luis. And I appreciate you getting over that whole coffee thing and being my friend."

"That whole coffee thing." Luis snickered. "You're like a fucking vengeful but superhot demon when mad, papi. Swear to God."

"I'm sorry!"

"Yeah, whatever. I'll get my revenge one day." He started rubbing my back again, but this time his hand was lower and his long fingers brushed my ass. "So, if we're friends now, does that mean you'll say yes if I ask you to come to my next show?"

"What show? The strip club thing—"

"No, Man-dated Attraction." He shook me a little. "I want you to come watch the shit we just practiced. It's next weekend."

"Um..."

"You don't even go anywhere, so if you don't come it's just because you're sitting home by yourself smoking weed and drinking cheap wine."

I snorted out a laugh. "Wow, way to call me out."

"Well, I'm saying though. I want you there!" He stuck out his lower lip again, giving me puppy dog eyes. "Please?"

"Ugh. *Fine.* I will go. But do not make a spectacle of me being there and force me to talk to anyone."

"I won't. I swear."

I eyeballed him suspiciously, but he smiled so brilliantly that I couldn't help but smile in return. When he kissed me, soft and gentle like he claimed to never be, I didn't want him to stop. I wanted to exist in the weird fucking bubble of the bathtub forever.

CHAPTER FOURTEEN
LUIS

"**W**hich one is he?"

I threw Gabe, my absurdly tall dance partner, an exasperated look. "Could you stop? Damn, you're going to fucking blow this for me, bro."

Gabe tossed his mane of long red hair over one shoulder, tapped his foot dramatically in his stilettos, then swished his butt over to the curtain. He was the swishiest motherfucker I'd ever met, and I spent a lot of time around queer dudes. If there was one thing I knew about Gabe, it was that his stage presence wasn't only an act.

He lived and breathed as Rox Off—the hilariously sassy gay boy with enough pizzazz to queerify a straight boy. His whole shtick was that he'd created an actual gay agenda during brunch with his equally gay and glamorous friends, and that agenda consisted of seducing straight men. It directly fed into my routine since my character would be his "seduce a straight athlete" check mark. Considering the way he'd hung all over me after I'd joined the troupe, I was convinced he had a similar to-do list in his real life. Especially since he'd lost interest after learning I wasn't straight.

"I wanna see him," Gabe whined, stamping his foot. He had his head sticking between the curtains and his butt wiggling around on our side. He was wearing the ring boy costume—glittery short shorts that only covered half his ass cheeks and a crop top with giant heels. "He must be a-maz-ing for your stuck-up ass to be sweating him this hard."

Rolling my eyes, I grabbed his wrist and pulled him away from the curtain. He did a little shimmy, growling like a kitten.

"I like it when you're rough, daddy."

"Oh shut up. You just want to piss me off because Marquis didn't approve any of your tweaks for choreography."

Gabe sniffed. "Yes, well, you may be correct about that."

"Can you knock it the fuck off, then? You're leaving anyways, dude. You don't need every fucking drop of attention on you in your last month of—"

"Whoa, babe, calm it down a bit." Gabe held up his hands, blue eyes wide. "I was just kidding around. What's up your ass? You don't bottom so I know it's not a butt plug."

I ground my teeth together. "Nothing. Just quit trying to make me nervous. We go on in like... ten minutes, and I think I'm going to fuck up."

"You're never nervous," Gabe said, eyes narrowing so I could barely see the blue beneath his extra-ass lashes. "Your cocky self has oozed confidence since you rolled into the troupe. This boy is who's got you nervous, and *I* want to see him!"

I looked up at the light fixtures on the ceiling, praying to God and my mother and the holy spirit that someone would give me the patience to deal with Gabe for another month. As much as I admired his talent, he grated on my nerves. Always in my business, always cyber stalking my shit to dig up info about my personal life, and always fixating on my personal life.

"Fine," I snapped. "If I show him to you, will you just chill?"

"Yup."

I glared at him and his innocent smile for a long moment before pulling at the curtain to scan the crowd. I'd peeked out earlier just to make sure he was there, and I'd spotted his curly hair at the back of the crowd. As soon as I'd gotten the confirmation I'd been hoping for, I'd felt like puking. Sure, I'd stripped in front of him, but this was different. This mattered to me. And I wanted him to respect me as a performer on stage, not just when I was in my damn dining room.

"There," I said, pointing. "He just walked up to the bar."

Gabe practically threw me out of the way in his haste to see Charles. He inhaled deeply, and I couldn't help a smile. Charles wasn't anywhere close to being my dude, but I still liked it that Gabe could appreciate how fly he was looking tonight.

"Metallic black leggings, Doc Martins, and oversized knit turtleneck?"

"Uh... I guess. Yeah."

Gabe bounced in place. "The one with the hair?"

I grinned. "Yeah. That one."

"Oh my fuck. That ass though. I wish my ass looked like that," Gabe moaned.

I looked out again and saw Charles was leaning on the edge of the bar just enough for his ass to be on full display. God, he was bitable.

"Can we say hi later?"

"No," I said sharply. When he gave me a hurt look, I raised a pacifying hand. "Look, he doesn't really like people. I promised I wouldn't make him talk to anyone."

Gabe rolled his eyes. "Whatever. Dramatic."

His annoyance wasn't promising. He tended to do the total opposite of what anyone wanted him to do if he was told no. Desperate, I held up my phone. "What if I show you the video I took of us practicing? He let me put it on my Instagram since you can't really see his face in it."

Gabe brightened, and I knew I'd made the right choice. For the next few minutes, he oohed and aahed over the video and quizzed me on Charles' training and background. I kept it as vague as possible, and Gabe seemed satisfied in what I'd shared by the time Marquis was hissing at us to get ready.

I dashed backstage to put up my phone and check my makeup. The makeup really wasn't my thing, but Donna kept it to some shit that made my eyes look even darker and my cheekbones look sharper. It was weird seeing myself looking so similar and yet so different with nothing more than powder, but donning my shiny robe that was basically a giant DR flag made it all better. It was my super hero cloak, and having it around me when the curtain went up simmered my frayed nerves.

I could do this. I would do this. The night was going to be just fucking fine.

 **CHARLES**

It began just as I'd envisioned.

The curtains rose to the sound of the Dominican national anthem, and Luis—or Punch Drunk Louie—strutted out. He was outfitted exactly as he'd been for his actual boxing matches from what I'd seen from my Googling. Red lo-top boxing boots, a DR flag robe, and red gloves.

A wide smile stretched over my face, and I whistled sharply as he strutted up to the stage as if he was trying to intimidate an opponent. There was enough swag and flex for ten boxers, but Luis was all by himself, and the crowd loved it. The club had capacity for a couple hundred people, and it was packed full of people who seemed delighted at the sight of him shrugging off his robe to display baggy trunks, fake belt, and his ripped torso.

Luis postured for the crowd, flexing his biceps while eyeballing an imaginary opponent. He bounced on the balls of his feet and threw a couple of playful punches at the air that looked dangerously real. The control he had over his body was incredible, and those punches could be deadly if he wanted them to. The contrast of what he was doing versus what he could be doing was... really doing it for me.

I bit my lip, told my dick to stay down, and focused on the performance. His solo dance was awesome, but it definitely wasn't the best part of the show even though it was key to sucking people in. It was the epitome of a burlesque tease—taunting and coy but in a very Luis way. He had people screaming for more by the time his partner strutted out onto the stage wearing blue glitter shorts, a crop top, and high heels.

The crowd whistled shrilly at the new guy—Rox Off—but an uncomfortable tightness formed in my chest. He was hot. Like really hot. Long red hair, a great body, and the way he walked in those heels was intensely sexy. He swayed like a daydream while holding a card with the number one on it, prancing around Luis who had stopped mid-dance, struck dumb by the sight of his ring boy.

Rox smiled big and faced the crowd, bending over right in front of Luis so his ass was pressed to Luis' crotch. Luis' jaw dropped comically, and Rox flipped his card. It read: *Gay Agenda. #7 – seduce a straight athlete.*

The crowd hooted. I downed my drink.

As they launched into the routine I'd helped Luis practice for the past week, the tightness in my chest turned to something more readily recognizable. A particular insidious burn that spread from my chest through my veins to infect the rest of my body before poisoning my brain.

I couldn't appreciate it when Luis was stripped down to nothing but a rainbow jockstrap, because Rox was the one rubbing all over that delicious bulge. By the time they were to the portion of the dance where they had to literally kiss each other, I was a simmering ball of irritation. My leg was hopping, my teeth grinding, and I had to look away repeatedly.

What the fuck was wrong with me? Why was I like this? It was a performance, for God's sake. And even if it wasn't a performance, we were just friends. I had no claims on him. He had none on me. We were f-r-i-e-n-d-s.

Friends who'd spent the entire morning kissing and dry humping after I'd lured him upstairs after ordering brunch from the Staten Island Diner. He'd tasted like French Toast and syrup, and I'd licked at his mouth until every trace was gone. Then we'd grinded until I'd been on the cusp of begging him to flip me over and nail me until everyone on the block heard me saying his name. But I hadn't.

Because friends. Friends who were comfortable enough with each other to make out.

So, we'd said our goodbyes, and I'd promised to come to Club Cumming to support him, and now I just wanted to set the fucking place on fire.

Who knew that my extreme jealousy wasn't only triggered by cheating ass ex-boyfriends.

I ordered another drink right as they ended the performance with his hand tangled in Rox's long red hair, and Rox gripping Luis' jockstrap. My brain was telling me Luis' dick had to be throbbing by now, and that they were probably pressing against together, and maybe they'd been turning each other on for ages during rehearsal even though I'd thought the flirtatious practicing had been limited to me.

My brain told me that I was delusional and stupid, and Landon was right about how people generally just used me for a good time when no one more interesting was round. Rox was definitely more interesting than me. He was a successful and popular burlesque dancer with over twenty thousand followers on Instagram. I'd just been fired from a gig on a crappy cruise that people went on with their spoiled children or for golden anniversaries. I was fucking trash.

"Hey, hon. Fix the frown and—"

"Why don't you shut the fuck up?" I snarled at the bartender. "And don't worry about how my fucking face looks."

The guy's head jerked back and the people around me stared. I stared back, challenging them to speak, and they looked away. I needed to get the hell out of here. After throwing back the rest of my second drink and wincing at the way it scalded down my throat, I pushed away from the bar and started for the door. It was so fucking packed in the small space that I had to literally elbow my way through the crowd. By the time I managed to get to the front of the club, another routine had started.

"Hey, where are you going?"

Luis' voice was closer than I'd expected it to be considering he'd just been on stage two minutes ago. I froze, staring at the door and my escape, but melted as soon as he grazed my back with his fingers. I could tell by that hesitant touch, by his uncertain tone, that he knew I was angry.

"I was leaving," I said, trying to sound normal. Everything was stilted. "You did a good job."

"Okay..." Luis said slowly. "Can you turn around so I can talk to you?"

I bit my bottom lip, closed my eyes for a beat, then turned to look at him with a forced smile. Up close, he was even more striking than he'd been on the stage. Someone had given him a smoky eye that made him look assassin sexy. "I'm fine, babe. For real. It's just crowded in here, and I only came to see you, so..."

Luis' mouth pulled to the side. "All right, but why did you look so stressed? Did I fuck up or something? I missed a step in the second half because I was getting nervous about all that kissing and shit. Gabe was on my last nerve before we went out, and I didn't think it'd look believable since I was supposed to be falling all over myself for him."

He kept going, explaining all the ways he'd fucked up, while I lost the ability to form words. They were right there waiting to blurt out—all the ways he'd been amazing, and how I'd noticed the missed step but had thought it was deliberate because his performance had been so seamless, and how it had been *very believable ha-ha*. But all I could do was replay the words 'Gave was on my last nerve' over and over again.

"Charles, what the fuck, yo? You're freaking me out!"

"I'm sorry," I said quickly. "I'm just... I was just... Fuck, Luis, you were amazing. And I got mad that it wasn't me up there with you."

The smile that broke out over Luis' face could have shifted us from night to day. It was beautiful. *He* was beautiful. I was super fucking falling for him. My God.

"I should go," I stammered. "It will take me forever to get home. The ferry is only running on the hour now."

"Wait for me. We can share a cab."

"Luis..."

"Here you are!" A voice rang out over the music, obnoxious and tacky and uncaring that other humans were now on stage. "Luis' leggy lover. Hey, maybe that can be your stage name, Charles."

I wheeled around to face the owner of the voice and saw it was Rox—or Gabe. Whoever. He was still wearing his ring boy outfit plus a long white satin robe. Even though he was apparently more of an annoying coworker than a rival for... whatever the hell I was now wanting from Luis, I as so on edge that I gave zero fucks about being nice to this person.

"Excuse you?" I asked.

Luis coughed into his hand to cover a laugh. "Charles, this is Gabe slash Rox Off."

"Nice to meet you." Gabe gave me a big handshake all while sizing me up. "You're smoking hot. Like fire."

"Yeah, I know." I pulled away. "Look, I'm about to go, so..."

"Marquis wants to meet you," Gave said, as if this made sense. "After seeing your videos, and that body of yours, I think you'd be perfect to replace me, Mr. Julliard."

Shock washed over me. Luis spoke before I could figure out a response.

"What the fuck are you talking about, Gabe? Who even asked you to get all up in our business like this?" he demanded, pointing at his partner. "What'd you do—look him up?"

"Yup. And I told Marquis about him having been in school, and he nearly had an orgasm." Gabe rolled his eyes at Luis before turning back to me. "*Anyway*, if you have interest in joining the troupe, you should talk to Marquis. I'm gone after a month, but you could spend the month rehearsing and learning my parts. Or coming up with new ones."

I didn't say anything. There was nothing to say. I was equal parts annoyed that this stranger had taken it upon himself to recommend me even after Luis had apparently told him to leave me alone, and... excited. The hum of jealousy transitioned to a throb of adrenaline as I pictured myself up there in costume, dancing before a largely queer audience. I didn't realize my hands were shaking until Luis grabbed one of them and squeezed.

"Okay weirdos," Gabe said, rolling his eyes. "My solo is in a bit, but Luis could probably get away with taking off to go fuck you somewhere."

"Ay dios mio, Gabe, shut the fuck up," Luis muttered. "Christ. You need a fucking muzzle."

"And you need some fucking manners," Gabe snapped right back. "I'm doing your man a favor, and you're acting like a nervous bitch. Go get some ass and lighten the fuck up before our show tomorrow."

Luis bristled, looking ready to say something reckless, and I grabbed his hand.

"Thanks Gabe," I managed. "Have a good rest of your show."

At that point, he was obviously irritated, and swung around so that his face nearly whipped me in the face. Annoying? Yes. Dramatic as hell? Fuck yes. But helpful? Shockingly... yes. I stared after him in a daze while Luis watched me intently.

"Listen, I'm gonna tell Marquis I'm leaving now, okay? Don't move."

"Okay."

"You promise you're not going to leave?" Luis demanded, voice rougher than he'd ever used with me. "I will be pissed if I come back and you jetted."

"Luis, I'm not going anywhere."

"Okay..."

He started away, but he looked over his shoulder repeatedly as if he was worried I'd disappear. Fortunately for him, I was too stunned to get even one foot off the ground and not just because of Gabe's unexpected offer. It was suddenly hitting me all at once that meeting Luis was turning out to be one of the best things to happen to me in a long fucking time.

CHAPTER FIFTEEN
LUIS

C harles was silent beside me, and it had me more nervous than the time my mother had caught me smoking weed out the bathroom window in ninth grade. She'd torn my ass up with her slipper then proceeded to make me watch fucked up documentaries about junkies to make me realize why I needed to live a drug-dree life.

As much as I'd sucked my teeth and rolled my eyes, arguing about how weed wasn't even that serious, that shit had worked. Goodbye marijuana, hello health nut. Although, she'd also sat my ass down and made me watch documentaries about people with brain damage after I'd announced I wanted to pursue boxing professionally and not just as an extracurricular activity. It hadn't deterred me that time, though.

For as long as I could remember, she was the only person capable of putting me on edge. She was the most important person in my life, even if that made me a mama's boy, and it was only her opinion that had mattered to me since my teenage years. No one I dated had even come close to making me doubt my choices or my attitude. They'd been blips on my radar in between one goal and the next, because I'd always viewed people outside of my close circle as temporary whereas the blueprint to my life plan was the real deal. But here I was, sweating in my white T-shirt and jeans even as the cab driver blasted us with too-cold air, because I couldn't figure out what was up with Charles. It was like sixty-five degrees outside and homie was trying to turn his cab into the arctic.

"My man, can you turn that shit down?"

The driver clicked it a notch lower without looking at me. I sneered. Charles kept looking out the window as we crossed the Verrazano. He'd been staring out the window since we'd entered the cab, and I was obsessively categorizing every detail about his body language to figure out what was going through his mind.

His body wasn't tight the way it got when he was consumed with anger, but he didn't look distant and sad either. I'd caught that expression a few times when we were sitting on the floor watching videos together. His eyes would lower and he'd go so quiet and still, like he was lost in a memory that made him want to detach from the present. I couldn't pick out any of those signs right now, though. He just looked pensive.

I reached over to rub the back of his neck, slow and careful like I might get bitten. He responded by scooting over and leaning against me, head tucked into the crook of my neck. Some of my worry faded.

We rushed over the bridge, moving over the East River as container ships and the orange blip of the Staten Island ferry passed below. The Statue of Liberty was dwarfed by the rest of the skyline, but it always drew my eye. In a city that changed every time I blinked, it was one of those symbols that couldn't be moved or modified even if half the people in the country didn't seem to understand what it stood for anymore.

Charles' lips brushed my jaw, drawing me out of my thoughts. I looked at him, startled, and was met with big dark eyes drilling into me with enough heat to ward off the air conditioner. My stomach flipped.

"See something you like?" I teased softly.

"Yes." One of his hands slid over to my thigh. He could probably feel my muscles tensing from the attention. "You were really great tonight, Luis. The crowd loved you."

"But did you? You acted so damn funny that I still can't tell."

Charles wrinkled his nose. "Must you always call me out?"

"Yes. You acted mad funny." I kissed the tip of his nose. "And you're still acting funny now."

"I'm just thinking." Charles pressed against me tighter, half turned in the seat so he could plaster his body to mine while holding my gaze. It wasn't the first time we'd sprawled all over each other, or tucked up into each other, but there was something different now. The wild gleam in his eyes, the way he kept dampening his lips, and especially his hand slowly rubbing up and down my thigh. "I got so caught up in my own head that I didn't really appreciate how amazing you were up there, so I was like... replaying it in my head and appreciating you all over again."

"Yeah?"

"Yup. It's not just your dancing that had that crowd drooling." He spoke with a quiet intensity that was almost too intimate for this cab ride. Even with the Plexiglass divider between us and the driver. "It was you. You're so authentic. It's a performance but never an act. When you threw those punches, everyone could probably tell you know how to fight for real. Same with everything from that tough guy glare of yours, to the way you strutted around like you're hot shit, and the way you moved your hips when you were grinding all up on his ass." Charles' hand moved up a little higher, his fingertips dragging along my groin. "Everyone was probably imagining what a hot fuck you are."

I inhaled sharply. "You be careful now." My thighs spread a little wider.

Charles' hand moved up higher, fingers tracing the shape of my dick beneath the fly of my jeans. My breath hissed out, and I widened my thighs as far as they could go. He responded by rubbing me in earnest, all while watching me.

"What are you doing?" I breathed. "Tell me what's going on."

"Me appreciating you." Charles kissed my jaw again then trailed damp little kisses down to my throat. "Is that bad?"

"Fuck no it's not bad, but..." My breath hitched when his fingers went from teasing to squeezing. "Just trying to make sure I don't randomly get cut if I wander into this uncharted territory without my Understanding Charles manual."

Charles snickered against my neck, shoulders shaking. "Can you not fuck up this vibe with your smartass commentary?"

"Look, I just don't want to die when you rapidly change your mind and get pissed at me." I tilted his chin up and brushed my mouth against his in a wet kiss. "You're like those gorgeous creatures who lure sailors in being all enchanting and beautiful, then you kill them."

"Mmm. A siren." Charles bit his lower lip, eyebrows hiking up, as he toyed with the button of my jeans. "I kind of like that. But you don't have to worry. I'm not in a bad mood. I'm just really into you right now."

The words resounded in the small space. They imprinted on me, burrowing into my flesh and manifested as hope that clashed with lust just enough to spark a fire in the center of my chest. I smiled, just a bit, and tilted his chin up so our lips were barely grazing.

"Yeah, I like you too, Charles."

I expected a wise crack, but he kissed me instead. I parted my lips for him, and he swept his tongue inside to slide against mine. We'd been kissing and feeling on each other nearly day for what felt like a month now, but this kiss was different. There was a hunger in the way he attacked my mouth, and an impatience in the way he restlessly shifted on the seat.

He wanted me to touch him. The way he moaned pleadingly when I gripped his hair made it plain as day. But if I went any farther than tugging his curls and sucking on his hot tongue, I was going to rip his leggings down and fuck him raw right in the back of this cab.

"Fuck, baby," I said, voice a hoarse whisper, when he kissed down and dragged his teeth against my throat. He sucked on the knot of my Adam's apple, all while rubbing the heel of his hand against the hardness trapped beneath denim. I arched into his hand, and he pressed harder, sending sparks of fire flying through me. "You're gonna make this hard to part ways when we get back to the house."

"So let's not part ways," he whispered against my throat. "I want to show my gratitude."

"For what?" I gritted out.

"For you being here. With me."

My brows twitched together, and I woke up just a little from my daze. "You don't have to—"

The cab came to abrupt stop. A quick glance out the window showed that we were home. I fumbled for my wallet, but Charles wasn't deterred. He was sucking on my throat then worked his way up to my ear, hand still sliding between my thighs. The cab driver studiously ignored all of this while I squinted at the meter and forewent a wad of jumbled singles, fives, and tens to swipe my credit card.

"Go open the door," I panted as Charles began rubbing my dick in earnest. "C'mon, baby."

Charles squeezed me one last time before sliding over to the door on his side. He left the cab, and I was so distracted by his metallic accented ass in those skintight leggings that the cabbie had to clear his throat so I could hit the right buttons. With my erection raging and my heart pounding out of my chest, everything was taking too long. It was an eternity before I signed the tiny slip of paper and shoved it at the cabbie and managed to escape the car.

I took the steps two at a time up to our front door, and stepped into the dark vestibule to find Charles leaning against the window sill with his leggings down around his hips. His thighs were spread, dick gripped in one hand, as he pressed his head against the window behind him. There was no shade or curtain, but he clearly didn't give a damn about someone peeping. I didn't care either, so I stepped between his thighs and sucked his lips into my mouth.

I kept one hand on his face, angling it up so I could tongue him, and used the other to get my jeans open. Once upon a time I'd thought I was pretty smooth with adequate game, but all that was nonexistent with Charles. I fumbled with my zipper, snapped the waistband of my boxer briefs trying to get them down, and nearly came as soon as Charles grabbed my dick. He wrapped his long legs around me, crushing our lower bodies together, and wrapped his long fingers around our cocks.

"Ahh...." I braced my hand against the window, hips jolting forward. "Yes...."

Charles squeezed our erections together and started pumping, causing pre-cum to ooze from my tip every time he pulled my foreskin with each upstroke.

"Fuck," I whispered. "Yeah, jerk us off. Make that dick drip."

Charles arched his back from the window, hips jerking as he went from using one hand to two. My dick in one, his in the other. I fucked his hand while my body overheated and my balls pulled up tight. I was unable to look away from his wild eyes and parted lips. He kept glancing between my dick and my eyes, his brows twisted together and hair everywhere. Eventually he abandoned his own dick to focus on mine, one hand choking my thick erection and flying over it so fast I was seeing stars.

"You're gonna make me come," I warned, eyes rolling back. "I'm so close."

"Not yet." Charles slid his hand away, eliciting a mournful groan from me. "I want to suck it."

My hand shot down to squeeze my base as an explosion of heat started in my belly. This was a fantasy, an actual fantasy I'd had about him some time in the past couple of months. I'd jerked off to a pretend scenario where we ran into each other getting the mail and wound up fucking around right in this exact same spot. It was nearly déjà vu when he reversed our positions so my back was to the window, and I swear it had happened before when he knelt between my thighs. The difference was that in my fantasy, he was smirking and teasing. Here, now, in real life—he was breathing hard and impatient to get me down his throat.

I was on the thick side, but Charles opened his mouth wide and took me in with a moan. His fingers tightened around my base, fingers pressed in the vein pulsing up the underside of my cock, and slowly pulled his mouth up and off. I could do nothing but watch dazedly as he flicked his tongue at my dick slit as it poked out from my foreskin. He pulled it down a little, revealing more and more of my cockhead, and lavished it in wet sloppy kisses.

My eyes rolled back. "God, I love your mouth."

Charles hummed against my dick, pulling the foreskin up again, then flicked his tongue at it. My thighs strained, trembling just slightly, as he flicked his tongue beneath the thin fold in a tease that sent more pre-cum sliding down my shaft. I pressed my hands against the sides of the window, tilting my head back, and unraveled as he played with me. Everything in my body was coming undone, seams unraveling and brain self-destructing, as he sucked the tip of my dick into his mouth again and pulled away with a pinch of my foreskin still between his lips.

"*Fuck*," I cried. "I'm really gonna come."

Charles pumped me faster, gripping me so tight I was stripped of the ability to think. Every thought narrowed to his hand, the pulse of my cock, and the feel of his wet velvet mouth sinking down to cover me as he jerked the base. I braced the back of his head with both hands and fucked into his mouth. A devil took hold of my hips and forced them to drove myself deeper down his throat.

I grabbed the base of my dick with one hand and a handful of his hair with the other. He looked up at me then, eyes twinkling and lips spread into a wicked smile, and it was just like my fucking fantasy. I flashed him a smile of my own. It widened when he pressed his hands to the floor between his folded legs, all demure and passive, and stuck out his tongue.

I tapped the tip of my dick against his extended tongue. "¿Quieres esto?"

Charles nodded, gaze never leaving mine. I pulled my foreskin back and dragged the sticky tip of my cock along his tongue before feeding it into his mouth. He never took his eyes off me. Not even when my balls were pressed to his chin and he had no choice but to breathe through his nose. I yanked my shirt up so I could see, unobstructed, the sight of him sucking my dick without use of his hands.

"Yeah," I hissed, rocking into his mouth. "Mi niño lindo." The moan that muffled out from around my cock prompted me to move faster, sliding in and out of his lips so that my balls slapped his chin. "Ahh..."

He wrapped his lips around my shaft just as I exploded all over his tongue. I grabbed the base again, working it with my fingers as my mind blanked out. I released spurt after spurt into his waiting mouth, ass cheeks clenching as I lodged down his throat. When I pulled out, it was with a shaky groan and a sloppy smear of my cockhead against his lips.

God, he was a mess. Saliva and semen all over his mouth and chin. I flashed back to that night in the basement, and the desire to kiss him overtook everything else. I yanked him up by his collar and slammed him against his door. He whimpered when I began giving him the exact same kind of tongue bath I'd given him that evening—licking all traces of saliva and cum from his face instead of ice cream.

"I want you in my bed," I said between licks. "I want to make you come. And then I want to fuck you."

"God, yes," he whispered. "I need that so bad."

"Yeah?" I licked down his throat, sucking the side of it. "Tell me why you need it."

"Because I need to be fucked. By you." Charles pulled me into a brief messy kiss. "Until I can't think about anything else but that fat cock deep in my hole, shoving so far inside that you might hit my fucking bladder."

My jaw dropped. "Jesus Christ."

He arched a sassy eyebrow. "You asked."

"Leave it to you to make it sound all... violent."

Charles smacked my ass. "Shut up and pick an apartment."

"Depends. What kinda lube you got?" I knocked my hand against his door, and my fingers brushed paper. Without thinking, I removed a folded piece of paper that had been taped to the door. "What the hell is this?"

Charles froze then burst into motion. He grabbed the paper and squinted in the gloom from the street lamps outside. It took all of a second for his posture to stiffen and him to inhale audibly.

Dread filled the tiny vestibule so palpably I could taste it.

Landon had been here.

CHAPTER SIXTEEN
CHARLES

I couldn't get my leggings pulled up fast enough.

All of a sudden, everything was a rush. The intimate moment was gone, my dick soft, and panic was choking me instead of a burning need to be manhandled and penetrated by the ridiculously sexy bastard hovering behind me.

I could only think of Landon having been in the house, of having a way inside the vestibule even if he couldn't get into the apartment, and maybe even lurking around. Having seen us through the window. Or having seen me and Luis some other time, maybe on one of the many occasions when we'd stood here kissing playfully and teasing each other. I wanted to vomit.

All of those special bits and pieces that had painstakingly added up to the whole that had made me deliriously happy only ten minutes ago were suddenly violated. By that motherfucker.

"Hey, hey..."

Luis put his hands on my shoulders, and I flinched away from him. The need to not be touched when I felt so small and fucking exposed was instinctual, and yet the automatic reaction made me feel like absolute shit.

"I need to go," I gritted. "I need to go upstairs."

I fumbled in the pockets of my sweater for my keys, hands shaking. They nearly dropped when I finally untangled them from the oversized knitted fabric, and I couldn't hold my hand still enough to get the key into the lock.

"Charles, please." Luis gently put his hand over mine, closing his fingers over my own. "Come to my place."

"I need to be alone."

"Baby, no. You'll just go take this shit out on your apartment, and then you'll be upset later." He tightened his hand on mine, his breath slow and even in my ear. "Just come inside with me, and we don't have to talk, or you can scream and curse and I'll sit there quiet. Or you can use my punching bag. Whatever you want."

I closed my eyes, sucking in deep breaths as my heart tried to pound out of my chest. He inched in closer, until we were so close I could feel his warmth, and smell his cologne and hair product. Over time, all of those things had become a comfort to me even though I'd rejected the dawning realization that *he* was a comfort to me. And I was so grateful for it. For him.

My throat locked up and my eyes burned. I pressed my forehead against the door, sucking in deep breaths but unable to stop the tears from sliding from the corners of my eyes. Biting my lip didn't stop the choked sob from trying to escape my throat, and it was loud as hell in the quiet room.

Luis put both hands on my shoulders, digging in tight, and held on even when I violently tried to shrug him off. I growled, but he ignored it and pressed his face into my hair.

"Just *leave*," I pleaded. "Go away, Luis."

"No. I'd rather get cut than leave you here like this."

Those words, spoken in that low fierce tone, totally broke me. I pressed my hands to my face, crying harder, and was too frazzled to stop him when he spun me around. He rubbed my back while I cried into his shirt, which just made it all worse.

"I fucking hate this," I choked out. "I fucking hate that you see me like this."

"It doesn't matt—"

"It matters," I shouted, pulling away only to find the door at my back. "I wanted—I realized I wanted... more with you. And then I fall to pieces as soon as his name pops into my head. I'm a fuckup and a mess, and I hate myself for being so weak—"

Luis jerked my chin up, hands rougher than they'd ever been on me, and kissed me so hard our teeth clicked together. I pulled away and tried to speak, but he shoved me harder against the wall and kissed me again. With his tongue lashing at me, and him effortlessly holding me against the door, it was almost too easy to go slack and part my lips. Even with anger and fear soaring through me and trying to make me their bitch, I couldn't stop from moaning against him. Or from frantically kissing back.

He could probably taste the salt from my tears, but it didn't deter him. He cupped my face with one hand and used the other to lift me up as if I weighed nothing. It another moment, another mindset, I may have been annoyed by the treatment, but now I wrapped my legs around him. He was so fucking strong, so hard and powerful, that my dick thickened against him again.

"Forget him. Focus on me," he whispered against my lips. "Come inside and let me treat you right."

I shook my head, panting and slightly out of my mind. "No, you—upstairs. I want you to fuck me in that bed. Make it mine again."

Luis' eyes slit open just enough for me to see the glitter of them, then he nodded once. He let me down and panted against my neck while I shoved the key in the lock. His hands were all over me, but not reaching down to grab my dick or yank at my clothes. He slid them up and down my sides with firm glides of his palms while tracing light kisses along the side of my face.

I'd never felt more cared for.

The key went into the lock with limited fumbling, and I led him upstairs like I had so many other times before. The only difference was that this time there was no flirtatious dissing and teasing, no banter or laughter. The stairwell was filled only with the sound of my heavy breathing and his footsteps behind me. We remained that way even after entering the dark apartment. It was surreal to bring him to my bedroom with Landon just lingering at the back of my mind. Over the past several weeks, he had become nonexistent to me. Now, he was a ghost hovering just at my peripheral vision. A reminder that I'd caught them in this exact same room, this exact same bed, about to bang.

Luis put his hands on my hips, jolting me from my reverie, and guided me down to the bed. "Stop thinking about him."

"I can't." I let him push me onto my back, my legs hanging off the side of the bed. "He's everywhere. All that note said was that he needed to pick up the rest of his shit, and I had a breakdown. He's a disease that spreads and turns everything rancid."

"Not everything." Luis knelt between my thighs, his big body pushing them further apart, and yanked off my barely tied boots. "So close your eyes and let me take care of you."

It didn't work that way. I wanted to snap at him, to bare my teeth and explain how fucking didn't wipe away bad memories. His dick wasn't magic, and it didn't contain a cure. Especially not when he had a habit of running from his own problems. But on the same token, I wanted him to fix me. To fix all of this. Or at least make me forget so I could enjoy all the feelings that had been swimming to the surface after we'd left Club Cummings and gotten into that cab together.

"Think about dancing, baby," he said as he pulled off my socks one by one. "It's what I do when I'm angry. I think about working out, or boxing, and how I can work off that anger and frustration so I don't put my fist in someone's mouth."

Dancing. Performing. Being on stage with Luis instead of Gabe or Rox or whatever the hell he wanted to call himself. Me moving with Luis in that slow grind, us side-by-side celebrating our queerness and our desire, and him giving me a worshipful kiss on stage in front of hundreds. Our choreography that we'd developed together. Us fucking hard and fast in a dressing room after an intense performance. Us going home together. Our plans twining together until they completed each other.

Was it possible?

One of my leggings skinned down, then the other.

Could it be real?

Did I have the courage to pursue this dream come true? The possibility was terrifying and thrilling, and enough to blight out everything but a reminder that Luis was the best thing to happen to me in a very long time.

"Luis..."

"Yeah?"

"I want to meet Marquis."

Luis pressed his lips to the inside of my thigh, and I could feel the shape of his smile. "There's my hardheaded pretty boy."

I closed my eyes as he trailed a line of wet kisses up the inside of my thigh and up to my groin. "Would that make you happy? If I was in the troupe?"

"It's not about me. Stop making shit about me and your...

gratitude to me."

"But—"

"Charles, it'd make me happy to suck your dick until you're so relaxed my cock won't hurt you when I shove it in your ass."

My dick throbbed, balls so swollen I reached down to pull on them only to find my hand slapped away. It was no gentle slap. My hand stung, and it only made me harder. I moaned, low and surprised, and lifted my bare feet onto the mattress.

"Spread your legs for me," Luis said in that same low serious voice. "Show me everything. I need to know what I'm working with if you want me to work it out."

I moaned again, louder this time, and lifted my legs so I could grab the back of my knees. Cool air from the window blew against my body, and the feeling of being utterly exposed in a way I hadn't been in ages hit me. My last few times with Landon before the cruise had always been with me face down in the mattress as he rutted against me until he came. It'd been hate fucking. And not the good kind. It'd been sad and—

"*Oh shit.*"

The feel of Luis' tongue circling my hole vanquished every thought. My eyes rolled back and my dick pulsed against my stomach. He pressed his big hands to my lower thighs, pushing them apart, and fucked my ass with the pointed tip of his tongue until I was undulating on the bed like a wave. After so long the sensation was unfamiliar enough to be exotic—something I'd received so rarely that the very idea was enough to make me come.

He ate me like I was the best meal he'd had in years, groaning with each lick and squeezing my balls as they grew tighter. I spread open wider, writhing, and started jacking myself the moment he went from licking my ass to sucking on my balls. When one of his fingers slid into my saliva streaked hole, I cried out so sharply it pierced the night.

It was the last sound I mustered. My voice caught in my throat and my mouth gaped, no sounds coming out except harsh gasps as I was triply stimulated—dick, balls, and ass. I was going to come in no time—it was a given. There was no other option with him using every body part he could access, and I could already feel it building.

"Yeah, like that," I whispered. "Please, just—just like that."

Luis moaned against me, a low anguished sound, and my hips jackknifed up. I could feel my peak about to hit just when he went from playing with my ass to restraining my arms. My body went into shock from the sudden lack of sensation. It was the worst kind of torture, and I could do nothing but squeeze my eyes shut and suck in sobbing breaths.

"Condoms," his voice filtered in. "Lube?"

I threw out a wild arm to point to the end table. I couldn't help any more than that. My entire body was rebelling against me, balls abandoned, ass clenching, and dick so hard the ache was on the verge of painful. The only thing keeping me from cursing him was the fact that I was going to have him in me soon.

"Fuck me," I pleaded softly. "Please fuck me. I just..."

Luis grunted above me, his breath hissing out. I heard the sound of something wet slicking, and knew he was lubing himself up. "You just what, papi? You want this dick?" The plump crown pressed to my opening, and my toes curled. "To pound that sweet ass of yours?"

"Yeah." My voice was nothing more than a breath, so I strained myself to look up at him. His head was bowed, full lips damp and parted, as he jacked his dick with the head pressed up to my hole. "Luis."

Those dark eyes rose and drilled into me, sending a chill down my spine. He was wearing the same expression he'd worn in the mock ring earlier this evening. The look meant to intimidate opponents, and to silently say *I'm going to fucking wreck you.* My body was molten lava under the weight of that stare.

"I want you to fuck me until you think I can't take it," I whispered. "Until I'm almost in tears because I'm stretched so fucking wide. Until you know I can't think about anything but the biggest dick I've ever had in me completely wiping out every thought."

Luis sucked in a deep breath. He just narrowed his eyes, upper lip curling just slightly, and pressed his dick into me in a slow invasion that sent every nerve ending alight. It burned, a white hot streak through my body, and I couldn't help another pointed cry. I cringed, and he pulled out. His breath tore out of him so violently I felt bad for the obvious lack of readiness even after my filthy plea. But I appreciated the feel of his fingers spreading into me while covered in another large dollop of lube.

He fingered me hard, three fingers stabbing into me and hooking up to brush my prostate. The veer between pain and pleasure was so abrupt that my body rebelled against me, twitching and jerking with each touch while my dick continued to throb. His painstaking patience was driving me wild, and by the time he slipped his fingers out of me I was in a daze. I'd fucked myself on his fingers so needily that dignity was out the window. I didn't care. Especially when he was murmuring in Spanish while playing with my prostate, clearly enjoying the process of turning me out so thoroughly I'd have crawled across glass to impale myself on his cock.

At long last he impatiently dragged me into a position that left him straddling one of my thighs while he lifted the other up with a tight grip on my ankle. It left me completely stretched open with his dick aimed right at my hole. It was so hungry for that thick intrusion that I didn't clench up this time when he fucked his way inside. My body accepted him completely and tightened only when he began to obliterate the muscles clenching around him.

It was everything I'd wanted from him. The pounding intensity, the feel of his deliciously talented hips relentlessly forcing that beautiful dick deep inside my body, and the way he swiveled them just enough to jam against my prostate. It was impossible to do anything but accept this brutal fucking, be humbled by it, and cling to the bedding as he flexed his hips in a way that made me want to shout.

Luis' grunts grew louder the harder he fucked me. I'd never heard his voice so high and agonized. Spanish words poured from his mouth as he defaulted back to his first language. "Si mi amor, cogelo. Este culo tan bello es mio."

The words translated and set me off like a firecracker. I was coming before I was ready, crying out into the night while he continued to saw in and out of me. Tremors took over my body, and they increased when Luis ripped out of me only to flip me onto my back. He jerked my legs up by the ankles, forcing me to lock them behind his neck, and lifted me off the bed in another casual show of power. He angled his hips and fucked into me again, holding me off the bed and slamming into my clenched ass repeatedly.

The feeling of being weightless and suspended only by his bulging arms while he powered in and out of me was incredible. I'd just come, but I was crying out again. I never wanted it to end. I could die like this—filled to the core and stretched incredibly wide by a man who had managed to overtake my mind and body.

Luis hips jolted hard once more before he cried out.

I blinked through the sweat trickling into my eyes, and watched his face smooth as bliss swept over it. His mouth gaped and he swallowed hard, rocking in and out of me until his brows puckered. He let me down gently after he pulled out, treating me with care after his relentless fucking.

Unable to stop watching him, I lay on my side as he shed and dumped the condom. I watched as he pressed his hand to the end table, eyes closed and breathing hard. He was trying to gather himself, I thought. To get himself together so he could face me. It was so fucking endearing that I grabbed his wrist and tugged him toward the bed.

"You're staying up here tonight."

Luis' eyes opened, and that big smile crossed his face. The intense fuckbeast he'd been a moment ago slipped inside his muscular chest, and the teasing joker came out again. He dove onto the bed, causing it to bounce, and dragged me against his sweaty body.

"That mean it worked?" He placed wet open-mouthed kisses along my face. "Yeah?"

"It worked." I rolled onto my back and took him with me, wanting the heavy weight of him pinning me to the mattress. "All I can think about is you."

CHAPTER SEVENTEEN
LUIS

I woke up to the feel of lips on my neck, trailing down slowly to my chest. My head was so fuzzy from the sudden hard sleep I'd fallen into that it took a moment for me to realize I was in Charles' amazingly squishy bed, and it was his mounds of wild cowlicks and curls dragging along my skin.

"Mmm." I put my hand on the back of his head. "Lower."

He sucked my nipple into his mouth, sparking a chain reaction of hot explosions that settled in my gut and hardened my dick. I felt him smile against me before slowly pulling away with one last flick of his tongue against my nipple.

"I didn't mean to wake you up."

I snorted. "I'm not a heavy sleeper. Any time you touch me, I'll wake up."

"Then do you mind if I wake you up by sucking your dick?"

My shoulders shook in silent laughter. "Why the hell would I mind that? The real question is whether you wondering about how to wake me up means we get to spend the night together on a regular basis?"

Charles pressed his chin into my chest, looking up at me with those incredibly dark eyes. "Is that what you want?"

I rolled my eyes, but couldn't stop myself from burying a hand in his hair. "Okay, time out. I need clarification on some shit."

"If it's about whether I enjoyed the way you fucked me?" Charles smiled, a slow dirty smile. "Yes. Very much. I don't think I've had anyone in me that deep... ever. I woke up horny from the memory of it."

My dick perked up, and I didn't hesitate to reach beneath the sheet to squeeze on it. We must have crashed soon after round one, but a long enough time had passed for my body to be raring to go again. It had to have been like an hour or two, but I only really needed twenty minutes. It was a personal goal of mine to take a day to spend riding him as many times as possible. He had the kind of body I needed to claim repeatedly, just to make sure he knew it now belonged to me.

"I know my dick is mad huge," I said, cuffing his chin lightly. "So nah, that wasn't the question."

"Ugh." Charles rolled over onto his back. "I can't even distract you with flattery, you smug asshole."

"Definitely not. There's not much that can distract me from what I want, and what I want now is for us to have real talk." I watched him watch the spinning ceiling fan, then shifted so I could straddle him. I was still hard, so my dick poked up through the sheets, but I ignored it. "You said some things that had me wondering, and I want you to explain them."

Charles' cheek clenched. The first sign of irritation or defensiveness. But instead of snapping at me or defaulting to sarcasm, he arched an eyebrow. "Okay?"

"First—you keep saying you're grateful for me. Or you keep thanking me. But for what?"

Even in a room only lit by moonlight, I could see him go ruddy. "Because," he said. "I'm an angry, ragey, sometimes irrational asshole who was shitty to you over something that wasn't your fault. And you stuck it out and put up with me long enough to get to know me." Charles snuck a quick glance at me. "And because of all that, I'm thinking about dancing again in front of an audience in way that... matters to me, for the first time in years. That wouldn't be possible without you, Luis. You fucking know it. And that's why Landon inserting his bummy self into our moment just... It just..."

"Made you want to slash and burn everything on the north shore?"

Charles' mouth twitched. "Yes. Pretty much."

"All right." I nodded, watching him from beneath my lashes and trying to stop myself from kissing all of his anger and self-doubt and frustration away. Mushy stuff later. We were laying the cards out first. "My turn to respond to item number one—"

"Oh my God, you're so weird.

"Uh-huh. The *weird neighbor*." I flicked his nose. "First off, I wasn't doing you some huge favor by being persistent. I already told you I felt that we had an instant connection even if you kept fighting it. I wanted to get to know you because of that, but also because you're talented and fly and funny and have a big culo."

Charles released a startled laugh. "You're *such* a top."

"Fuck yeah, I am." I bit my lip and leaned forward to drag my dick against his belly. "But more importantly—do you believe me when I say all that? Or do you think I'm just saying it to get my way with you?"

"No." It left Charles' mouth so fast, even he looked surprised. "I believe everything you say when you say it. You're the most honest person I've met, Luis."

"Mmm." Unable to resist, I leaned down to kiss him. Our tongues slid together briefly, and his hands came up to grip my waist. "I love it when you say my name."

He moaned against my lips, shifting his hips restlessly. "What's your full name?"

"Luis Wilberto Ramos."

"Wilberto?" Charles grinned against me. "Cute."

"Shut the fuck up." I softened my growl with another long kiss. "I already know your last name, Mr. Jovanovic. What's your middle name?"

"No middle name. Sorry to disappoint."

"Unfair." I sat up again. "But let's get back to item number two— in the cab you said you wanted more with me. What did that mean?"

"Oh dear God, he remembered every word." Charles threw out his arms out dramatically. "What does it *sound* like?"

"It sounds like you wanna be my man. Is that what it means?" Charles pressed his lips together. I rocked against him again. "I'm serious. Just tell me what it means. I don't do vague."

"Well I don't do causal," he grumbled. "I've never done causal, even as a teenager. Every relationship I had was intense and I focused all of my being on that other person, etcetera. So, unsurprisingly, I caught feelings for you pretty fast."

"Hey, it's been like two months. Not *that* fast." I tried to school my face into a serious expression, but I couldn't help the grin wanting to take over. I'd been in relationships before even if none of them had been very serious, but nothing had compared to this feeling of satisfaction at Charles confessing he wanted me. "So, you know I like you a lot, right? Like even when your ass was throwing coffee at me? It's not news. So, can we just say we're dating?"

"What are you gonna do, run to change your status on Facebook?" Charles ask scornfully even as he smiled. "Because I want no part of that."

"I'd settle for you just telling me you're my boyfriend without being a smartass."

"Oh." Charles cringed. "Sorry, I'm bad at this."

"What, like, being nice?"

"Yes. Confessing my feelings and trying to have deep talks about the future of relationships historically has not panned out for me." Charles blew out a breath and returned his hands to my sides. "I want to date you. I want you to be my boyfriend."

"Bet." I leaned down for another kiss, lazier and wetter this time. We were grinding together slowly when I pulled away, my dick sliding precum all over his tight stomach. I was so ready for round two. "One more question, lindo. Then I need to fuck you again."

Charles bucked his hips up then proceeded to position himself so his long legs were thrown over mine and spread open. Wide. "How do you need it?"

"I need you to ride this," I rumbled, grabbing my dick and tapping it at his hole. "But not until we finish talking. And not until you calm down from how pissed this next thing might get you."

Charles collapsed against the bed like his strings had been cut. "What now?"

I searched his face, those sparking eyes and pursed lips, all evidence of his quick temper and short fuse. How much did I want to potentially piss him off versus how badly did I want to feel him riding my cock? In the long run, answers were more important.

"Look, I'm only asking you all this shit because I really like you, baby. I want us to be good together for a mad long time. For you to dance in the troupe, and for us to practice together, for you to meet my moms, and for you to fucking trust me. Right? But first that means

I have to figure out what it looks like when you trust someone."

"I don't trust any—"

I shushed him with a finger to his lips, closed my eyes, and prayed to Jesus for some patience. "That's not true, okay? And if I'm your boyfriend, and you don't trust me, that's a problem. It basically means boyfriend translates to you riding my hog and us hanging out, but we can be friends-with-benefits without the official title if that's all you want."

For a moment, Charles gave me that same furrow browed annoyed look he used to give me whenever I showed my face on the block. But then his face cleared, and he let his eyes slide shut. "I don't do casual. I go in when I like someone. All the way."

"Me too, so please tell me how we can make this work so your first instinct isn't to kick me out or tell me to fuck off when you get upset."

"Luis..."

"No, I'm serious." I ran my fingers down the side of his face, tracing his nose and lips. "You said Landon's note was just him demanding the rest of his stuff? Okay, but the way you acted had me thinking it was a threat. I was ready to call my boys and go find that piece of shit. Or call the cops, if you wanted to play it that way. You freaked me out, then told me to leave."

Charles' eyes snapped open and widened, horror washing over him. "Oh, God, I didn't even... I'm sorry. I just get so angry that I want to hide before anyone can see how emotional I'm getting. I just hate... people seeing me that way."

"But I'm not people."

"I know, but that doesn't change my need in *that moment* to be alone. To isolate myself until I can—I can just deal." Charles balled his hands into fists and closed his eyes for a moment. "I need you to understand that, Luis. I need you to understand that sometimes I just need some time to remember how to breathe."

I opened my mouth to tell him that I could help him remember, that I could be there for him when he thought he wanted to be alone, but I closed it. How could I tell him not to look for an escape when he felt overwhelmed, when I'd been hiding and escaping my problems in the Bronx for months? My own parents had been offering to help me all that time, and I'd demanded they let me deal with it my own way.

"I get it," I said. "And I'm not trying to act like I'm the solution to all your problems. Or that I know how to fix them even if you wanted to."

The relief that crossed Charles' face told me all I needed to know about his desire to have me swan in and shut down his coping methods. "I appreciate you saying that. You honestly have no idea how many people think they can do plug-and-play therapy with dicks."

My mouth twitched, but I swallowed the laugh. "Nah, that's not why I'm here just like you're not here to force me to go back to the Bronx. But... I'm your man now. Right? So, if you need to be alone, I get it, but please let me know what's up so I don't panic and assume the worst. I am all about giving you your space, but there's a difference between that and just being shut out in the dark so that I'm reminded that I'm only the weird dude who lives under you."

Charles was looking at me like I was a fucking unicorn charging out of a magical forest by then, but there was fondness in his expression too. He'd started sliding his hands up and down my sides, a soft smile forming on his face. "I like how straight forward you are, so I'll be straight forward too. About what I need."

Relief blossomed in my chest. He wasn't mad. He was listening. We were talking. No beverages were thrown or shivs whipped out. I wanted to shout hallelujah right before sucking his dick. Instead, I asked, "What do you need from me, gorgeous?"

Charles exhaled slowly and made a face like he thought his own request was ridiculous. "I need you to keep doing what you're doing. Calling me out. Pointing out when I'm being guarded and paranoid. You have to understand—this shit is deep in me now after so many years of being with Landon. My trust is... I mean, I was blind with jealous bitchiness after watching you dance with Gabe. I didn't want him touching you. I created this whole paranoid thing in my head where you treated him the way you treat me—and no, don't make that face," he said when I frowned. "Because I know it's not true. But it's... my self-esteem. Which is kicked in and stomped down and dusty. Okay?"

I almost mentioned how badly I wanted to kill Landon all over again, but only nodded. "What else?"

"Just don't change after a few months." His voice was lower when he said it, and the vulnerability twisted my guts. "It always happens to me. I trust someone, I fall in love with someone, and they change on me. And then I'm caught out there all devoted and stupid and desperate for it to work while the person I want is... checked out."

"That would never happen," I said fiercely. "I swear to God, Jesus, my mother, and Daddy Yankee."

Charles burst out laughing. He reached up to embrace me, squeezing tight and kissing the side of my neck. "God, you really did bring me back to life, Luis. That's why I'm so glad to have met you. I felt like I was going to be in that depressed dark place forever, and you revived me with this fucking... nonstop laughing. Every time I think of you, I smile."

"Can it be that way forever?" I asked, kissing him back. "Me being dumb, you laughing, us dancing, and maybe someday you going in with me on renting a studio that I can use for personal training, and you can use for like... dance lessons, while we do Man-dated Attraction on the side?"

Charles jerked back, eyes going wide. "Oh my God. What?"

"Am I jumping the boyfriend gun?"

He thwacked my arm. "No, that is brilliant. Even if I didn't want to kiss your face constantly, that would be brilliant. Romantic stuff aside, we could create a contract to share a space and make that work. And I—" Charles stumbled over his words and shook his head. "That's something I'd... actually want to do. And I know a lot of people who can help us with setting up businesses and the legalities."

I beamed. "Good, because that shit legit just came to me, and I think I'm a genius. Let's talk more about it after I fuck you."

"Talk over midnight post-sex dinner?" he asked hopefully, eager as ever for food.

"When else would we have serious conversations about business ventures?"

Charles smiled wider than I'd ever seen, and he looked so much younger and sweeter in that moment. It was like a light had been turned on inside of him.

"I love how weird we are together," he admitted softly. "How we made up all of these weird habits and traditions. It feels so real. So unique."

"We are unique. That's why we make so much sense together."

It was probably the cockiest shit I'd ever said, and I was definitely feeding into the mindset so many of my Man-dated Attraction troupe members shared when it came to dating people who understood your art. But as pretentious as it sounded? It was true.

CHAPTER EIGHTEEN
CHARLES

Marquis was everything I'd ever wanted in an entertainment manager. As soon as I'd slunk into his Williamsburg loft behind Luis—which was fifty-percent hardwood floors with mirrored walls and floor-to-ceiling windows—and laid eyes on his fabulously gay aesthetic, I'd felt tingly. It was very old Hollywood, with living spaces swathed in soft velvety fabrics, shimmering curtains, and gorgeous paintings of Marilyn Monroe, RuPaul, Lucy Lawless, and EJ Johnson.

I wandered up to the enormous painting of EJ, hands to my mouth to hide my huge grin. "Oh my God. Where did you get this?"

"I painted it," Marquis said, smiling around his straw. Luis had suggested I bring him Starbucks to get brownie points. "Luis didn't tell you about my many other talents?"

My smile faltered, Marquis' eyes twinkled, and Luis called from across the room, "Why're you making it sound like you've sucked my dick?"

Marquis snorted, and I relaxed. Holy hell, my jealousy gland was pulsing and we'd only been officially dating for two weeks. Two glorious weeks of dancing, sex, and sleeping in the same bed. And no word from Landon to ruin it.

"As if I'd ever touch a sweaty jock like you," Marquis drawled. "No thanks. I'll stick to letting Gabe seduce me."

Luis quit raiding the racks of costumes in the far corner, and muttering and complaining about each one, before joining us near the wall of art. "Heeeey, is that why he's leaving? Because you won't screw him if he's in the troupe?"

Marquis gave him such a dull like that I couldn't help but laugh.

"Not everything is about sex, Louie. Now sit there, be buff, and let me talk to your honey."

Luis grinned broadly at the title and threw himself into one of the velvety sofas. He grabbed a zebra patterned pillow, buried his face in it, and watched me with warm brown eyes. I tried to focus on Marquis, but Luis was a nonstop distraction. The way he looked at me all the time...

"This is gonna be pretty informal because I already know I want you based on your training and background," Marquis said to me bluntly. "I'm glad you came in real dancewear unlike your man who thinks appropriate attire is baggy sweatpants, so we're gonna do a few demos. I'll show you one of Gabe's pieces, and you perform it for me. Simple?"

Luis had been practicing Gabe's parts with me for the past couple of weeks, and it *still* sounded nerve wracking. Even so, I unzipped my hoody, tossed it at Luis, and gave Marquis one of my huge flashy smiles—the smile that helped me fake the kind of self-confidence I hadn't felt in years.

"Let's do this."

He clapped, looking genuinely excited. "You better kill this shit, Chuck. I want you in my troupe."

No pressure or anything.

The next hour or so was one of the most exhilarating stretches of time in my life since my shows and performances while at Julliard. We watched Gabe's parts on Marquis' 4K projector a couple of times, then I stood in the middle of his studio space and did my best to mirror the performance I'd just watched. I forgot about Marquis, about Luis, and even about the end game of this goal and focused on nothing but the beat of the music and the movement of my own body.

We did the dances from Gabe's Queer Agenda bit, his part in the new duet with Luis, and the political Rainbow Mafia performance which was basically an ode to resistance against intolerance with him leading the rest of the troupe in rainbow colored tactical gear. It wasn't perfect, none of them were, but I tried to roll with my screw-ups while sweaty and full of adrenaline in a way that showed I was flexible and thought on my feet.

By the time we were done, I was full of energy. I'd already felt like

Luis had breathed life back into me, but the audition had me walking on fucking sunshine. I whipped wet hair out of my face after the final piece, smiling widely at having nailed something I hadn't even practiced much.

"That was un-be-fucking-lievable," Marquis breathed. "Don't tell him I said it, but you move better than Gabe. Doesn't he, Louie?"

We both looked over at Luis and found him slumped on the sofa with his gaze running all over me. He was biting his lower lip and so visibly turned on that my body heated in response. Considering I was already sweaty and exhausted, my insides became an inferno.

"Oh Lord." Marquis rolled his eyes. "Okay, love birds, we can finish up so you can go home and fuck—"

"Can't do that just yet," Luis complained. "He has brunch with one of his pals."

"And you have to work at Male Revue later," I countered. "Sooo... It's not all on me."

"Work is money. Brunch is you spending money."

Marquis looked between us. "Are you really bickering because you have no time to fuck?"

"Yes," we both said, then grinned at each other.

"Lovely. Seriously." Marquis pointed between us slowly. "The chemistry between you two will be off the charts in Punch Drunk Louie Comes Out."

"Speaking of..." Luis pushed himself up off the couch and sauntered over me in his shredded jeans and oversized hoodie. He grabbed me from behind, uncaring about my sweat, and nuzzled the back of my neck. "He needs a name."

"Oh shit," I said. "I hadn't thought that far ahead."

"Mmm." Marquis tapped his chin. "Chuckie Two-Timed."

My eyes just about popped out of my head, but Luis cracked up.

"How the..." I looked at Luis dryly. "Seriously? You told him about that?"

"It was before I knew we were gonna be a thing," he said quickly, still snickering. "I swear to God."

"And Daddy Yankee?" I made a face. "You're so lucky I like you."

"I think it's a good name," Marquis said. "Brilliant really. Not surprising considering I thought of it."

Good Lord. If the rest of the troupe had egos as big as these two fuckers, it was a good thing my general lack of confidence would potentially even things out. But I was getting ahead of myself. Luis' happiness and optimist was so contagious that I'd started leaving the safety of pessimism behind.

"Hold up," I said. "I haven't even been officially—"

"Congrats." Marquis wiggled his fingers at me. "It's official! I want you. We can get the paperwork signed. There's a contract that breaks everything down. And I hope Luis explained the money to you..."

I managed to nod while practically vibrating with excitement. No matter how hard I tried, I couldn't stay still. Even with Luis attaching himself to my back, I was nearly bouncing in place or shifting from foot to foot.

"We get a cut from whatever intake we get from each show after all fees are paid, which sometimes doesn't amount to much?"

Marquis winked. "It may start amounting to a little more, sugar tits. We'll be at the Highline Ballroom this summer."

My jaw dropped, and Luis stood up straight behind me. "No shit?"

"No. Fucking. Shit. Our show is moving on up, babies." Marquis held up his hand for a high-five and scowled when Luis smacked his hand so hard it echoed in the loft. "Savage."

"I really am." Luis wrapped his arms around me, squeezing tight and lifting me up. He was jittery with excitement, just like me, and wasn't deterred even when I elbowed him so he'd let me down. "I'm so fucking excited!"

"I'm... honestly speechless, and that doesn't happen a lot," I said. "When do things start happening?"

"As soon as possible. Gabe's last show is next week, and we need you practicing. Come by the practice space first thing Monday, and we'll get this thing rolling." Marquis beamed at me. "Congrats, Chuckie. You're soon to be officially Man-dated!"

We said our goodbyes, and I walked out jittery with a mind full of racing thoughts. When you were the type of person to generally be shit out of luck at every attempt to get ahead in life, a streak of fortunate events tended to seem mad suspect. A few months ago, if I'd found a sweet guy who liked me, come up with a potentially feasible future business plan, *and* scored a spot in a popular dance troupe... I would have frozen in one spot and waited for my luck to run out. Or, on my worst days, I'd have given up on these ventures before attempting them. My traitor brain who fell victim to imposter syndrome would have told me there was no way I would succeed, or live up to expectations, so why try?

But now? My heart was pounding out of my chest. I was squeezing Luis' hand like a child on Christmas morning as we bypassed the freight elevator and headed for the stairs. Marquis lived on the top floor of an old factory, with long staircases between each floor. I was a bundle of energy and I needed something, anything, to work it out so I could think rationally.

"You look so fucking happy," Luis said, pulling me to a stop on the first landing. He scrutinized my expression. "Are you? For real. This isn't, like, you being mad fake and your face got stuck?"

"No. I'm legitimately in a great fucking mood." I tried to school my expression to be serious, but a smile broke out again. "I probably look like an idiot, don't I?"

"Mmm... no, but you are cheesing pretty hard."

I smacked his shoulder. "Shut up. I'm just... I don't know. I feel invincible all of a sudden? And it's so fucking scary because everything always goes wrong, but I also feel like things have to be right because—" Self-preservation threw a life raft at my head to stop me completing that sentence. Unfortunately, it was Luis I was talking to, and he was never going to let me get away with not telling him everything that was on my mind.

"Because what?"

"Ugh. Why are you so persistent?"

"Because I'm Luis." He winked, then buried his hands in my hoodie and pulled me closer. "For real, what were you gonna say?"

"Just that..." I spread my hands helplessly, searching for a way to say what I wanted to say without being over the top mushy. It wasn't possible. And disgustingly enough? That didn't stop me from blurting it out. Because it was Luis I was speaking to, and he was safe. "When I'm with you, I feel like nothing can go wrong. You're my walking lucky charm. Or some shit."

Luis' face softened. He took a step closer to me, then another, until I was standing against the railing with him pressed against me. "Don't give me all the credit. I had the connection, but you had the chops. That audition was all you, lindo. And you were amazing. You were also so fucking hot that my dick was throbbing the entire time." He pinned me to the wall until our bodies were crushed together and his lips brushing my own. "I don't know how I'm ever gonna get through that duet without getting hard."

A breathless sigh escaped me as I thrust my hips against his. "Considering how hard you are from talking about it, I don't think you'll be able to stop yourself."

"Mmm." Luis skimmed his eyes over me before briefly drawing my lower lip into his mouth. "Think the audience will be offended?"

"By seeing the outline of your huge dick in your rainbow jock?" I grinned, slow and dirty, and rotated my hips. "I think they'd love it."

"But would you love it?" At my nod, he thrust his hips against me again. "What would you do about it?"

"Suck your dick backstage," I said, dropping my voice to a husky whisper. "And considering that cock is practically begging at the moment, I should probably do the same right now."

Luis' eyebrows shot up. "What—here?"

"Yes." I reversed our positions and slammed him up against the wall. "Here."

That rakish grin, the one that used to infuriate me, appeared on his handsome face. He folded his hands behind his head, fingers threaded together, and leaned against the wall. "We're on the top floor and Marquis isn't going anywhere. I'm not stopping you."

My heartbeat tripled. A staircase blowjob shouldn't have me questioning just how deep my feelings were for a guy, but here they were—doing just that. I'd never had this kind of easy relationship with anyone. It had never been this fun.

I pressed a kiss to Luis' lips, then his jaw, the hollow of his throat, and worked my way down. He stood admirably still, even when I descended to my knees and looked up at him through my wild hair. I knew he loved that look—the one that spelled out promises for what I would do once I had his dick out and in my hand. So far, it hadn't gotten old. Every time I made the first move, he was as shocked as ever.

"This is my favorite thing about you," I mumbled, kissing along his happy trail. "This line of dark hair leading like a fucking arrow straight to your cock."

"I think that's why God put it there."

This time, the look I shot him was withering, even as I tugged down the waistband of his sweatpants. "Do not bring religion into my cock sucking."

"Mmm." Luis thrust his hips forward to rub his bulge against my face. "I love it when you talk about sucking me off. And I love how much you enjoy doing it."

One day I'd be able to respond to Luis without constantly comparing him to the previous asshole, but that day hadn't yet arrived. So, I couldn't help but flash back on my ex's "teasing" about how much I'd liked sex and giving head. Teasing that had bordered on slut shaming. And there had never *ever* been a time when my enjoyment had mattered to him.

"Take it out," I said, kissing his abdomen and jutting hipbones. "Now."

He complied instantly, dropping one hand to pull down his sweats so they sat around his hips. He was wearing a jockstrap, something that got me unbelievable hot, but he tugged his dick out of it. I ran the tip of my tongue up the shaft, taking my time as his dick swelled thicker so the head pushed past the foreskin.

I glanced at him once more, grinning at his dazed expression, then planted one hand behind me for support while gripping the thick base with the other. Just as I started to take him down my throat, he shook his head.

"Hold up."

Pouting, I dropped my hands and expected him to back out. Instead, he edged around me, moving carefully with his pants around his hips, and gently nudged me so it was *my* back to the wall as I knelt before him. My heart accelerated, breathing coming out harshly, when Luis gave me another of those slow devilish smiles. I tried to think of something funny to say, or something bratty, but I was struck by his dark eyes.

"You're really beautiful," I blurted.

Luis blinked, startled, then laughed. "Hands up, Chuck."

I complied instantly, and crossed the backs of my wrists before pressing them against the wall. Still leering, he grabbed them both with one large hand and held me there, pinned and helpless against the wall. My dick was throbbing by then, my balls heavy.

"Open your mouth," he whispered.

I did it with zero hesitation. He slid his thick length past my lips, and I never broke eye contact. When he began flexing his hips and thrusting into my mouth, I relaxed my throat so he could plunder it at his pleasure. Him taking what he wanted from me while gazing down at me with this a sense of wonder in his face was incredibly hot. And when he used his free hand to brace heavily against the wall while barely swallowing deep groans, my dick pulsed.

"So good at taking that dick," he mumbled, pupils fully dilated. "I love watching those big lips stretch around me."

I hummed, and it came out wet sounding. He seemed to like it, because his eyes briefly rolled back before he fucked my mouth faster. I didn't stop watching him. I was obsessed with his expression when he came, and how he sometimes unraveled and cried out so loud he seemed startled by it. We were heading in that direction now. I could tell by the way he bit down on his plump lower lip and began to hump my face urgently. The sound of his dick sliding in and out of my mouth was obscene in the quiet staircase. It fucking echoed, and I loved it. I loved how brutal he was using me while still being mindful of not making me choke.

"Yeah, baby," he hissed. "Gonna come."

I moaned again, loving the way he rode my face, and the sharp groan when he exploded in my mouth. It was a big load, big enough for some to slide down his shaft and get on my chin.

"Clean that cock up," he whispered, still fucking my mouth. "Yeah, lick it all, baby."

Even if I wasn't in such a compliant mood, I'd have licked up every drop. I looked up at him while sucking him clean, finally ripping my arms free so I could grab his round ass cheeks and hold him in my mouth.

"Fuuuuck, Charles."

I released him from my mouth. He looked starstruck and infatuated, and it was a fabulous look on him. My chest swelled. Warmth filled me and sent me surging to my feet so I could grab the back of his head and yank him into a kiss. He slanted his mouth, letting me lick into it, and moaned against me. We crashed back against the wall, locked in an embrace that made me want to rip my clothes off and have him fuck me right there. Or in a few minutes when his dick got hard again.

"I can't get enough of you," he mumbled, kissing down the side of my face. "I just want to fuck you constantly."

"Mmm. Funny, I was just having that same thought." He dragged his teeth along the side of my neck, and I shivered. "Buuut we should probably go."

"I have a condom."

"Of course you do." I pulled away from him, laughing. "I'm gonna be late for brunch with Caleb!"

Luis smirked as he fixed his pants. "It's cool. You just ate."

"Nasty."

"Sucio," he corrected. "And you like me that way."

I couldn't help it. I kissed him again. He said he couldn't get enough of me, but I had zero desire to try getting enough of him. I was content to bask in his arm, and his kisses, for as long as I could get away with it.

CHAPTER NINETEEN

CHARLES

L uis had no reason to travel with me to where I was brunching with Caleb at High Street on Hudson, but he did anyway. And because I was aglow from the audition, fantastic thoughts of a future where dance was a staple in my life, and the reality of Luis being part of that life... I didn't roll my eyes or joke about him escorting me to the West Village. Not even when he left the subway and walked me to the restaurant, our fingers locked together.

"You could just come with me," I said. "I'd love for you to meet Caleb."

"Hmmm." Luis leaned against the side of the building, arms loose around me as he gazed into my eyes. He was so affectionate it was a little mind blowing, especially since I was used to being kept at a distance in public. "Maybe I want you to meet my mother."

My jaw dropped.

Luis laughed. "Your face right now... Holy shit. It's fine if you don't want to—"

"No, I didn't—" I shook my head. "That's not it. I just... I'm just surprised."

"Why? I told you my mother has been an ally way before I even told her I wasn't straight."

"Not that... Just." I waved vaguely to myself. "I'm kind of a loser, boo. In case you haven't noticed."

He rolled his eyes. "I noticed you say stupid shit sometimes, but that whole loser thing is make believe. She would love you."

"*Why*? I don't even have a job."

"Okay, but it's not like you're hitting me up for cash. You're living off your savings until you get your shit together." Luis flicked the tip of my nose. "And now you have actual plans to start giving dance lessons and working for the troupe. Speaking of, please don't forget to ask your boy for biz advice."

"I won't," I promised. "And you're positive you want to do that with me?"

"I want to do everything with you."

The words dried out my mouth and caused my stomach to flip. There was a part of me, the cautious part still lurking in the shadows after years of being with Landon, that thought this was moving too fast. Not just his declarations and affection and desire for me to meet his family, but my own feelings as well. When I looked at him like this, so content and happy to be in his arms, it was hard to deny this was escalating into something much deeper than us casually dating.

"What are you doing to me, Luis?" I asked in a whisper. "Tell me."

"You tell me," he countered, brushing his lips to my own.

"I don't fucking know."

I inhaled and exhaled slowly, then wrapped my arms loosely around his neck. There were scores of people on the sidewalk next to us, and neither of us paid them any mind. It was just me and Luis, the bright sunlight, the warm breeze, and the beauty of New York City in the spring around us.

"I think I like you too much," I said. "It's scaring me."

A brilliant smile broke out on his face. "Well, it's making me thrilled."

Because you're normal, I wanted to say. *You know how to experience life without a constant low grade thread of anxiety and fear about the next bad thing cropping up.* But, I didn't say that. Instead, I leaned in for a sweet kiss and kept the pessimism and worries to myself. For just a little while, I could pretend to be a normal guy who was capable of dating and PDA and falling in love.

"Charles?"

I broke the kiss to look over Luis' shoulder, and saw Caleb standing by the entrance to the restaurant. His head was cocked, and he was in typical Caleb day-wear with perfectly fit jeans, loafers, a cozy sweater, and a suede blazer with a color blocked pocket—the exact contrast to me and Luis in our dance and workout gear.

"Caleb!" I cringed at the sound of my own chipper voice. Luis burst out laughing, and I shoved him slightly before he let me go. "Hey," I said in a far more normal tone. "Sorry, I didn't notice you."

"So it would appear," Caleb said, smiling a little. He took a cautious step forward, as if he was intruding. "Are you Luis?"

"The one and only." Luis reached out a hand and squeezed Caleb's when he did so in return. "Nice to meet you, man. Charles talks you up nonstop."

Caleb's face brightened. "Oh, that's lovely to hear. I'm not very cool, so I wondered if I was a secret boring friend."

"Wow, that's such a Caleb thing to say." I rolled my eyes all over the place. "Caleb is super cool with his trendy jacket."

He smoothed his hands over it. "Oli made me buy it because I tried to get more corduroy."

"Hey, cords are legit," Luis said. "I used to wear them all the time before I started living in workout clothes."

"Now his big ass won't fit into anything," I confided.

Luis smacked my butt. "You should talk."

Caleb looked between us, a tiny smile on his face and curiosity blatant in his expression. "Luis, why don't you join us?"

I looked at Luis, suddenly hopeful, only to find him shaking his head. "I need to go home and sleep," he said, sounding regretful. "I work late tonight at the club, and I can't function without a long nap beforehand. Maybe next time?"

The mention of Male Revue niggled my brain, but I tried to sweep it away before Caleb noticed. My feelings about Luis stripping were mostly nonexistent until it cut into my time with him, and then I hated it. Someone else was getting to enjoy his beautiful body, and that didn't sit right with me. Because apparently, my territorial mess was already in full effect.

"Next time for sure," Caleb said to Luis. "Maybe for dinner. Or I can come to Staten Island."

"Oh man, you're willing to commute to the island?" Luis whistled softly. "You must be an amazing friend."

"He is," I said.

Caleb's face reddened, but he seemed happy. We said our goodbyes, him excusing himself to get our table while Luis kissed me once more before walking away. By the time we were seated in the most secluded spot they could offer—because Caleb had the power to request such things even at trendy brunch spots—my good mood had not dimmed. I was unselfconscious in my tank top and leggings with my miles of scarf wrapped around my neck, peering at the menu as my stomach growled. I didn't notice that Caleb hadn't glanced at his own until a waiter came by with water.

"I think I'm getting the meatpacker," I said with a leer. "Is it really extra if I get fried potatoes and sausage on the side? I just danced forever, and I'm fucking starving."

"We can get a toast board too," Caleb suggested. "I'm pretty hungry myself."

"Ohhh... Oli helped you work up an appetite?" Judging by the return of ruddiness to his fair skin, I was right. "You two are ridiculously attractive together. Your Instagram is adorable."

"I thought you hadn't gone back on social media?"

"Meh. I wasn't planning to, but Luis started uploading videos of us practicing, and I wanted to see." I withheld the part where me being on social media again had led to me being bombarded by a fresh wave of subs from former friends who had taken Landon's side in the breakup he'd performed for them so publicly. I'd had to unfollow multiple people who seemed to enjoy being snide. I knew Caleb would defend me, but part of me would always wonder if those snide comments were correct. I forced a smile and sipped my water. "He has *so* many followers. I mean, nothing like Ashton or Mere, but I was amazed because they're people who went from being fans of his boxing to fans of just him as a person. Brands have even been reaching out to him to start pimping their products on his page—workout gear and supplements and shit. He says no, but I think he should sell out like a motherfucker. Money is God unless you already have it."

The waiter returned to take our orders—Caleb of course ordering a spread because his mission was now to Feed Charles—and I chattered the entire time. I was aware that I was on a wicked adrenaline high, and that he was leaning against his closed palm and watching me with an amused smile, but I couldn't stop myself. After so many weeks of keeping everything close to my chest, I had so much to say.

I spelled out our amazing plan to save money—him at Male-Revue and me hopefully giving lessons to reach Staten Island kids in my apartment or their homes or last resort bartending again—to rent a gym space for a few months while we worked on building clients. We were both savvy enough to know we would need to stack our schedules with potential clients to even get this thing up and running, so not having to worry about rent for a few months would be perfect.

"This honestly sounds great, Charles. You've reached out to Clive, right?"

"Yes, but it seemed early for us to start talking about our contract before we even have a solid business plan and money saved. There's no point in getting hyped about this until we have the cash, which is why we haven't even begun brainstorming about a name."

Caleb pressed his lips together and toyed with his fork. He was likely refraining from offering to fund the whole project, and I was grateful for it. "I think it will be wonderful."

I beamed again. "Thank you. God, I was so worried you'd awkwardly tell me I'm a giant moron."

"Dearest, I jumped into business with Aiden and Oli before I really knew them. Sometimes you have to take chances. I just wish your chances didn't depend on you working yourself half to death to save so much money."

"It is what it is," I said. "And I'm just like you in that I don't like accepting money from people. No investors, no Go Fund Mes, no anything from people who might throw it in my face later. We're doing this on our own or not at all."

Caleb nodded slowly. "There was a lot of 'we' in your talk about the gym. Just how serious are you about Luis?"

The question startled me out of my full and sleepy lull, and I straightened. "What do you mean?"

"Don't be alarmed, Charles. I'm just curious. When you first came back, you were so lost and detached. You seemed defeated, honestly. And now?" Caleb reached out to poke my neck, where Luis had left me a super immature and somehow ridiculously sexy bitemark slash hickey the other day. "Dare I say that you seem smitten?"

Heat rushed to my face and a touch of defensiveness swarmed everywhere else. Smitten? I almost demanded. I'd just gotten out of a multi-year relationship with someone who'd treated me like an object to be ignored or used when convenient. I wasn't falling in love with anyone else so soon. I wasn't that stupid. And I wasn't that desperate to always be in a relationship.

I mashed my lips together, stared at him, but couldn't make myself speak. Every response sounded demeaning when contrasted with the way I lit up like a fucking street lamp whenever Luis rang my doorbell or appeared outside the house. Dismissing our connection—everything we had in common, our long late-night talks over late-night meals, the dancing, the way his touch set my body on fire—felt disrespectful.

The spitfire faded to a lighter with a low flame. I sagged against my seat with a sigh. "I have feelings for him," I muttered. "I can't even deny it. Is that totally pathetic?"

"Why would that be pathetic?" Caleb asked, sounding incredulous. "I think it's great. He seems equally infatuated with you if I judge by the way he looks at you and touches you."

This time when my face warmed, a smile accompanied the heat. "I know this is so fucking cliché, but I've never had anyone treat me the way he does. He's so patient and sweet and... God, he is fucking *hot*. The way he touches me is intense. Every single time, I feel like I'm going to come so hard every braincell will explode."

Caleb cast a furtive look around at the words, sighing.

I laughed. "It's not just the sex, though. It's everything. We have a lot in common. And his passion for dancing is basically equal to mine, which pretty much makes him a unicorn. Since leaving Julliard, I've rarely met people as emotionally invested in dancing, and it's like... this one last component that makes us *click*."

"It sounds perfect," Caleb admitted. "The fact that you haven't used the word *but* just yet is incredible, Mr. Pessimism."

"Ha, well, my pessimism is still present and accounted for. I've already accepted that if something goes wrong between us it will probably be my fault."

Caleb's smile wilted. He looked at me sideways. "Excuse me?"

"Caleb, you know how I am."

"Umm... charming? Funny? Intelligent? Talented..."

I made a face. "You saw how I was with Lan—"

Caleb held up a hand to stop me before I could go on. "That was a different issue entirely. He was cheating on you and gas lighting you for years. He drove you to... to extremes."

"I know, but maybe he wouldn't have been able to drive me to extremes if I wasn't already so close to the edge? I've been that way since I was a kid. I can look back and see all of these signs that my tendency to go dark or be explosively angry have been there since I was a teenager." I shrugged helplessly and toyed with the coffee mug. "I accept that. I also accept that Landon could identify how on edge I always was, which is why he knew... how to get to me. Also, he knew what to do to control me for so long."

"Because he's predatory?" The quiet fury in Caleb's voice caused me to look up at him again. "If I ever saw him again I don't know what I'd do."

"Oh, he'll be around eventually," I said darkly. "I just don't know when. He vaguely told me he'd be by to get the rest of his belongings sometime soon. When I tried to pin down a time, he refused. Just another way to keep me off balance and constantly worried about when he'll barge back into my life."

"Did it work?"

"No, and it's because I've been so at ease lately. This sounds like total bullshit, but... for the first time..." I hesitated, frowning at my own train of thought. My inner cynic wanted to smack me, but there was truth to where I was going with this statement. "I love my friends, and I've enjoyed... *parts* of my life for the past fifteen years or so, but this is the first time since I was in school that I've realized that happiness can be a thing. And the really fucked up thing is that I'd never noticed before now. Like, I thought it was normal to always be on edge or worried or upset or disappointed. This is the first time in a while I've been consistently... content."

Caleb, the sap that he was, looked close to crying. He grabbed my hand and squeezed it.

"So, I don't want to fuck it up," I finished.

Caleb's sighed. "You're not in danger of fucking anything up, Charles. For goodness sake, you're not someone who has difficulty keeping friends! It's not like everyone you've ever had a connection with has inevitably wound up backing away from you because of you 'fucking up.'"

"No, but maybe that's because I dial back my bullshit around everyone," I countered. "My temper? It's *bad*. I shut people out. I ignore them and blame them and stonewall. I evade my friends and bury my head in the sand. And I know for a fact I can't get away with that shit with Luis. He wouldn't put up with it."

"Are you implying that Landon *put up with you*?"

It should have been an easy no, but the comments I still saw on social media came back to me. They should have been nothing. A joke. And yet enough people subtly making the same jokes and cold comments, with my ex-boyfriend, about my erratic behavior was enough to make me marinate in doubt every time I glimpsed them.

What if they were right, and I had been a large part of the issue?

The restaurant seemed to quiet at the exact moment I stopped speaking. I cringed, because I was already on surround sound without public places falling into sudden hushes.

"Charles, Landon was a blatantly bad person. The way that relationship ended was his fault, not because of your anxiety or depression. It was him cheating on and abusing you."

"I know, but..." I curled my hands into fists. "That anxiousness? It's already starting to seep into me because I don't want to lose Luis or what we have."

"I get that, Charles. I do." Caleb seemed to sense I was getting worked up, because he held up a cautioning hand. "I'm just trying to tell you that those feelings, and the way you deal with them, aren't things someone is *putting up with*. It's not a reason for someone to walk away from you. The longer you're away from people who manipulate you and treat you badly, the more confidence you'll have in yourself."

When put that way, I knew he was probably right. A large chunk of my fears were connected to my relationship with Landon, and the disaster area of my confidence. Maybe they *would* fade over time. But, unfortunately, being logical about why those fears existed didn't force them to disappear.

CHAPTER TWENTY

LUIS

"You should come tonight." I zipped my gym bag and glanced over to where Charles was doing crunches on the floor of my studio. "You can give me a sign every time I fuck up and slip in some of our Man-dated Attraction choreography."

Charles paused mid-crunch to throw me a serious stank face. "You better not tease your slobbering fans with our shit!"

I slung my bag over my shoulder with a laugh. "My slobbering fans? Babe, it's been over a month since Ashton came through, and my supervisor has gone right back to treating me like some person who wandered in accidentally."

"After he stole your idea for dance lessons and gave it to those straight bitches," Charles muttered, still doing crunches. "Fuck that place."

"Agreed, but I need the cash." I tickled his side with the tip of my sneaker and smiled at his fierce warning glare. With his curly hair sweaty and skin flushed, he was utterly fuckable. Summer had come in like an inferno, and we'd both been sweltering while practicing together. It should have been uncomfortable, but seeing him red-faced and drenched was a turn on and a half. "Dame un besito, lindo. I'm late."

Charles heaved a big sigh and drew up to his knees. He pushed his lower lip out, gazing at me coyly from beneath his lashes. "Are you sure you don't want to just... tell them you're physically ill and stay home with me?"

"I'd love to stay home with you." I ran a hand through his damp hair before twisting it between my fingers. "I'd fuck you and feed you all night. But money is a thing, doll face. You should know. You've been busting ass giving lessons to the little mafia prince on Todt Hill for the past few weeks."

He snorted out a laugh. "Yeah, but that might slow down. His mom fired his old instructor, and he has some recital soon. Although, she's been bragging about me on her social media."

"Yeah, I think she wants you to be her gay bestie."

"I can be her best gay dance teacher for her and her rich friends." Charles rubbed his face against my t-shirt, looking like a cat begging to be pet. "I know the cash is good. I'm just needy."

"I like it when you're needy." I tilted his face up and my playfulness faded when I saw his moodiness was legit. "You could come, you know. I love it when you watch me perform."

Charles shrugged one shoulder. "I dunno about all that."

"C'mon. What else are you gonna do tonight?" I pressed my thumb against his lips. "You're still on a commuting strike so I know you won't be going into the city to see your friends."

"I'm going to practice, for your information," he huffed. "Have you forgotten my first show is next week?"

"How could I? Literally all you do is teach tiny mafia spawn to dance, workout, and practice."

"I also suck your cock quite a bit."

My dick twitched at the words. Because... yes. Yes, he did. I was halfway surprised he wasn't trying to get my shorts down so he could blow me right now, because that had become our routine. It was usually so standard before I left for work that I'd started wondering if it was his way of branding me before I went to get naked for other people.

I kinda liked the idea.

"Kiss me," I repeated, voice gone hoarse. "Before I fuck your brains out and end up late."

Charles sighed heavily and rolled his eyes, but leaned up to brush his lips to mine. One touch, and I dug my fingers into his hair even tighter so I could slide my tongue into his mouth. He went from lazy to attentive in an instance, and kissed me like there was a war on the other side of my apartment door. Like he'd never see me again, and he had to pour his everything into this last embrace.

"You're fucking addicting," I whispered. "And a menace. Now I'm gonna be at work all fucking turned on for the next few hours."

Something flickered in Charles' expression. "I guess you'll have to hold out."

I looked at him sidelong, then flicked his nose. "No shit. What else would I do?"

"I'm sure some thirsty fuck would love to have you grind all over—"

I shut him up with another kiss, and bit his lower lip as I pulled away. "You behave yourself, and I'll eat your ass later."

"You'll do that anyway."

He had my number, so I just flashed a smile and stepped away. "See you later, sexy."

Charles flopped back on the floor and crinkled his fingers in a wave. He watched me as I shut the door, and I felt a little twinge at closing it on him. And what a weird ass thing to feel bad about. We weren't that codependent already, were we? My reluctance bordered on '*no, you hang up first!*' lovesick nonsense.

I pondered on whether this was a terrible thing as I jogged towards the bus stop, and decided that it wasn't. Considering I'd never been this into someone, I was going to enjoy every second and symptom ranging from my ridiculous joy of sharing meals with him to cuddling him when we fell asleep together after sex.

My entire commute to Male Revue was spent with me thinking of Charles instead of my routines. After being iced out by my supervisors when it came to my own idea, I'd pretty much ran out of fucks when it came to putting real effort in. My new plan was to save my energy for Man-dated Attraction, and give my supervisor what he wanted at MR. Instead of rocking the stage with actual dancing and real showmanship, I'd twerk my way to dollar bills like the rest of the bros and stop trying to reinvent the wheel by turning Male Revue into a burlesque show.

The upside was that I was spending less time practicing for this instead of the burlesque performances that required me to always be on my A-game. I'd even redone my stripping schtick so my boxer routine was exclusive to Man-dated, whereas I now wore whatever costumes looked good on me when stripping. Well, except for hot cop thing. I wasn't ever gonna go down that fucking road.

My routines were less exciting to me personally now when I stripped, but there was no way to deny that the customers liked it. My whole bit was more sensual and tempting, and the bills thrown on the stage and tucked into my jockstrap had grown larger. Also, I was guessing the pole dancing and fake humping made me more inviting because I suddenly had way more requests for lap dances and private performances in side rooms.

It really was not my thing, but my money had tripled and my savings for the gym were growing. I was starting to think we would have enough saved to rent a place by the fall instead of the end of the year like we'd initially projected. The very idea of it caused a flood of excitement to go through me. What had seemed impossible by myself was not an actual reality with a partner.

It still bugged me to have watered down my act, though. It reminded me of what Charles had described about his experience on the cruise, despite my life now being easier. Riley, my Male Revue manager, and the other dancers had quit passive aggressively commenting on my performances, and I was less exhausted after work.

The commute passed quickly, and then I was at the club and changing into some random firefighter getup Duffy had procured for me.

"You look like you're in a good mood," Riley said, appearing in the grungy locker room. "I like the suspenders."

"Thanks bud." I snapped one at him, grinning. "The crowd seems into seeing me in uniform."

"That they do." Riley looked me over slowly, glanced around, then stepped closer. "Listen kid, I like what you've been doing lately. Talk to me later about those dance lessons you mentioned before. I did a test launch with Mitch and Abel, and I've had people request you."

Dollar signs exploded before my eyes. I nodded vigorously, trying not to smirk too obviously at him finally acknowledging it had been *my* fucking idea. "Hell yes. I could really use the extra cash. I was going to ask you about picking up another day."

"This might make you more money than dancing," Riley admitted. "You were right—it was a good idea. And people are into your salsaton thing."

I totally ignored his horrific pronunciation and flashed a thumbs up. "Just let me know when."

We parted ways with me feeling fucking buoyant. For the first time in a long time, I told myself that things were fast tracking in the right direction. I was always confident, but now I was feeling it for reasons other than my own belief that things would be okay if I busted my ass with the right kind of energy.

With my mood bolstered, and hope putting a smile on my face, I was in rare form once it was my turn on the stage. Instead of worrying about steps and moves and timing, I put on one of the filthiest shows I'd performed since I'd started working at the club. And the audience ate. it. Up.

If all it took to get hundreds thrown at me was me humping the stage and grinding my dick against the pole after twerking in people's faces with my jockstrap nearly pulled off, I could do it. It helped that I now tended to blank out the crowd and think of Charles while I was dancing. I thought of what I'd do if I was dancing for him, and I did it, even if it meant pushing the boundaries by fondling myself every now and again. Fantasizing about him while caressing my bulge was enough to get me hard in an instant, and the audience liked seeing my erect dick print.

At the end of my second set, one of the suits was panting like a dog at the edge of the stage. He was younger than most of the usual suit crowd, and kind of reminded me of Charles' friend. He'd also been the one throwing hundreds at me, so I wasn't surprised when one of the shot boys tracked me down to inform me that the guy had requested a lap dance. Cha-ching.

I agreed to do it after my break and peered out into the club to find where the guy was sitting. Instead of setting eyes on him, my gaze magnetized to someone leaning against the bar. Charles. He seemed to glance in my direction then pushed away from the bar to head to the bathroom.

Surprise mixed with excitement. Aside from that one time with his friends, he'd never come to a show no matter how many times I'd invited him. It was probably a bad idea to follow him into the toilets, especially since I had a customer waiting on me for a lap dance, but I had zero ability to resist greeting my man. We'd been in each other's lives for over two months now, and seeing him jumpstarted my heart with just as much electricity as it had the first time I'd pressed up against him.

I took a detour around the club, trying to stay discreet, and followed him. Two dancers had hit the stage together—Bruno and Isaak, the queer twins—so the audience was suitably distracted and the bathroom was empty except for me and Charles. I leaned against the door, grinning at the sight of him leaning into the mirror to examine his face. He probably wasn't trying to look like porn, but the sight of his ass in his usual tight pants gave me instant wood.

"Hey beautiful," I said, coming up behind him. "Fancy meeting you here."

Charles' dark eyes flicked up to my reflection. He didn't smile, but there was fire in that gaze of his, and not the sexy kind.

My hands froze on his hips, my smile fading. "What's wrong?"

He stood up straight and turned so he was leaning against the sink. I could see him trying to force his face into a grin, to put some lightness into the thunderclouds gathering on his brow, but there was no point. By now, I knew him. I possibly even knew him better than friends he'd had long before we'd met. And I could sense that the tension crackling between us had nothing to do with our usual clothing-optional attraction. This was anger. This was jealousy. This was a potential disaster.

"Nothing," he lied, finally managing a taut smile. "You were—"

"Don't lie. What's wrong?"

A muscle in his cheek ticked. "Why bother to push me into something I obviously don't want to talk about?"

I pressed my body to his, bracing my hands on the sink behind him. "Why bother to lie when I can see the pending explosion behind those pretty eyes of yours?"

Charles glanced at the door then back to me. His nostrils flared on an exhale that was slow enough to spell out just how much he was trying to control himself. "I shouldn't have come here. I knew it was a bad idea, and I still did it because I'm a fucking idiot."

"Or because you want to support your man." I scanned his face as the music pounded on the other side of the door. "Why're you mad? You knew what I do here."

Charles clenched his jaw again. "Right. I did. But I was picturing the type of dancing you did when I first came with Ashton and them, not you basically fucking the stage and jerking off for them."

Defensiveness cracked through me in a lightning bolt. My head jerked back. "Wow. Okay."

"Am I wrong? Is that not what you were doing?"

"No, you're not wrong."

Charles took another deep breath. "So, what's next? Private dances in the back? Lap dances?"

Each word came out in a low deep growl that punched into my chest with every syllable. I couldn't think of a response at first, not while staring into his pissed off face. And when he clamped his hands on my shoulders, fingers digging in possessively, the ability to speak further fled. His territorial rage was having an odd effect on me. As in, I wanted to be defensive even while my dick hardened.

"Charles—"

"Just answer."

I licked my lips nervously. Fuck, he was *mad*. And now I was doubting myself. *Should* I have told him I'd changed my act? That I was now writhing against strangers while they basically creamed themselves in response? Why had I invited him here without warning him of what he'd see? More importantly, how would I have reacted if I'd busted in on him doing the same with no warning?

"Baby, I'm just trying to make money to get the fuck out of here," I said softly. "You know that."

The tension in Charles' lean frame released so rapidly that he slumped against me. He was a marionette with its strings cut, his face falling and eyes dropping to the floor. Embarrassment and shame practically oozed out of him, and I hated it. I hated it so much that I lifted his chin and kissed him despite knowing this was the wrong place and the wrong time. Or was it? Was there ever a bad time for me to remind him that I would do anything for him? That he was my number one? That I was falling in love with him?

After a beat of resistance, Charles opened his lips for me. We kissed sweetly, like we were introducing ourselves to each other for the first time, while holding each other in a loose hug. Then he flicked his tongue against my lower lip, and my dick woke up yet again. A sweet kiss caught fire, and then we were all over each other.

I forgot that we were in the dim bathroom of Male Revue, that the booming bass from the music beyond the door meant I was at work, and that losing myself in Charles' touch wasn't the best plan. I moaned into his mouth when he scraped his short blunt nails down my bared back, and thrust against his crotch when I felt his dick getting harder.

We'd just been together earlier, just fucked this morning, but the red tide of jealousy and rage had washed those recent memories away. My body reacted to his like this thing between us was new, and I had to show him just how much I needed and wanted him all over again. I tongued him until I was panting harshly, and didn't stop him when he reached down to fumble with my borrowed firefighter pants. They were already too large on my narrow hips, so they sagged below my ass once they were undone.

A breathless groan caught in my throat once he shoved my jock to the side to free my erection and swollen balls. He grabbed my shaft with a grip so tight that my eyes rolled and my toes curled in my boots. I wanted to touch him too, to jerk him while he choked my cock in his strong hand, but I lost my mind as he pumped while sucking on my tongue.

He jacked me so fast and viciously that it was clear he was trying to get me off quick. I was so focused on the electricity racing through my veins, and the climax building in my gut, that I forgot why. It wasn't until I came with a loud *oh fuck, yeah* as the door swung open did I remember why this was a really bad idea.

CHAPTER TWENTY-ONE
CHARLES

I *got him fired.*

The thought had been on repeat in my head since Luis had been dragged to the office by his manager and dismissed from the club's premises not even fifteen minutes later. It'd gotten louder as he'd quietly told me that he'd broken the rules by having sex in the club, and that having sex with a "customer" had been the nails in his coffin.

When he'd stared at the sidewalk, hands in his pockets and jaw clenched, and let me call an Uber instead of commuting, my brain had started screaming.

Your fault, jealous bitch.

Your insecurity is why he even felt like he had to touch you.

You knew you shouldn't have gone.

You knew he'd stepped up his game to make faster money.

You know Luis would never sleep with someone else, and you acted like a fucking idiot anyway.

You got him fired.

You're a piece of shit.

You should end this now.

That I was going rancid from guilt and stricken silent from self-loathing instead of apologizing to Luis on the ride home was yet another ticked box on the "you're fucking worthless" checklist.

One glance at his tense body, his eyes slit and focused out the window while he rubbed his stubbled jaw, seemed enough to confirm all my doubts. I'd fucked up beyond all repair. I'd ruined everything. My jealous had gotten him fired, cost him a job that had allowed him to bring in nearly two thousand a week by dancing four days a week. I had no idea how any of this worked, by my brain was cranking out all the ways this was a disaster.

Could he get a job dancing somewhere else?

Would his manager even give him a reference?

How would he make money now? What were his other answers?

Was his dream of having his own gym indefinitely on hold?

By the time the Uber pulled up in front of the house, I was ready to puke. I needed to get the fuck away from everyone, hole up in my apartment, and never look anyone in the face again. I practically jumped out of the car, ran up the stairs, and fumbled with my keys to unlock the door. My hands were shaking again, just as badly as they had the night Landon had left that note, but this time Luis didn't come up behind me.

He didn't speak or touch me. He didn't do anything, even when I barreled into the vestibule and immediately went to my own apartment. We'd stopped locking the bottom doors since we'd basically been going between our apartments interchangeably for the past month, so there was nothing to stop me from sprinting up the stairs.

Luis did not follow.

My breath ripped out of me in harsh pants as self-loathing tumbled downhill and slowly became rage. Pure blinding rage aimed at myself.

I ripped off my scarf and discarded it violently, and kicked off my boots so they slammed into the bookcase. Books and knick-knacks clattered in the rickety piece of furniture, and I had to bite my bottom lip to keep myself from tearing it apart. The negative energy was building inside of me until my brain presented only one way to release it: complete and utter destruction.

Holding myself still, I squeezed my eyes shut and clenched my hands tighter.

I could calm down.

I could escape this nightmare merry-go-round thought process that everything I touched turned to shit.

I could let go of this anger, this hatred, without taking it out on my apartment.

I could—

He probably hates you.

"Fuck," I shouted. "*Fuck*."

Hands landed on my shoulders, and I nearly jumped out of my skin. I hadn't heard Luis come in behind me, or the door creak open, over the freight train of negativity powering across my brain. Fuck a freight train, it was a tornado. Shrieking wind and destruction capable of making me spin out of control until there was nothing left in my wake but dust.

I opened my mouth to croak at him to just go. To go downstairs and not bother explaining to me how badly I'd ruined his plans. Our plans. Everything. That I already understood what would happen from here on out, and he didn't need to explain why he didn't want to deal with me anymore.

But the words wouldn't come.

Luis wrapped his arms around me and yanked me to his chest. He was hugging me, but the drawstrings holding me so tight wouldn't release. I stood there tense and stiff, staring blindly at the dancing boy figuring in the bookcase, as he squeezed me tight.

"Charles..." His voice was low, gravely. "I need you right now, baby. C'mon."

My heart cracked in two.

I did not deserve him.

But because I was incapable of denying him, I turned to pull him into my arms. It was my turn to hug him as he released shuddering sighs and buried his face against my neck. To rub his back and try to think of comforting words. It failed. I couldn't think of anything other than a plea for him to extradite himself from a relationship that, in my mind, would go downhill from here. My ability to function normally was apparently capped at a month or two, and now it was fucked.

He sighed slowly and leaned away so he could see my face. I tried to look away, but he captured my chin with one of his large hands and held me still. It was dark, but his scrutiny burned away all my armor. He could see through me, I was willing to bet. Past my looks and talent to identify the small scared person burrowed way down deep.

"We need to talk," Luis said after a long silence. "For real."

A chill swept through me. I managed a nod while shivering. "Okay."

Luis propelled me away from the door and to my bedroom, not releasing me until the door was shut and we were sitting on the bed. He sat on the edge, twisted so we were facing, but I bowed my head to stare down at the chipped black nail polish on my fingers.

"Listen, I need you to look at me."

I flinched, shoulders rising, and didn't do any such thing.

"Charles." He spoke my name like a command. An order to get my fucking shit together. "Dude, this isn't you going through something. I'm the one who got fired. Not you."

I bit my tongue so hard I tasted iron.

"This is the thing that's getting me," he said, voice steady and hard in the dark room. "I feel like shit right now, papa. And I know you do too, but this isn't about just you and your feelings right now, so I'm gonna lay it down so you hear me."

My breath picked up. I nodded. Kept staring at my fingers.

"I've had this endgame way before I met you, dude. I used to want to fight, yeah, but the idea of having my own place has been a tickle in the back of my mind ever since I saw how shitty Tony ran Cadet's. It was always this *maybe* that seemed impossible. But guess what?" A rich sardonic laugh left Luis' mouth. "I'm a fucking millennial, and I told myself I'd make that shit happen. So I got the certifications, and I figured out a way to make money. I sold out at Male Revue to make even more money, to speed this all up. And then I fell in love with you, couldn't keep my hands off you, and threw that part of the plan away."

It was true. And even though it was true, defensiveness ran up my spine like a spear someone had shoved up my ass. "Sorry I ruined it for you," I said flatly. "I already—"

"No one is saying you did a fucking thing," Luis snapped. "Look at me."

I refused long enough for his arm to dart out and grab my chin, forcing me to meet his gaze. My heart fell to my shoes. His eyes were red-rimmed in the darkness, his wide mouth pressed into a slash.

"I'm sorry," I said hoarsely. "I'm *sorry*."

"For what?" Luis dropped his hand abruptly. "This. Is. Not. About. *You*. Yeah, I saw you looking uptight and angry about me shoving my dick in some dude's face, but you know what? I would have had the same reaction if I hadn't expected it. I was the one who like, *needed* to reassure you by getting all up on you because, in case you misheard, I'm all in love with you."

I flicked a glance up at him.

"I know it's really fast for me to be saying that," he said quickly. "But, fuck man, that's how it feels. And everyone always says love makes people do mad stupid shit, so me deciding kissing all over you and messing around in the bathroom at work was worth the risk of getting fired is sure as hell a stupid thing." A wry smile crossed his handsome face. He raised an eyebrow. "Do you not agree?"

I didn't know what I agreed or disagreed with. I was hung up on him saying he loved me. On bloodshot eyes. That smile.

"How can you—" I cleared my throat and shook my head. "Why are you smiling? How is any of this funny?"

"Because it's ridiculous," he exclaimed. "Is this entire thing not totally absurd to you? We're having a fight, or whatever this is, because I invited you to the strip club I work at then tried to de-jealous you by making out in the bathroom knowing damn well I'd get in trouble if the wrong person walked in. The guy who'd tried to get a lap dance from me walking in and throwing his own jealous fit just makes it even more weird and stupid."

He was right. This was absurd. It was as unlikely and ridiculous as me walking in on him with my boyfriend, wanting to *murder him*, then falling for him a month or so later. Our entire relationship was one burlesque act after another.

"You're not angry at me?" I asked quietly. "For luring you into the bathroom because I was jealous?"

"Oh, I'm pissed at you, but not for that."

I balled my hands up again. "Then why?"

"Because, you were so busy worrying about how this situation would affect you that you totally forgot I was the one who just got fired—"

"That's not true."

"—and stormed up here without saying two fucking words to me. You didn't even try to console me. I had to walk up here and console *you*." Luis leaned forward, invading my space so that I could smell his cologne. That irresistible scent that turned me into a walking, talking Axe commercial where the smell of a man made me want to get naked.

"We talked about this before, and you did it *again*."

"I know!" I squeezed my eyes shut and took a deep shaky breath. "I don't know what to do sometimes, Luis. I just don't know how to handle things, so I *run away*. And you told me you understood. You told me—"

"I do understand, but there's a difference between you asking me for a moment and you closing the door in my face when I need you! The way you shut me out when you're feeling some type of way is really fucking cold, Charles. And if anything makes me want to walk away from you, it's the fact that you knew I was feeling like shit and still chose to ghost on me with zero words."

I watched him and waited for more. More justifiable descriptions about my failings as a boyfriend. About my selfishness. I waited for his anger and disappointment. I waited for the moment where I'd either fly into a defensive rage or feel like crawling in a hole with my head in the sand to deal with the fact that I'd fucked up yet again.

Luis searched my face, anxiousness making itself evidence in his own, and frowned. It was that slight downward curve of his generous mouth that snapped me out of my slide down a shitty spiral.

He wasn't Landon.

He wasn't going to spend the next two hours reaming me.

He was just as freaked out as I was.

"I'm sorry," I said again, louder this time. "I don't know how else to explain except to say that I'm so used to a fight or a misunderstanding or a mistake turning into a disaster that my first response is to run and hide." The roiling in my stomach calmed as he nodded and watched me, his hands reaching out to grip mine. "And I *know* you're not Landon. I fucking know that. But my relationship with Landon was the only real relationship I've ever had, and ninety percent of that was him making me feel like shit. I got into the habit of wanting to escape at the first sign that I've fucked up or let someone down."

"You didn't do anything wrong at the club," Luis insisted. "It was my choice to start that. I wanted you. I *always* want you."

"And I always want you," I said with a harsh laugh. "That's why I was like *livid* at the thought of anyone else touching you. God, I was so angry. And I knew it was ridiculous but I couldn't stop being angry. It was almost like... like I couldn't talk myself out of thinking about all the ways you could hook up with someone else even though my actual brain kept trying to remind me that you would never do that."

"So, you trust me?" Luis brought my hand up to his mouth, kissing the knuckles. "Or you trust me but don't trust yourself about whether having faith in some dude you just met a couple months is a good idea?"

I winched, but nodded at the latter. "Is that shitty?"

"It hurts a little, but after everything, I get it. I'm not trying to tell myself that us being together is going to magically put Band-Aids on everything that's happened to you in the past several years." Luis raised our locked hands to press them against my chest. "Those battle scars are gonna be there for a long time."

"They are. And I'm not always going to react the way someone else would. Or the way you would. I'm going to do things that seem irrational or rash or plain-ass fucking stupid." I scanned his expression again, pessimistically searching for a sign that he wasn't as understanding as this whole conversation felt, but found nothing. "I'm sorry that me being this way hurts you, but you have to know that's the last thing I want. I..." *I love you too.* "I... I'm still trying to adjust to being with someone who isn't a total nightmare."

"I get it, Charles. I really do."

If Luis was disappointed in my lack of a declaration, he didn't show it. Maybe he hadn't expected one. Maybe he hadn't even wanted one. Maybe he didn't need one. There was a chance he had no qualms about throwing his feelings in the air while expecting nothing in return. I wasn't like that. Even now, with his words branding my heart, I was on guard.

"Charles, I just need you to try something for me, okay?" Luis scanned my face and seemed to choose his words carefully. "When you feel like you need to run and hide, will you give me a heads up? A simple warning. I don't know what you're thinking or feeling, baby. For all I know, you're pissed at me, or scared about something, and I have no way to figure it out."

"What if I make that promise and then I'm so far gone that I can't?"

"I'm just asking you to try," Luis said. "And I'll try on my end too. To give you space when you ask for it, and to stop running from my own problems in the Bronx."

I put a hand over my eyes. "That's what I want or expect. You don't have to go back there."

"I do, though. That's my home. My people are there." Luis flopped back onto the bed, sighing. "And this whole conversation just reminds me of the fact that I need to handle my shit too."

Maybe, but I wasn't going to push him. As far as I was concerned, he could avoid that neighborhood forever. "Did this ruin everything in terms of saving for the studio?" I asked after a beat of silence.

"Heh. Maybe? I don't know." Luis sighed, low and shuddery. "It took me a long time to get that much stage time at Male Revue. Months and months of racking in enough tips for the club to earn a decent percentage for it to be worthwhile. If I start over somewhere else, it will take a while before I'm earning enough to save. And if I get a normal job?" Luis said *normal* with the same disdain as I'd always used when thinking of nine-to-five positions. "Who knows. It's most definitely a monster of a setback. Maybe until next year."

"Fuck."

"Exactly," he said. "This is a mess, but at least we have burlesque, and the show next week. Things will suck for a while, and it's a setback, but the bright side is that I at least *have savings* to pay my rent and bills for a minute. If this would have happened to my parents back in the day, we'd have been fucked. They had no savings."

I let myself fall onto my back, causing the mattress to bounce beneath me, and covered my face with my hands. The unsteadiness of my anger had faded, but uncertainty remained. In some ways, not knowing was worse than being certain that things were over. At least with certainty, I could plan. Even if that plan was usually to retreat entirely.

"How can I fix this?" I asked from behind my hands, because I was incapable of his glass half full approach. "Help you find another job? Pretend to be your manager if someone calls for a reference? We were *so fucking close*, Luis."

Luis snorted softly. "You let me worry about that. It's not your job to fix it."

"Even if it's not my fault, I can still help you. That's what—" My brain stuttered. I dropped my hands, and quit holding back. "We're lovers but also business partners, right? We help each other."

Luis grew quiet beside me. When I glanced over at him, he was gracing me with a slight smile.

"What?" I asked, frowning. "I'm not just being a sap. It's true."

"I know it's true, but I like hearing you say it. And..." Luis shifted so he was stretched over my body, his knee between my thighs and his muscular torso pressing me to the bed. "I'll expect you to act like my lover and my partner going forward instead of shutting me out when shit gets heavy. ¿Oíste?"

"I hear you," I mumbled. "But I need you to hear *me*, and give me time to figure out how to relationship."

"I can do that." Luis kissed me softly. "We can do this, man. We can't fucking give up."

His we sounded like 'you' in my head, but there was no sound of an accusation in his voice. Only a plea. To work with him, be with him, make this fucked up patchwork of a relationship work despite all of the messiness and drama. It didn't seem possible. Not reasonably, anyway.

But when the fuck had I ever been reasonable?

I could do this.

We could do this.

Landon hadn't ruined me. I wouldn't let him.

I arched up to catch Luis' mouth in another kiss. This time, neither of us pulled away. His tongue lashed mine, demanding and forceful, as if to seal the deal on our words. A groan poured out of me from deep inside my chest because his touch was a salve on my battered body. The raw wounds I'd inflicted with my own doom and gloom scenarios healed and vanished with every handprint he left on my body.

"I'm going to fuck you." Luis ripped my pants open while sucking on my lower lip. "Like I wanted to fuck you in that bathroom. Take these tight fucking things off."

He rolled off the bed to shed his clothes in quick efficient movements, never taking his eyes off me the entire time. It didn't seem like he was watching the way I had to shimmy and buck to get out of my pants. It seemed like he was afraid to look away, as if I'd disappear before his very eyes. Or run out the room the moment he shifted his gaze.

I hated his uncertainty.

I hated that I'd planted it there when we'd been unwavering for the last few weeks.

"Fuck, you're so gorgeous." Still staring me down, Luis stepped around the bed to yank a string of condoms from my drawer. There was a mix of older condoms, from my time with Landon, and the Magnums I'd bought for Luis. He found one, and the sticky bottle of lube, never looking away. "Do you know what I wanted to do to you when I walked in that bathroom and saw you bending over that sink?"

I watched him slide the condom over his cock, mouth watering, and shook my head.

"I thought about that delicious ass of yours. Always wrapped up like a present for me to unwrap. To bite and eat and fuck."

My heavy breathing filled the warm room. I hadn't turned on the air conditioner, and the breeze drifting into the window with the beats of a distant salsa song was hot.

"I think it would have been worth it to split you open right then and there," Luis said as he knelt on the bed between my thighs. "Imagine his face if you'd come from being pounded hard, right after he walked in?"

"Fuck, that's so wrong and yet it's making my dick so hard it could cut glass." I reached down to stroke myself, unable to look away from his smoldering stare. "How are you so magical?"

Luis jerked my knees up then shoved them open. He drizzled lube in his hand then swept it over his dick, hissing at the contact. "Am I, baby?"

"Yeah." I was transfixed by his hand sliding over his length, and began pumping my own faster in response. "You make me forget I'm a walking disaster."

"If that's true..." Luis angled my hips up. The blunt head of his dick bobbed against my ass. "You're the most irresistible, talented, goddamn beautiful disaster I've ever seen."

I squirmed on the bed, overheated and wanting and ready to feel nothing but every inch of him searing into me. "Sweet talker," I whispered. "You're so good at this. Like disgustingly good."

Luis flashed that rakish grin of his and pushed into me with one clean deep thrust. "I know."

My head fell back, mouth falling open in a soundless gasp. The initial push of his dick sliding into me would never not hurt, but the pain promised pleasure that obliterated everything else. It took over me, *he* took over me, and left no room for doubts or worries once his big body was pinning me to the bed.

He held my wrists again, crisscross over my head, and moved against me in a slow unceasing grind. With my legs held open by his broad body and my hands useless, I was there for his taking, and I fucking loved it that way. Every blunt thrust, every low growl, and the drip of his sweat onto my chest and stomach as he moved his hips in a way that allowed him to slide inside of me deeper.

I was overwhelmed by him in all the best ways. The ways that drew agonized moans from my mouth and likely spilled them out onto the streets, and the ways that filled my head with a thousand incoherent pleases for him to never stop. Even when I went off like a geyser from one touch to my erection, I didn't want him to stop. I prayed that he would hold my thighs open forever, stay so impossibly deep in me forever, because fucking had never been like this for me and I never wanted it to stop.

I wriggled my hand out of his grasp only to clutch the back of his neck as he hunched over me. Our gazes locked, foreheads pressed together, the next time he thrust into me. I squeezed him as tight as I could, loving the way his eyes unfocused and the way he bit his lower lip.

He was gorgeous. He was magic. And he was mine.

When he came, Luis was lodged deep inside me and my heels were digging into the small of his back. I held him to me, not letting him pull out or move away, and kept my thighs locked around him in a Street Fighter grip until he collapsed on top of me.

After a second, he chuckled in my ear all deep and throaty. "Is this stage five or stage six clinger status?"

"Stage ten," I breathed. "I'm physically incapable of letting go of you right now."

"Good." Luis grinned against my face. "Don't. And keep that shit in mind next time something goes down. Because you know it will."

I laughed quietly, my chest moving against his. He was right. There would be a next time. There was always a next time. And maybe when it inevitably came—that next scary moment when the world seemed to fall down around me with bits of hope sifting between my fingers—I'd remember how good this felt. I'd remember that I didn't always have to be scared.

CHAPTER TWENTY-TWO
CHARLES

I threw up twice on the day of my first show with Man-dated Attraction. Not only because I was a nervous wreck, but because I'd had a couple of drinks on an empty stomach and puked like a kid who'd just downed their first red cup.

To me, it was an omen.

To Luis, it was hilarious.

I supposed it was good at least one of us had maintained our sense of humor in the days since he'd lost his job.

"It's going to be fine." He watched me sit down heavily on the studio floor in his apartment. "You've been practicing nonstop with both me *and* Gabe while Marquis breathed down our necks. You know this routine like the underside of my dick."

Half-laughing, half-snorting, I flopped onto the floor in a spread eagle. "It's different in front of an audience. Do you know when was the last time I performed in front of actual people?"

"Gee, I dunno, like three months ago?" Luis kicked my bare foot with the tip of his Nike. "You performed for a ton of people for six months on a wack boat. Stop acting like you're old and rusty."

"That was different!"

"How?" he countered. "Because they were just there because it was a free event, instead of paying to see your *art*?"

A smile nearly stole from my lips before I remembered I was supposed to be serious about my artist convictions. "Maybe."

"Maybe you're a snob. Which, I can be too, but you still entertained someone on that ship, you know. It's not like your ass was doing the shuffle for an audience of three."

"Sometimes I was," I said sullenly.

Luis arched an eyebrow. "Stop. You're gonna be awesome. My mom is psyched to see us dance together." The look of horror I aimed his way brought about a sheepish expression, and he smiled. "Oh, forgot to mention that, eh?"

"Luis!" I sat up straight. "What the *fuck*? How are you going to A—not tell me, then B—tell me right before the show."

"Technically, this isn't right before the show." He looked at his watchless wrist. "The show is in like eight hours."

I put all the power of Stephanie, Jace, and Mere combined into my glare. "Dude. You have to prepare me for meeting the parents stuff! I am not a parent person. Parents have not liked me since I was in junior high when they knew me as the giant queer kid who cursed too much and had no manners."

"So, not much has changed?"

I started to kick his ankle, thought better of it, and stomped my foot.

"Yeah, that's right," he jeered. "Be easy on the merch before the big show."

"I'll be easy on something, all right. Like..." I ground my teeth together. "Like... *fuck*, I don't know. Insert something witty. Does this mean I have to meet your parents?"

"Uh-huh. And my cousins. You think my fam was gonna miss my biggest performance yet?" Luis snorted. "I honestly thought it was common sense."

"My parents literally threatened to send me to live with distant family members in Serbia if I didn't stop being gay," I said scathingly. "How the fuck would it ever occur to me that other people's family would jump at the chance to see their son dance in a rainbow jock strap?"

"I dunno. 'Cause my parents are as awesome as me?"

"I am going to kill you."

Luis gave a long suffering sigh and plopped down beside me, appearing physically unable to bite back his cute little grin. "Okay, I'm sorry. I am. But... is it so bad that I'm hella psyched for you to meet my folks? My mom has been stalking your Instagram for two weeks, and she's all the way into this relationship as long as you pass her tests."

A cold sweat was on the verge of breaking out on my forehead, and now he was talking about tests. "Luis."

"I'm playing!" He knelt in front of me and braced my face with his hands. "Seriously. It's fine. She just wants to support us, and they both want to meet you. Man, we've been talking about renting a space together for our businesses. Even if we weren't fucking like eight times a day, they'd want to meet you based on that alone."

This oddly calmed my nerves. I wasn't just the boyfriend who'd gotten him fired with bathroom sex. I was a potential business partner. The person he'd be signing a lease with. I was more comfortable trying to convince her to trust me with paying half the rent and filling a space with clients than trying to convince *anyone* that Luis could trust me with his heart. I mean, I thought he could, and he thought I could, but did other people? Did I care what other people thought?

I wanted to say no, but I did care. I cared what his parents thought, and also what the other dancers at Man-Dated Attraction thought.

"I just want people to not think I suck," I said finally. "Since high school, I've been *that* gay dude. The loud dramatic one. The one who alwaaaays had a problem. And I've been stuck in that role for-ev-er."

"My parents won't think that. I'm the one dramatically flinging off my boxing trunks to shake my ass in a rainbow jock. How's that for drama?"

I couldn't help a smile. With him, I never could. "Do they know why you got fired from Male Revue?"

"Uh. No." Luis did a full body cringe. "I just said I had it out with my manager and dipped. They don't need to know that I was trying to get busy at work. My mom will tear my ass up."

A laugh popped out of me, and my shoulders loosened. "Okay. I'll calm down. Maybe before the show, I'll do one of those meditation tapes Ashton gave me."

"Do it." Luis kissed my forehead. "I'd stay and chill out with you, but I promised my parents I'd meet them before the show. They want to say good luck and everything."

"Where are you meeting them? By Highline? It's so early."

"Nope." Luis hesitated briefly then grinned. "I'm going to the Bronx."

My eyes opened wide. "Luis, what the hell? You're going to do that before the show?"

"Yeah, I have plenty of time."

"That's not even what I mean. What if something happens?" I nearly bit off my own tongue, and rushed to add, "Not that I think something bad will happen, but won't you get stressed?"

"Maybe. Or maybe I'll feel like I conquered my fear and will be ready to take on the audience at Highline?" Luis smiled, and it wobbled a little. "It's just something I want to do for myself. I want to show my parents I can make the step to go see them again, and I thought it would be pretty cool if they showed up with me to Highline. Is that cool?"

It was actually adorable. His love for his family was one of those things I'd known early on, just judging by how frequently I'd catch drifts of his conversations from downstairs, and it had charmed me. I'd never been close to my family, and so many of my friends had issues with theirs. Seeing him being lovingly embraced, and cherishing that bond, was special. I just hoped no one in his old neighborhood tried to ruin it.

"It's very cool. Just be careful, babe."

"Always. I'll see you tonight."

We kissed again, longer this time, before he reluctantly retreated out the door. Once it shut, clicking loudly in the old frame, I rolled onto my side to watch him through the windows as he descended the porch and headed down the street. For some reason, I wanted to freeze frame that moment. The sight of him with a gym bag over his shoulder, smiling to himself and striding away from our house, warmed me all over. He'd left happy because of me. And I was here laying on the floor, gazing after him with an answering smile that he would never see, because of him.

Was this what it felt like to be in love? And if so, why was the feeling so goddamn unfamiliar? It was odd to imagine that all the things I'd thought I'd felt in the past, the intensity and passion and heart wrenching angst, hadn't ever amounted to anything close to happiness or completion.

Exhaling slowly, I grabbed one of the foam rollers from the corner and shoved it under my back. Stretching, yoga, then meditation. If that didn't relax me before trekking to Chelsea, then nothing would. And wine was officially out of the question.

I cleared my thoughts by sitting on the floor and breathing naturally while trying to focus on nothing but my own breath and how good my body felt with each inhale and exhale—all techniques Ashton had taught me after multiple pleas for him to share the self-care methods he vaguely discussed on Instagram—and quit obsessing. Not just over meeting The Parents, but the show, the other dancers, and of course Luis and my future plans. How would we get back on track? Could we get back on track? And how much would it affect our relationship if things never panned out? Doubting him felt wrong, but people tended to underestimate the power of disappointment and how it could rot even the deepest of affection.

Those concerns plagued me until I found a calm center and slowly felt the worries ease. It wasn't perfect. I wasn't on a Scientologist level of *clear*, but I was definitely less weighed down by a thousand worries. And my body felt limber and flexible enough to put on a good show.

Excitement spun up in my gut, golden threads and silver sparkles that had been rusted over for years. Instead of focusing on my doubts, I thought about my costume. About inviting Luis' parents for dinner after the show. Of slyly asking them embarrassing secrets about him, and then shyly avoiding questions about how we'd met. Of celebrating our success, and potentially asking them for advice on how to get our plan back on its feet. That was what family was for, right? To help.

Feeling upbeat, I got to my feet and stretched one more time. The sun was gleaming through the window in deep golden rays and, when I followed them outside, all of my feelings of positivity extinguished. I cried out, jumping backwards with my hand flying to my heart.

Landon was looking at me through the glass. His pale eyes roamed my body in a way that made my skin crawl. I needed to put on more clothes. To lock the doors. To call Luis. To fucking hide. I needed to run.

He made a face at me. "Open the door! I'm here to get my shit," his muffled voice came through the window.

Right. His belongings. He'd warned me he would be showing up soon. That he'd show up when he was ready. And that time was now. Now, of all times. Today, of all days. How could it be? How could it be that coincidental?

Unless it wasn't one.

My stomach twisted as we stared at each other through the glass—me stricken, and him raising his eyebrows in impatience. It was the possibility of him being in a hurry that got my ass in gear, and forced my feet to take me to the door. I'd only truly been afraid of him a few times before because I'd been so hellbent on the idea that I could handle myself. I could *defend* myself. But now my hands were shaking. Everything was misaligning.

"Took you long enough," he snapped, shouldering past me once the door was open. "You're not the only one with a life, Charles."

I didn't know what that meant, so I said nothing. I watched him look towards Luis' apartment as if waiting for him to materialize, before scoffing and heading towards my place. The one we'd once shared. There was a moment of panic when I realized the wastebasket in my bedroom had empty condom wrappers, that there was lube on the side table, and that there were signs of Luis everywhere, but the concern was stupid.

He'd just seen me doing yoga in Luis' apartment. He knew. And I shouldn't care that he knew, but my stomach still sank.

"What do you even need?" I asked woodenly. "I looked through everything, and there are literally none of your belongings in this house."

Landon cast me a disparaging look. "If you took it, we're going to have trouble."

"What are you talking about?"

I trailed behind him as he went into the living room and jerked open the tiny closet inside. It was so narrow it was basically useless except for the drop-down staircase leading to the attic. I thought there was no way he'd be going to that, except for the part when he did. I watched, mystified, as Landon clambered up the rickety wooden staircase and stomped around.

With certainty, I knew he'd stashed something illegal up there. What other reason could there be for him to find such a remote hiding spot? We'd had access to the attic forever but had never been willing to clean it up. Even when my landlord had suggested I use it for a dance studio, the urge to fix up someone else's property had not been strong. But Landon had had other ideas.

Once he dropped back down to our apartment, a little dustier and a lot out of breath, I was not surprised to see a chunky manila envelope in his hands.

"Money?" I guessed. "Or pills."

"None of your business," he countered. "But if you keep trying to make me sound like a criminal mastermind, you're going to find yourself in a world of trouble."

"You doctor shop and resell Xanax while living in your parents' basement," I said flatly. "I would never mistake you for a mastermind."

Landon's jaw clenched. Instead of tearing into me, he cast a long slow look around the apartment. The wooden floors, the artwork, the sun making it look homey and cozy. Everything that was no longer his, including me.

"So, you're taking your turn with the stripper."

I raised my lip in a snarl. "You never got anywhere with him, so don't even try to talk shit. He's too good for you."

"You're probably right." Landon stopped scanning the space and focused his laser focus glare directly on me. "He's too good for you too. And he won't take your shit."

"*My* shit?" I demanded. "That's how you remember everything that happened between us? Me starting shit with *you*?"

"More or less, yeah." Landon never started with a raised voice. Oh no. He went in exactly like this—calm and methodical as he took me apart word by word. "Our relationship was fucked, I don't deny it. No one could deny it, babe. Not even our own friends. But it wasn't just me who was the problem. My main problem was not leaving you sooner, and dealing with it by fucking around with other people just so I could feel normal for a little while at a time."

I expected a lot of terrible things from Landon but this stunned me. It reminded me of all those comments people had said on social media—the subtle jabs and snide subs. The people who had said "good for you" after he'd posted about walking out on me. I'd been seeing it for months, and yet it still struck me. "Wow."

"You always do that," he said, shaking his head. "You always act shocked or hurt when someone points out the truth, and then we feel bad and bite our tongues, so no one ever takes the time to tell you the shit you really need to hear."

"Such as?" I asked, voice lowering. "What do I really need to hear,

Landon?"

"That you're toxic, Charles," he said, mimicking my tone. "You're needy, and you shut down whenever things don't go your way. Then you blame everyone in a fifty-mile-radius for yet another bad thing that has happened to you. Yet another misfortune, another string of bad luck, because bad things always happen to Charles, right? And it's never your fault. It's a coincidence, or someone mistreating you, or a conspiracy. Whether it's your parents, your high school friends, your Julliard friends, or even me—there's always *someone* who has wronged you, right?"

"How..." I had to blink and shake my head. This was surreal. This was unbelievable. And yet this was souring my stomach and making the hair on every part of my body stand on end. "You isolated me," I managed to grit out. "You made me believe my Julliard friends hated me—"

"I pointed out that they likely didn't give a shit about you. That's not the same as hating you. It just means they don't care. Just like your other friends went on with their lives when you were on that stupid-ass cruise ship, and just like your parents when you iced them out just because they wouldn't jump up and down with a pride parade when you came out."

My gasp was so sharp and audible that he immediately rolled his eyes.

"Come on, Charles. Did you really think they wouldn't need time? You could have kept trying, but instead you went into professional victim mode and shut them out entirely. It's the same shit you did with me, babe. You got all jealous and crazy, dramatizing everything that happened between us, and would wind yourself up until it was WWIII. And because you were so fucking much, I'd get drawn in and end up acting crazy right along with you."

Brick by brick the foundation I'd started building for myself was coming undone. The stabilizing layer that let me walk around without feeling on the verge of a tumble was going all to pieces. Had I shut people out? Had I failed to give them chances? Had I fought hard enough?

Was I the one with the problem? The toxic one?

Everyone but my immediate circle seemed to think so. Even

former coworkers who'd claimed to like me.

"I'm going to give you a piece of advice," Landon said, pointing at me with the envelope as he headed for the door. "First—be glad we're done. I feel free now that I know what it's like to move on without having to make due with the bullshit I had. And second?" Landon paused, frowning a frown of the truly concerned. "Don't ruin Luis the way you did me. He's actually a decent person."

And with that said, Landon was gone.

No violent screaming.

No fighting.

No insults or slut shaming.

Just cold hard facts.

I sat down in the middle of the studio, stared at the floor, and watched as the sun rays receded and the room darkened around me.

CHAPTER TWENTY-THREE

LUIS

I jogged up the subway stairs at 167th street like someone was gunning for me. Arms loose at my sides and trying to appear calm while looking around so much people probably thought I was paranoid.On the entire ride up to the Bronx, I'd worked hard to convince myself that everything was going to be fine. I wouldn't see anyone I knew. Most people who knew my name by heart were cashiers, the guy who sold pastelitos through a store window by Grand Concourse, and the people who lived in my building. Who was to say Bronson and his boys would even be out and about? If I had to guess, I was willing to bet they would still be loitering at Cadet's. Trying to pretend they were somebody due to the proximity to real talent.

For the most part, it panned out. As I walked up the hill towards my old block, I was just as invisible as every other average joe. Sure, a few people looked at me. A couple of teenage girls even hollered a "god bless you, papi" at me from the corner, but no Bronson. No homophobes. No boogeymen.

Somewhere between Domino's and my favorite Chinese restaurant, I realized that by speed walking straight to my parents' house, I was still holding back. I wasn't facing my real fears—which were mostly confined to returning to the boxing club that had let a bunch of phobes chase me out.

I paused by the park, right across the street from the building I'd grown up in, and stared at it. Technically, I had time. If I really wanted to, I could kill twenty minutes to swing by Cadet's just to rub it in all their faces that I hadn't let them run me out. I wasn't quitting my dream because they couldn't handle sharing space with a guy who loved every gender. That I was gonna be better than everyone with a fly-ass boyfriend and a part-time job as a dancer.

It was so delicious in theory, but... it was just a theory. An idea.

One that could go wrong.

I'd promised Charles I would be careful, not go straight into the hornet's nest to start a bunch of shit. If he'd decided to pick today to go confront Landon, I'd have taken his temperature. I'd have told him that wasting his time trying to prove anything to someone so toxic made no sense. On the same note, going to Cadet's made no sense. Especially when I hadn't faced my fear to save face at the club. I'd come for my family.

The tightness in my chest loosened, and I jogged across the street. Fuck Cadet's.

"Hey papi," a singsong voice called. "Where you going?"

I came to such an abrupt stop that my body rocked forward. Of course, Bronson would come out of nowhere and find me as soon as I'd decided to avoid him. Life was just ridiculous sometimes.

Sighing, I stopped walking by the gate surrounding the building. He was leaning against the Welcome to Butler Houses sign, wearing his usual try-hard outfit of every name brand known to man complete with a Supreme hat. In fact, he kind of reminded me of Landon.

"You still trying to pick up fourteen-year-olds who walk by?"

Bronson's nostrils flared. "You really want to come straight out with bullshit as soon as you see me?"

I shrugged. "Seemed like the right call."

"Because you must have no fucking common sense."

Yeah, that was an understatement. I wished I was one of those people who spent time preparing a speech for their enemies, one to unleash in case I ever came face-to-face with them again, but I wasn't. When I was done with someone, I was done. I acted like they didn't exist and avoided the confrontation unless it really mattered.

"Can I help you with something? I'm trying to see my mom."

"You should have let her keep coming to you." Bronson pushed away from the sign and crossed the few steps so he was in my face. His eyes did a circuit of me as he sneered, like my existence sickened him. "I can't believe you showed your face."

I lifted my chin, waiting for him to do something, but I never got the vibe that he was going to try. Usually in a fight, I could sense the energy in my opponent, and I could identify the twitches and tells that immediately proceeded the swing. But Bronson? He wasn't squaring up or even thinking about it as far as I could tell. He was all talk.

As usual.

Apparently, he could only beat up a queer dude if he had backup from his friends.

Sucking my teeth, I glanced at my mother's building again. "You know son, I don't have much time to waste on you today, but let me tell you one thing—you're exactly the scumbag everyone always said you were. And I never should have defended you."

"Defended me?" Bronson scoffed. "You think I need you to fight my battles?"

"That's not what I'm talking about, jackass." On a whim, I raised my hand and pointed at his chest. Still cautious, still waiting for a sign that he was gonna swing, but picking up on nothing. "When we were kids, you always used to get your ass kicked because you talked so much mess. Remember? It's why you started hanging out at Cadet's. You thought you'd somehow learn to fight just by watching other people do it."

"That's bullshit," he snapped. "And I don't know why you're acting like you know so well."

"Because despite your revisionist history bullshit, we do." I scoffed, and hoped I was exuding the exact same disgust he was showing me. "Whenever someone messed with you, I was there. All through high school and junior high. It wasn't until I got a little older, and I realized how hateful you were, did I take a step back. The only time we hung out was so I could make sure you weren't doing something stupid, and you used to straight up thank me for it. You said I was like your brother."

Bronson's jaw tightened, but he didn't deny it. Instead, he looked over my shoulder and pretended to be bored. "You done with your bitch ass reminiscing?"

"Almost." I stepped to the side so he was forced to look at me. "I'll just put it to you like this, bro. If you'd turn on someone you considered a brother just because I'm bi, something I hid so well you *never* knew in all those years, I guarantee you'd never make it outside of this micro world you made for yourself in the Bronx. You're too fragile to handle differences unless they're the ones you approve of, so you'll never amount to shit."

Bronson pushed his shoulders back, but he was stock still. "And you think you're gonna amount to something? Stripping and fucking guys?"

"Yeah, pretty much. I'll strip my way to owning my own gym, and fuck my hot boyfriend every night when I come up." I shrugged. "Sounds good to me."

"Sounds fucking disgusting."

"Mmm. Well, I'm personally disgusted by the fact that you're still leaning against that same sign scoping girls the age you were about a decade ago, but that's just me." I stepped around him like he meant nothing. Because he was nothing. And he wasn't gonna do nothing. "Have a nice life, motherfucker."

I kept my body loose and ready the entire time I walked away, but he didn't follow. He didn't even call after me. I had the feeling he was watching me walk away, but a glance over my shoulder showed he was back to looking down the block.

Maybe my words hadn't mattered to him, shit maybe *I* didn't matter that much to him now that our initial beef had grown cold, but the fact that I'd gotten to tell him how I felt... that mattered to me.

As soon as I was in the building, I pulled out my phone before inevitably losing service in the elevator. I shot Charles a text telling him I was in an even better mood than I'd been in before but even after I was on my mother's floor, he didn't respond.

 **CHARLES**

In the past, my anger had usually been directed at other people.

My parents, Landon, random assholes who pissed me off and made me feel small at one of my many jobs. Sure, I'd hated on myself and felt hopeless, but I'd never felt the same level of vision darkening rage about my own actions.

Now, I did.

After spending a hours falling into a deeper and deeper pit of despair, a text from Luis had woken me from the fog. He was at his mother's house, and he was happy. He was looking forward to seeing me soon.

A follow-up text showed a selfie of him and his mom. The message said she was excited to meet me. That she heard I had hair just as curly as hers.

They looked so happy. So excited. yaayAnd here I was in a tailspin over Landon.

The contrast of him and me, in that specific moment, had only sent me in another tailspin.

How the hell had I ever thought I could have a normal relationship? Who had lied to me and told me I could manage stress? Why had I ever made promises to take on something as huge as a performance at Highline Fucking Ballroom when, in the deepest part of my gut, I'd always expected something to go wrong. And I'd known that if something did go wrong, I wouldn't have been able to handle it.

My usual self-loathing escalated until I wanted to punish myself. It got even worse when I looked at the clock, over and over again, only to see that my struggle to calm down was getting slower. It was only getting later.

I was never going to make to Chelsea on time.

A sob tore out of me. I pressed my hands to my face, trying to muffle it, to stop myself from falling further to pieces, but I couldn't do it. Thinking about being late, of letting Luis down, only forced me to realize how badly this would damage our relationship. It would be over. And it was inevitable now.

I was already late.

I was a *wreck.* There was no way I could dance in this condition.

My phone chimed with another text message. I ignored it, and focused on unwinding from the knot I'd curled into while calling myself every name in the book. While telling myself that Landon, and all of his friends, were right.

"Get up," I whispered, trying to make my body obey. "You can do this."

A shudder ran through me, but I forced myself to sit up. The sudden movement caused my head to swim. I'd been down there for hours. Crying, hating myself, and causing my head to pound so badly I practically had to squint to see straight.

It didn't help, so I closed my eyes and forced myself to breathe. Breathing naturally wasn't possible when I was on the verge of coming out of my skin, so I sucked in deep breaths and pushed them out. I tried to find a calm place, something peaceful or happy, and could only think of Luis. Not just of his mouth or hands, or the way he made me feel, but the things we'd talked about. The life we'd planned. That future that seemed so out of reach and impossible late at night when it was just me and my fears, but looked reachable in the light of day when he was at my side.

It's reachable, I told myself. *If you get up. If you don't let him and yourself down.*

If you don't shut him out again.

"Fuck!"

My voice was monstrously loud in the silent apartment.

I sucked in another deep breath.

I could do this for him. I could show up, even if I didn't get to dance. And it wouldn't just be for him—it would be for me. To prove Landon couldn't control my actions. He couldn't mindfuck me and shut me down.

I could do this. I could get up.

My body felt heavy and exhausted once I got to my feet, but the simple act of pulling myself together even that much freed some of the weight from my shoulders. I took another deep breath, a slower one, and felt my heartbeat begin to slow. So, I did it again. And again. And went back to picture a studio that half belonged to me while the other belonged to Luis. I pictured us doing burlesque on the side. I pictured us moving in together.

I thought about an entire life that didn't include someone who appeared to get genuine joy out of sucking me dry. Someone who loved me as much as I loved him, with an apartment we shared, and a business of my own.

I can do this.

One exhale later, and my phone was in my hand. I cringed at the dozens of messages from Luis, and balked at responding. What did I even say at this point? How could I explain without freaking *him* out before his performance? A performance Gabe might have to stand in for if I was fucking late.

The self-loathing swelled inside of me again, but I punched it down. If I was going to get out of Staten Island and away from this damn apartment that had become my cave, I couldn't think about Landon. I couldn't think about lateness or how this was going to go wrong. I just had to fucking *go*.

I texted Luis a quick *"Don't worry. Something just came up. Running late"*, and hurried to my bedroom to get changed.

Twenty-two

Luis

The Highline Ballroom was packed with my parents front-and-center in the first row. So far the troupe's sets had been met with a level of enthusiasm from the crowd I wasn't quite accustom to, and I should have been ecstatic about my chance to walk on stage. Unfortunately, everything was wrong because Charles was a no-show.

"Where the fuck is that big-haired queen?" Marquis hissed. "You go on in ten minutes."

"He'll be here," I snapped. "He's coming from Staten Island, and the bus or ferry is probably being trash."

"Are you sure?"

"Yes," I snapped. "He told me he's running late."

Marquis' gaze was cold enough to freeze the Arctic itself, and I could read all the accusations he was throwing with his eyeballs. That he'd let Charles audition because of my recommendation, that I'd sworn he was reliable and professional, that it had nothing to do with the fact that we were together. That we could count on his first show being at our biggest gig yet because his talent was legit and he didn't really get stage fright.

I could see how Marquis was going to put this all on me if Charles bailed. And I could see how this would then become my last night with the troupe. A cold sweat broke out behind my neck, and I could feel it trickling along my spine beneath the satiny robe custom made to look like the Dominican flag.

Jerking my attention back to what I could see of the crowd, I felt sick. No matter how many times I scanned the back entrances as if Charles would try to come through the front instead of the back, he didn't magically appear. And no matter how many times I called him, his fucking phone went to voice mail. I tried again anyway, knowing it was probably the thirtieth time, but panic shot through me yet again when the automated message picked up.

"*Fuck.*"

"Luis."

I looked wildly back at Marquis. "What, man?"

He pursed his lips and looked around at the other dancers. Everyone was excited and happy, no backstage drama or sniping like I'd seen at so many other shows, and yet folks were still throwing side eyes at me. My energy was all wrong, and I wondered if it was throwing everyone else off too. Like my funk was dampening their hype.

"If he doesn't show—"

"He's gonna fucking show," I all but snarled at Marquis. "Dude, he would never—"

"Luis, you barely know him."

My head snapped back, and my brows crashed down, but before I could launch into a defense Marquis put a hand up.

"Just hear me out," he said. "I like Charles, and I think he's a beautiful dancer, but I've known you since you shifted from boxing to burlesque, and I've never met anyone with as much drive and raw talent as you. I'm not gonna fire you because of your flake boyfriend."

Relief sang through me, but I still shook my head. "He's not a flake. If he isn't here, it's because something happened."

"Look, unless he's dead—"

I threw up a hand to stop him talking. "Don't even fucking play."

Marquis huffed out a sigh and put his hands on his hips. "What I'm trying to say is that I won't fire you," he said sharply. "But if he fucks this up, he's done here and I strongly consider you rethink a relationship with someone who ghosts on you on the night of one of the biggest performances of your new career. You go on in a couple of minutes, and to him you didn't even warrant a courtesy call after that initial text."

Those words, more than any, sank my stomach.

Part of me could imagine several scenarios that could have led to Charles bailing on me. Nerves. His own doubts eating away at him and totally killing his confidence. Illness. The commute. Even Landon. I could fill in all the blanks with a ton of details and what-if scenarios to make plausible excuses for why he wouldn't even call me, tonight of all nights, to let me know in advance that he wasn't coming.

But unless he was physically unable to give me a heads up, I'd have to live in a world of make believe to convince myself that him blowing this off, of all things, wouldn't have lasting damage on our relationship. Because why didn't I warrant a courtesy call if his lateness had turned into a no-show?

That question ping ponged in my mind until I pictured him hunched over his sink with a bleeding hand, him trying to open his door but unable to due to his fingers trembling, and how long it had taken him to unfurl from the knot of pain he'd been in for weeks.

My chest tightened, and I blinked rapidly before quickly averting my gaze. "I get where you're coming from, dude, but not everything is that simple. Yeah, this sucks, but I know Charles. And I know there's a reason for this. And even if I get mad at him, I'm still in love with him, and if I'm being honest it makes me sick to even consider going out on stage instead of running to Staten Island to make sure he's okay." I took a deep shuddering breath and ran my hands over my short hair, feeling ridiculous in my robe and trunks while panic twisted my guts. "It's only the slight chance that I might *miss him* because he's on his way here that's stopping me."

For a moment, Marquis continued giving me that scornful glare. Then, he rolled his eyes and sighed. "You're so fucking sweet. That speech almost made my bitter ass fall for *you*. Luckily, I'm your boss and am primarily concerned with how you're going to modify this performance if he doesn't show up."

Forgetting twisting in knots, my stomach sank. "Marquis..."

"I'm not pulling your performance," Marquis said flatly. "The show would end too early. Ad-lib your fine ass across that stage."

"I can't—"

Thunderous applause exploded on the other side of the curtain, and I cringed. "Fuck, okay. I'll... I'll mix it up with the schtick I did at Male Revue."

"Atta baby." Marquis smacked me on the shoulder. "Don't screw up."

"Gee thanks."

Marquis jerked his chin at me as the dancers from the prior performance left the stage. The cold sweat had upgraded to a monsoon raining down my back, but I closed my eyes, bounced in place a couple times, and tried to find my calm center. In my boxing days, this had been simple. I'd focused on the win, the end goal, and remind myself that I was a boss who knew my opponent's weaknesses and how to exploit them.

But this was different. At the moment, I was my own biggest opponent. My head and my heart were both trying to psych me out because it was undeniable that Charles was more important than going out on that stage. It was only my gut feeling that he would be here, that he would not miss this, that allowed me to release a big exhale and put on my boxing gloves as the music began.

Cat calls rang out as soon as I strode from behind the curtain, glaring around like an opponent was waiting for me in an imaginary ring. I raised my gloved fists, pumping the air, and let my satin robe fall open to reveal my trunks and abs. A shrill whistle rang out across the huge audience and oh-my-*fuck* there were nearly one thousand people staring me down. I'd never performed *or* boxed in front of a crowd this large.

My heart hammered in my chest. I couldn't think about them. Or the fact that I was here alone with no set plan on how I was going to modify this dance. If I considered the reality of winging it in front of an audience this large, I was going to keel over right in front of my mom. And I could not do that to her.

"You rock that flag, baby!" a voice hollered.

I almost cracked a smile at Yaneris, but didn't. I was Punch Drunk Louie right now, and I was trying to scare the fuck out of my rival. For yucks, I pretended my rival was Valdrin and not my nerves.

As the national anthem of DR began to transition to the song Salgo Pa' la Calle by Daddy Yankee, my strip tease began. I channeled my Lou persona from Male Revue to keep them titillated. It also kept my brain calm as I did steps that came naturally so I could frantically plan for the next part of the performance which I would now be doing solo.

It took no thought to flex my hips in a serpentine rhythm while dancing to choreography I'd used while stripping for years. The crowd screamed when I threw each boxing glove, they went wild when I whipped my robe into a twisted rope while grinding against the air, and someone shouted a thank you to Jesus after I threw the sweat-damp cloth into the audience and allowed them to scrabble for it.

To slow things down, I did a slower tease with my belt. Instead of dropping it to the side and flexing my biceps which was supposed to lead to my partner strutting out, I worshipped that damn thing. It only added a bonus twenty seconds as I kissed the belt, did the sign of the cross, and then carefully placed it to the side as if it were made of glass, but... it was enough time for me to decide to say fuck it and do the whole strip tease instead of trying to account for Charles' part. There was no way I could think of a better way around it now. Punch Drunk Louie would just have to queer it up on his own. Maybe to psych out my fake opponent.

I turned to the audience, keeping my ice glare in place as I flexed and postured for the start of a fight. Just when I was planning to desperately throw myself into a half-assed plan, a new series of sharp whistles turned my attention to the other side of the stage.

I nearly wept from relief.

Charles strutted out in his glittery booty shorts, shirtless minus the sparkly powder that should have covered him, and in blue chuck taylors instead of the sky-high heels, but still holding his card. His hair was wild as fuck, and I knew that was likely from his rush to get here, but it made him look sexily unkempt. The flush of his face and the lack of make-up was a huge change from what the troupe usually went for, but no one in the audience noticed. He was beautiful with or without make-up, but I didn't miss those red-rimmed eyes.

Tear streaked face aside, Charles was in full character. He sashayed in a way that would have normally made me want to fuck him right here in front of a thousand people, and held up the Round 1 card to the audience before coming to stand in front of me. I remembered my part only after he shot me a quick glare. I snapped to it.

The crowd laughed when my mouth fell open. They hooted when I ran my eyes all over his long lithe body. And they whistled again once he bent over while holding the card, big ass pressing to my crotch, and flipped it to show them his "gay agenda" to seduce me. I hovered my hands over him, making them shake comically, and shot the audience a helpless look. They laughed, thank God. They were into this. We were good.

Charles tossed the card to the side and whirled to me. "Good luck, sugar," he said loudly enough for his voice to carry. The slow wet kiss he pressed to my lips was unscripted, unrehearsed, and it was exactly what I needed right now. Especially when he mouthed 'I love you' right before sashaying away.

I wasn't feigning the expression of shock on my face right before I dramatically dropped to my knees. I held out my arms for him, and he threw a coquettish look over his shoulder. This time, his eyes widened even as a naughty smile crossed his face.

Me? he mouthed, turning again.

I knee-walked closer, pressing my hands together in supplication. The crowd ate it up as Charles tapped his lip with a finger, cocking his head and pretending to think even as he winked at them. After a moment, he gestured for me to stand, and I did so with just enough wiggle for my trunks to fall to my feet. Once the rainbow jockstrap was out, everyone was in.

The rest of the performance was solid.

I danced for him at first, expressing my love with each move, as he paced around me as if trying to figure out if I was worth his time. When I did the splits in my jock, Charles fanned himself as if he was going to die. Then it was his turn to dance for me. His routine was part of choreography we'd rehearsed together more times than I could count, but seeing him put his heart into a performance while the remnants of tears clung to his face made me love him so fucking much I felt like my heart would burst.

When I dragged him up into a dramatic kiss for the crowd, I couldn't help the desperate way I held him to my chest. His fingers dug into me as he lashed his tongue against mine, tempting and sensual and delicious. Forget fighting nerves, I was now trying to control my fucking hard-on. Charles grinned against my mouth. I pulled away just enough to mouth *you okay?* He nodded and mouthed *I'm sorry* right before we transitioned into the dirty dancing part of the routine.

We moved together, kissing and groping frequently for the hysterical crowd, then facing each other while mirroring the moves. By the time we finished, we were both streaked with sweat, but the audience gave us a standing ovation as he gripped my jockstrap and I tangled my fingers in his hair.

We kissed, unscripted yet again, and pulled away laughing.

"I love you," he said, but this time it was too loud and the words carried.

The audience went nuts.

"You better," Yaneris shouted.

I burst out laughing. So did Charles.

We bowed for the crowd and ran backstage where I once again swept him up in my arms. The applause was still thundering as I held him close, and felt the tension slowly return to his lean body.

"What happened?" I asked between breaths. "You look wrecked. I was so worried."

Charles pulled away, worry crossing his face. "Landon showed up and got all in my head," he said over the applause. "He—I don't know, Luis. He—"

"Did he fucking touch you? Because—"

"No." Charles shook his head vehemently. "But he said some things that made me think... He just made me think the wrong things. I freaked out so badly. Totally went to pieces. Even after I finally got dressed, I was sure that I would be too late." Charles inhaled deeply before speaking again. "I thought about calling Caleb, but I didn't want him to rescue me again. I don't want to always call other people to bail me out when I fuck up—"

"You didn't," I said softly. "You were freaked out and panicked. It's different."

Charles squeezed me tighter, his eyes glittering. "I tried to take a cab to the ferry, realized I'd miss the ferry, and ended up asking the cabbie to take me all the way here. But there was traffic, and my phone died—" Charles sucked in another breath. "It was just a mess. Part me wondered if I should bother to come at all if I was going to make a mess of it, but I didn't want to let Landon ruin this for me. For us."

My heart dropped to my boxing boots, and I pulled him to my chest again. "I knew something was wrong. I fucking knew it."

"I shouldn't have let him get to me," he whispered in my ear. "God, for those first few hours I was so messed up thinking I should stay away from you, and I'm bad luck, and it would be better if I blew off the show so you could see how unreliable and shitty I am."

"That's not true. It's *not*."

"I know." Charles pulled back, wiping his face. "It took me curling in a ball for three hours for me to be able to think rationally again. But... then I forced myself to stop thinking about how much better off you'd be without me, and I got mad at myself for letting him manipulate me again. I pictured this whole life we planned, and remembered how you asked me to stop leaving you out in the cold." He shook his head, eyes damp. "I figured even if I was late, at least I wasn't shutting you out or leaving you hanging. You'd know I tried even if my usual bullshit caused me to mess it up."

"No, dude. Don't insult yourself. It wasn't bullshit." I kissed his forehead, unable to stop touching him. The fact that he relaxed each time I put my hands on him only encouraged me further. "Whatever selfcare you need to use, you fucking use it. Yeah, it sucked not being able to get in touch with you, but I knew there was a reason. I trust you. And I know you."

Charles stared at me, blinking and silent.

"I'm serious," I said. "Marquis came at me with some bullshit, talking mess, and I told him—"

"I know," Charles said. "He reamed me when I sprinted in, and then he told me what you said. And... I just, I don't know. It meant a lot."

"Is that why you finally said the three words?" I asked, flashing a tiny grin. "Or was that for the crowd?"

"That was for you," he said sharply. "Fuck the crowd."

Another laugh burst out of me. "Nah, I think I'll take your fine ass somewhere and fuck you."

Marquis appeared at our sides, rolling his eyes but smiling grudgingly. "Not before you go out there for another round of applause, fools. They're demanding to see your mushy asses again."

I blinked, astonished. "Did anyone else go out twice?"

"Nope," Marquis said. "And... a certain casting director for the Broadway version of Charlie and the Chocolate Factory is lurking around and waiting to speak to you, Luis. Apparently, he's been coming to all our shows for the past few months, and he's interested."

My jaw dropped just as comically as it had out on stage. "You're fucking with me."

"Holy shit," Charles exclaimed. "That's amazing!"

"Mmmhmm. He needs strong dancers with comedic skills for the ensemble, so…" Marquis jerked his head at the stage. "Go bow again, soak it up, then go impress the man."

When I continued to gape, Charles grabbed my hand.

"Let's do this," he said. "Everything is going to be all right."

"How do you know?" I asked, breathless and wide-eyed, and feeling like someone was playing a trick on me.

"Because if you get a part on a Broadway show, you'll have the money to save for the gym. Your dream isn't thwarted!"

"*Our* dream," I corrected. "We're in this together, lindo."

As bloodshot as they were, there was happiness in those big brown eyes of his. "We are."

"You sure you want to go back out there? We can say fuck this and—"

Charles shut me up with another firm kiss. "No. I need this right now. That crowd? Dancing with you?" He shivered. "God, it brought me back. I loved it. I love you. And I want more clapping."

I grabbed his hand. "Then let's go get it."

Marquis shoved us towards the curtain, muttering about our over-the-top sap, but even his grumpiness couldn't ruin the moment.

After everything Charles and I had gone through in the past, this all should have felt like a fantasy, but it didn't. This was as real as it got, and so was our future together.

CHARLES

"Wait, we need a picture!"

I groaned from where I'd collapsed on the gym floor in a pile of sweaty and aching limbs. "Ashton, come the fuck on. That workout was brutal."

Ashton kicked my foot with one rainbow colored running shoe. "It was brutal because your boyfriend is an *amazing* trainer, so now I need to tell all my Instagram followers about it and direct them to this gym, kay?"

Who could argue with that argument? Also, how could I be the only one in a ball of pain while he and Val strutted around like the brutal lower body workout we'd just endured for an hour hadn't been literal torture? My boyfriend may be amazing, but he was also killing me by drawing me into his early morning pre-client training.

My ass was looking quite delicious, though.

"Okay," I whined, crawling to my feet. "I'm up. Picture time, and then I get a mimosa."

"Pretty sure mimosas aren't in our nutrition plans," Ashton said sweetly.

I gave him a death look. "I'm not on a nutrition plan, pal. I dance all day with my clients, so I get to eat like a horse. Give me my alcohol."

Luis came up behind me, rubbing his face all over my sweaty neck. "I'll give you something all right."

My body immediately reacted to the feel of his crotch fit to my ass and his rock-hard chest against my back. We'd merged apartments to share his (since he had access to the backyard) a few months ago, but even though now lived together *and* worked side-by-side in our gym, we still could not stop touching each other. Not even in front of other people.

"Okay," Val groaned, interrupting our slow kisses. "Just take the picture and quit your PDA."

Luis pulled away, scoffing. "You should talk, Mr. Caught Macking on A-Town Against a Tree in Page Six."

"Why do you stay reading gossip columns?" Val wondered. "That's the real issue here."

"No, the issue is my lack of a mimosa," I grumbled.

"Okay everyone," Ashton sang. "Shut the fuck up and do your sweatiest, toughest, mean mug for the selfie!"

He swung out a long arm, gathering us around him, and I had zero issues glaring at his giant phone. He snapped a million pictures in like one second, then instantly frowned down at the screen before carefully selecting the perfect image.

Unable to help it, I peered over his shoulder. As grumpy as I was now that our brunch routine had been pushed back for our group training with Luis, I couldn't deny the picture was grade A adorbs. Val and I were glaring at the camera as if our lives depended on looking super pissed off about having to be in this picture, but Luis had stuck out his tongue so it looked like he was licking my ear, and Ashton's mean face was just sultry and fuck-me-now. He literally could not help it, and it was funny because he was the biggest dork.

"Okay, how's this caption," he asked. "Just finished a brutal workout at #SavageEleganceStudios with my beautiful boyfriend, bestie, and @trainerluisramos. Guys, he is LEGIT. I was already in okay shape, but I'm seeing definition in eight weeks that I haven't seen in my LIFE. If you're down to make the trek to the north shore of Staten Island, I can totally put in a good word so you can get on his list!"

Luis' eyes nearly popped out of his head. "What if people actually come?"

"Babe, that's the fucking point," I said.

"But..." He looked from Val to Ashton. "What if—"

Val gave him a side eye. "Are you seriously being insecure right now? Because I might record this to memorialize it."

The sudden streak of nerves vanished from Luis' expression, and he flashed his brilliant smile. "You're right, that was dumb. Bring on the rich clients!"

As Val teased him and Luis rolled his eyes, I glanced around our space. It definitely wasn't large or fancy like the resort gym Ashton and Val went to, but it was efficient. And ours. That was the important part. The space had two rooms—one with rubber mats on the floors and professional weight training equipment for him, and a room with mirror lined walls and hardwood floors for me.

It had originally been a small gym with a strength training section and aerobics section, so it suited our purposes just fine. We'd cobbled together our business plan, did a huge grand opening with incentives and raffles, and had barely kept things running on a handful of clients for the first few months. After that, the miracle of Google and Yelp reviews had kicked in along with word-of-mouth, and we'd had an influx. Now, Luis had a solid fifteen clients, and I taught two classes at a larger dance studio and had eight of my own clients who I saw regularly in our space along with people who hired me to come to their homes. We weren't living large, but we were comfortable, and I fucking loved it.

"Why are you grinning over here?" Luis asked, pulling me against him again. "Dreaming of that mimosa? We're about to go to brunch so you can eat."

I snorted, glanced around, and saw Val and Ashton had gone to the other room to wash up and change. "No. Well. Yes, but mostly I was being mushy."

"Ohhh..." Luis kissed my cheek then trailed his lips down. "Tell me more."

"I'm just proud of us?" I wrapped my arms around in him return. "We're good right now, but I think things can only improve from here. Not only is Ashton pimping the gym, but the dancers you performed with in that run of Charlie and the Chocolate Factory have been inboxing you too. Everyone wants to be your client ever since you did that body transformation contest after the grand opening."

"Yeah, but I'm worried about being stretched too thin." Luis glanced at the door leading to the other room then back at me. "I know the extra money would be dope, but we both already work twelve-hour days sometimes, and I kinda miss our late-night dinners and dancing for fun."

"And lying in bed together while discussing supplements and watching YouTube dance and workout videos?" I asked, smirking. "Our version of romance is super fucking work oriented, babe."

"And?" Luis bit my earlobe. "Work aside, we have a lot in common. And you know you love my rants about supplements and whey isolate."

"I love it more when you feed me Dominican takeout right before sucking my cock."

Luis' booming laugh exploded in my eardrum. He pulled away, holding up his hands when I glared. "You'll forgive me when I tell you my really good idea."

"Mmk. Does it involve alcohol and food?"

"Fuck yeah, it does." Luis kissed one of my hands. "My fam is going to DR this winter for the holidays, and they want us to come. So, there'd be family, food, and alcohol. Also, an island instead of some wack snow. I want us to go and have a real vacation."

It sounded magical, actually. "They really want me to come?"

"Uh, yeah. My mother loves you, and Titi Yaneris thinks you can do no wrong. I try to tell her you're wrong, like, a lot of times per day, but she isn't trying to hear that shit."

"Because she knows you're slandering me like an asshole," I said, whipping my sweaty hair at him. "That sounds amazing. Of course, I'd love to go. Especially if we can take a couple of days to be alone and fuck really loudly on some excessive beach house."

Luis bit his lower lip, eyes sweeping over me.

I snickered. "I take that as a yes."

"You can take that as a hell yes."

I draped my arms over his shoulders, smiling, and brushed our lips together. "I love you, Luis Wilberto Ramos."

"I love you too, Charles Big Booty Jovanovic."

I pinched his side just as Ashton reappeared in a floppy black hat, slinky black dress, and giant shitkicker boots. "How do I look?"

"Like a vampire with badass delts," Luis said.

Ashton beamed. I snorted, and Val squeezed said delts when he came up behind Ashton wearing his usual hoodie and jeans. "We ready to eat?" he asked.

"I'm always ready to eat," I informed him. "As soon as I slap on some deodorant and a sweater."

"Mmm, but I don't mind you sweaty," Luis said.

Val made a face. "Dude, can I stop knowing things about your sexual desires?"

Luis grinned wickedly. "Not anymore. Just wait until brunch."

"I'll put on my headphones and ignore you," Val deadpanned. "No lie."

"He will." Ashton shook his head mournfully. "If Angel or Aiden isn't there to bro out with him, he literally ignores us and listens to music."

"Val couldn't ignore me if he tried," Luis said with full confidence. "And he has tried a lot in the past decade."

I shook my head, walking out of the room and laughing as they continued to banter. For the hell of it, I checked the post Ashton had tagged me on, and grinned at the first comment.

Amazing group shot. Your insta is my daily queer affirmation. I hope to someday have similar friendships and as satisfying a life as you all seem to have!

Not all days were as good as this one, but... I couldn't deny that I hadn't felt as good in my own skin for a long time. My life wasn't just satisfying, it was happy. And it would be even happier once I had my mimosa in hand while I daydreamed about going on vacation with my beautiful lover.

Explore more of the *Five Boroughs* series at:
riptidepublishing.com/titles/universe/five-boroughs

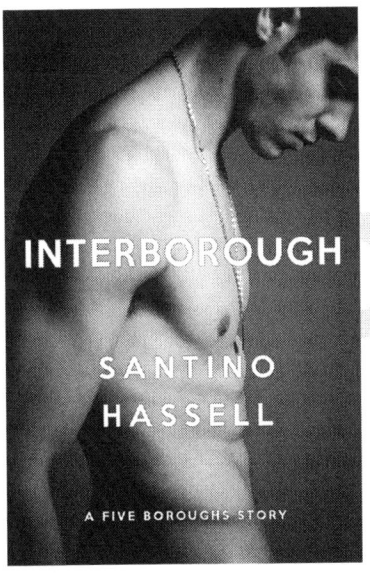

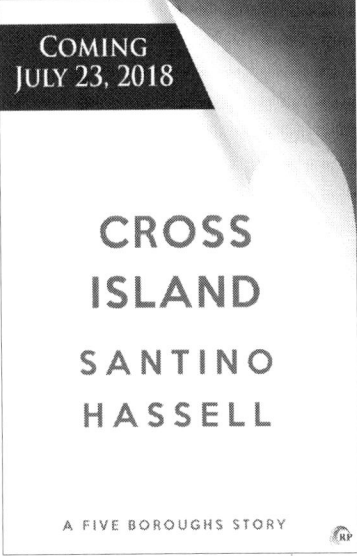

Dear Reader,

Thank you for reading Santino Hassell's *North Shore*!

We know your time is precious and you have many, many entertainment options, so it means a lot that you've chosen to spend your time reading. We really hope you enjoyed it.

We'd be honored if you'd consider posting a review—good or bad—on sites like **Amazon, Barnes & Noble, Kobo, Goodreads, Twitter, Facebook, Tumblr,** and your blog or website. We'd also be honored if you told your friends and family about this book. Word of mouth is a book's lifeblood!

For more information on upcoming releases, author interviews, blog tours, contests, giveaways, and more, please sign up for our weekly, spam-free newsletter and visit us around the web:

> **Newsletter**: tinyurl.com/RiptideSignup
> **Twitter**: twitter.com/RiptideBooks
> **Facebook**: facebook.com/RiptidePublishing
> **Goodreads**: tinyurl.com/RiptideOnGoodreads
> **Tumblr**: riptidepublishing.tumblr.com

Thank you so much for Reading the Rainbow!

RiptidePublishing.com

ALSO BY
SANTINO HASSELL

ABOUT
THE AUTHOR

Santino Hassell was raised by a conservative family but grew up to be a smart-mouthed, school-cutting grunge kid, a transient twentysomething, and eventually transformed into a grumpy introvert and unlikely romance author with an affinity for baseball caps. His novels are heavily influenced by the gritty, urban landscape of New York City, and his desire to write relationships fueled by intensity and passion.

He's been a finalist in both the Bisexual Book Awards and the EPIC Awards, and was nominated for a prestigious RITA award in 2017. His work has been featured in *BuzzFeed*, *Huffington Post*, *Washington Post*, *RT* magazine, and *Cosmopolitan* magazine.

You can find him at santinohassell.com, in his reader group on Facebook—Get Hasselled, on Patreon, and on Twitter as @santinohassell.

Enjoy more stories like
North Shore
at RiptidePublishing.com!

87745626R00155

Made in the USA
Columbia, SC
26 January 2018